Praise for

Her Infernal Name & Other Nightmares

"A bold, new voice in dark fiction, Robert Ottone breathes genuine life into the stories collected in *Her Infernal Name* with vivid characters, deft plot twists, skin-crawling creatures, and weird supernatural entities that will haunt readers long after the story ends."

James Chambers
Bram Stoker Award-winning author of *On the Night Border*

"Ottone hits every mark of a genre-bending writer at the top of his game. The subtle build of each story, the rich and dark depth of each character, and the imagery so sharply brought to life, it left me both terrified for humanity and hopeful for a brighter tomorrow. Whoever says horror can't be beautiful has clearly not read this book."

Ryan Sprague
Author & host of the *Somewhere in the Skies* book and podcast

"Rob Ottone is a talented writer with a cinematic imagination and a fine ear for dialogue. His dark stories have charm, originality, and an understated humor, and his dialogue is just about word-perfect."

Josh Gidding
Author of *Failure: An Autobiography* (Cyan, 2007)

"I like when people can take established horror tropes and just change them slightly this way or that and it feels like a completely new and fresh thing."

Julian Titus
Host and producer, *Nerds without Pants* podcast

Her Infernal Name
& Other Nightmares

Robert P. Ottone

Edited by Louis Maurici

Spooky House Press

Scan this QR code for a Spotify playlist of songs curated by the author.

ISBN: 978-1-7340445-3-9 (Paperback)
ISBN: 978-1-7340445-4-6 (Ebook)

Acknowledgments

This is my first time writing an acknowledgments page, so bear with me.

To begin, this book couldn't have been written without the guidance and skill of Louis Maurici, my editorial Sherpa. His notes and enthusiasm are invaluable, and he's a heavenuva guy.

I'd be remiss if I didn't thank the Sand Sharks. James, Frank, Lou, John, Allan. What was easily one of the scariest things I ever considered doing has turned into a monthly gathering I actively look forward to. Thank you all.

I'd like to thank my beta readers Ashley and Amanda for giving me different feminine perspectives on a character I didn't want defined by her femininity.

Thank you to everyone who bought my first book. The reactions from so many inspired me to continue, and for that I'm grateful.

To the janitorial staff at the middle school I worked at that did nothing about the gnats infesting the teacher's lounge, you'll know which story is for you.

To my niece and nephew, I adore you both.

CONTENTS

Her Infernal Name 1

The Monitors.. 83

Elevator of the Dead 109

Kelly, Watch the Stars 127

Full Understanding.. 141

Green Gospel 147

The Sugar Bowl 151

Panels 155

Support.. 161

The Arborist.. 165

You Can't Walk It Back 173

The Nebulous They... 177

Apple Valley 189

Playing God 217

Gnats in the Teacher's Lounge 239

The World Whispers Madness................................... 261

The Final Goodbye 269

Miscellaneous Ephemera 277

HER INFERNAL NAME

Shoshana graduated early, earning her four-year degree in only three by taking multiple summer and winter classes. She received her master's degree in education, and started teaching high school social studies. When Shosh (as her friends called her) went to work for a large public school in Queens, she found herself nearly able to make ends meet. Her salary was barely $60,000 per year, nowhere near enough to afford her the life of leisure and excitement she saw on TV and on Instagram and Snapchat. Shosh was a hard worker and smart as a whip, but she couldn't figure out how young teachers were expected to make it in New York, especially New York City. Administration was surely making six figures, but they had been teaching for a long time, and they deserved it, right?

Shosh was barely able to make ends meet between her college loans, rent, car payment, car insurance, utilities, and other expenses. She was lucky if she found herself with an extra hundred dollars per month, all said and done. Living in the city had always been expensive, and even though she never saw her roommate, Shosh wondered if she should get a second job. When she finally did, picking up a couple extra shifts as a bartender at the terrible biker bar down the street, Shosh was pulling in an extra couple hundred dollars per week, but even then, as quickly as she made it, it seemed to fly out the window just as fast.

Her college repayment plan was structured in a way that, over time, her monthly payment would increase slightly. What started as $220 per month had ballooned to around $800, which was a lot for anyone to afford, let alone someone just starting out in the world. Shosh refused the help of her parents, who were having difficulties of their own, as the property taxes at their home on Long Island had shot past $18,000 per year, a kingly sum for such a small piece of property in Nassau County.

Shosh didn't know what to do, as all of her extra money was being poured into her college loan. Eventually, cutbacks at the school resulted in her being excessed, which is just a nice term for laid off, and even though Shosh was able to collect unemployment for a time, the $400 per week wasn't nearly enough for her to survive. With a few years of teaching under her belt, Shosh began seeking employment outside of education. Some smaller schools, mostly Charters, showed interest but ended up going with younger, newer candidates. They also paid about $10,000 less than what Shosh had been getting at her first teaching gig. After a bit of time, she found herself employed at a small marketing firm, one of those boutique places that afforded her more freedom, but also paid her about twenty thousand dollars less per year than she was making previously. She felt the sudden dip in salary immediately, and after numerous calls to her student loan servicers, she began receiving pieces of mail indicating that she was in collections for both her personal and federal loans. The company, Irwin Agencies, kept up a steady stream of mailings to her apartment, with each letter increasing how much her minimum payments had to be.

In the little free time Shosh had, she found herself watching Instagram and YouTube videos, since all she and her roommate could afford was Internet service. They made a point to tell others that they were "cutting the cord" in an effort to stick it to the cable companies, but the reality was that they just couldn't afford television any longer. Shosh found herself watching makeup tutorials, listening to teenaged Instagram influencers discuss the injustices of the world, and absorbing as many reaction videos as possible, all featuring thumbnails of well-maintained people with expressions far too excited or scared to be reacting to whatever it was they were reacting to. *They couldn't possibly be making those faces in reality, could they?* she often thought to herself.

A particular favorite influencer of Shosh's was a girl named Royce who lived in Manhattan and seemingly never stopped partying. It was the kind of life Shosh envisioned for herself upon graduating from school. She worked her ass off in college, but since graduating, she didn't have a lot of time for fun. Watching Royce allowed her to live vicariously through this young girl, who couldn't have been older than fifteen. Royce had a legion of friends and fans around her at all times and was always at movie premieres, record release parties, concerts, on vacation in various tropical countries, and more.

Royce had become something of a "wellness guru," often featuring recipes and other "healthy" pieces of advice that were geared toward nurturing the body. With a heavily female focus, Royce seemed poised to take her social media influence and to transition into one of those talking heads you see on daytime television, discussing the latest trends in healthy eating or espousing the benefits of kale. Royce always had an "obsession," something she dedicated multiple posts to, often with the hashtag #RoyceObsessed, and typically, it was some kind of natural oil or product, mostly paid advertisements.

In a few videos, Royce featured a fertility expert talking about the benefits of eating apples, far beyond the traditional apple a day to keep the doctor away, as well as maca root (which Shosh had never heard of), coconut oil (which Shosh slathered herself in every morning, post-shower), and the benefits of eating something called crappit heid, which Shosh refused to eat based solely on the name alone. When she finally looked the strange-sounding remedy up, she nearly puked, but in a follow-up video, watching Royce and the fertility expert (whose name was Abda, because *of course*) enjoy slipping pieces into their mouths, Shosh's interest was piqued, but she was never brave enough to give it a go.

One evening, Shosh went back to Royce's first ever upload, among the thousands, and found that the uploads dated back to when Royce was twelve. Her first ever video had received ten million views, and her average views per video hovered somewhere around the 25 to 32 million range. This seemed insanely high, but Shosh was impressed. Royce happened to be a pretty girl, youthful in appearance, with a strong anime-inspired aesthetic. Her hair color changed with almost every video, and she was decidedly pale compared to your average person. Royce's body was also remarkably developed for a girl her age, something Shosh thought was just part of growing up these days. Shosh's own body was nowhere near as developed as Royce's, so she thought maybe the kid was just blessed with great genetics.

Royce's early videos were covers of popular songs, as well as her thoughts on school and what she was doing that weekend. At twelve, Royce didn't have much going on outside of her friends (who never appeared in the early videos), her parents, and her lo-fidelity covers of Sia tracks. Royce in the beginning wasn't the anime character come-to-life she was now. She was a simple girl with brown hair, sad eyes, and a pretty voice.

Unable to make the full amount per payment that Irwin Agencies was demanding, Shosh called them, begging to be put on some kind of smaller repayment plan. Shosh's debt had begun to grow, courtesy of interest and more, resulting in a remarkably high debt-to-income ratio. While on the phone, Shosh felt as though the agent she was speaking to was in a tunnel, the voice slightly echoing as it spoke. Shosh also heard a low hum in the background, rhythmic, sounding more mechanical than static.

"We're happy to work with you, Shoshana. In certain circumstances, we can send an agent to better assist you in-person to go over options once we research your particular case," the agent on the phone told her. "In the meantime, we'll put your loan on hold for a financial quarter. Interest will continue to accrue, but you won't need to make payments in the meantime. That way, our team can put together a few options for you, and you can help by getting your financial affairs in order. Is the address we have on file for you in Brooklyn correct?"

***

After about a week, Shoshana was returning home from a four-hour shift at the bar, after having already worked ten hours at the office (with no overtime pay), when she found a tall man standing outside her building, holding a briefcase. He introduced himself as Gary from Irwin Agencies, and when Shosh asked how long he'd been waiting in the area, he informed her that Irwin takes their accounts very seriously, and that he was happy to come by later at night, knowing her work schedule.

Even though that didn't answer her question, Shosh welcomed the agent into the apartment, and once inside, she poured herself some coffee, as well as some for him. He reviewed her repayment options, as well as potential options for her to make more money, through a variety of additional revenue streams. Shosh informed him that she already had two jobs, and he nodded, saying "Yes, yes, I see."

"Are you familiar with our client named Royce? She's a YouTuber, pretty famous," he asked.

"Sure, yeah, I watch her stuff sometimes," Shosh lied, ashamed that she was secretly obsessed with this child of the Internet.

"She does promotion for us at a variety of events through our parent company." He produced a card that highlighted the parent company, a massive New York-based corporate entity known to have its tendrils in a variety of enterprises. "She's always looking for good help. You're a smart girl, Shoshana. I could possibly make a few calls and see if she'd be interested in bringing you onto her staff."

"What would I be doing?"

He shrugged. "You'd effectively be her tutor among other assorted duties. She's home-schooled. You'd make more than you do currently, that's for sure. Our previous placements with our clients typically saw their debt reduced either entirely or substantially in a year or two of work. That said, it will be very demanding of your time and energy."

Shosh nodded. "Yeah, I mean, if gets me out of debt, I'll do it. Please let me know."

He smiled, shook Shosh's hand, and left, after letting her know that he'd be in touch in a few days. Shosh wondered what this kid could need help with other than her education. Basic secretarial type work? Answering phones? Shosh had friends who worked as assistants to actors, lawyers, and more, so she imagined she'd be making reservations for Royce at a variety of restaurants, picking up her dry cleaning, cleaning her fancy penthouse apartment (which seemed always void of any parental figure), and other basic tasks not suitable for a star of her caliber to do herself.

Jeez, making reservations for a fifteen-year-old kid at restaurants I couldn't afford on my best day, that seems fair, Shosh thought to herself.

***

Time passed quickly, and finally the agent from Irwin called Shosh back. He had set up a time and day for Shosh to head to Royce's apartment and meet with "her people" to discuss the position. Shosh obliged and used a sick day to head to the interview. The building Royce lived in was never mentioned in her videos, and even in accepting the interview, Shosh had to sign a non-disclosure agreement that would result in a multi-million dollar lawsuit were the information ever released to the public, with proof that Shosh had been the one to leak it. The building itself, a modern high-rise in Manhattan, the *Balaam,* featured spectacular views of the city, and impossibly high prices, the likes of which Shosh could never afford herself.

In the elevator, the lights flickered quickly when Shosh pressed the button for the penthouse. As the elevator sped skyward, Shosh felt a sudden feeling of nausea and gripped the wall-rail to steady herself. She glanced at her reflection in the steel doors of the elevator, and thought about how she should've dressed cuter for the interview. She was wearing a black pencil skirt and a gray jacket.

Comfortable, yes, but she knew that if Royce was actually *at* the interview she might judge her for not dressing funky enough, since Royce always had the latest, most stylish outfits, with hair to match.

She pushed the thought of Royce judging her based on her outfit alone out of her head, and when the doors opened Shosh was greeted by a small woman of around seventy who welcomed her warmly. The woman, whose name was Inge, had a thick German accent, but it was decipherable if one listened carefully. Inge wore thick glasses ("Coke bottles" as Shosh's dad might say), pink sweatpants, sandals, and a gray sweatshirt that had a picture of a kitten wearing electric green sunglasses on it. *Even this broad's dressed funkier than me*, Shosh found herself thinking as she followed Inge deeper into the penthouse Shosh had seen so many times on YouTube.

Shosh recognized the entire apartment for the hours she spent watching Royce live her life. In one corner was the amp and guitar Royce would play. There was the balcony Royce would dance on, usually wearing as little as humanly possible, with a tripod set up to catch the amazing NYC skyline in the background. There was a telescope nearby that was featured in one of Royce's earlier videos, where she talked about how one of her favorite pastimes was staring at the night sky and dreaming of being in another place to escape her life. *Escape this? Why?* The walls were littered with diamond play buttons, gifts from YouTube for having millions of subscribers and views.

In the living room, which was also the site of so many of the videos, sat the girl herself, Royce, in the flesh. She had a pair of Airpods in her ears, her hair in two explosive pink ponytails. She had a pair of glasses on, something that was never featured in the videos, as well as a lime green tank top, with strategic slashes in it showing off a hot pink bra. She wore a pair of pink running shorts that were impossibly small. Royce smiled widely when Shosh walked into the room, stood up, and walked over to her.

"Hi. I'm Royce," she said, extending her hand. Shosh shook it. The girl must've been freezing, as her hand radiated ice. "I make YouTube videos that are like, all about who I am as a person, but also, about my hopes and dreams."

Inge smiled, adoring the young girl. "This is Shoshana. She's very interested in the job we talked about."

"Yeah, yeah, very cool, very *real*, you know?" Royce said, sitting back down. "Take a seat. Can I call you *Shosh*? Like on that old show, what's the one?"

"I'm not really sure, to be honest," Shosh admitted. *First mistake, not knowing pop culture.*

"Meh, it'll come to me. They always do, you know what I mean?" Royce said/asked, laughing. She was as high-energy off-camera as she was on. Shosh wondered if the girl was on cocaine.

"So, I'm interested in learning more about the position, I'm not entirely sure what I would be doing other than tutoring, should I get the job, of course," Shosh began.

"Let me stop you there," Royce interrupted. "I basically just need someone to help me with my everyday-type shit. Inge is great and all, but she's getting up there in years, and honestly, my style just doesn't allow for her to be seen with me all the time. No offense, sugar mama."

Royce blew a kiss at Inge, who smiled and nodded in agreement. Shosh glanced at Inge uncomfortably, then back to Royce. "Gotcha."

"Good. So like, you have a degree in teaching, according to your resume, which I read last night, of course, what else are you good at? What's college like? Did you fuck a lot of guys? What was your GPA? Were you in a sorority?"

Wait, what?

"I'm sorry?"

"You must excuse Royce, Shoshana. It's easy to forget that she's just a child. Her mind runs a mile a minute. You know this new generation. They're so easily distracted and all over the place with their thoughts," Inge said.

Royce smiled, "Totally, I love that, I love *her*, you know? She keeps me totally grounded."

Shosh nodded. "College was great. Met lots of people. No sorority, though. My school didn't allow Greek culture on campus."

"Aww, that's gay," Royce sighed. She leaned back on the couch and sat, her legs open. Shosh looked away when she noticed Royce wasn't wearing underwear. "Do you have a cigarette?"

Shosh shook her head. "I do not, sorry. I don't smoke."

"Good, me neither. Just a little pot. That was a test, Shosh, and you passed it! I love you for that!"

Shosh nodded. *Where the fuck am I?*

"Royce, you silly girl," Inge smiled and patted Royce on the leg. As a reaction, Royce closed her legs.

"When can you start? I've got a weird vibe off you that I'm addicted to. I can't get enough. You're really cute if you weren't wearing that lame AF outfit, you know? I bet the guys blast in their pants over you. They do for me, usually," Royce said, jumping up and standing on the couch. She extended her hand and Shosh shook it.

"I can start whenever, I suppose," Shosh said.

"Good shit. Inge, show her the benefits package on her way out, and also, call Abda, I need my happy juice," Royce said, walking away and peeling off her clothes as she walked down the hall toward what Shosh knew to be a bedroom that also featured prominently in her videos.

Inge walked Shosh back to the elevator and explained payment, benefits, and more to Shosh. While the entire interview experience was bizarre and manic, Shosh couldn't deny that the money she'd make was astounding. She'd also have benefits, which was something she never had before, really. She'd also be able to give up her bartending job, which she'd have to do anyway, as the position working for Royce meant she would have to be on-call 24/7.

Most importantly, her debt would be wiped out completely. As part of Royce's deal with Irwin Agencies, any debt accrued to that point would be wiped out entirely after six months of service under her contract with Royce. Shosh read over the contract briefly, and signed. She was to start the following week. When she got home, she called her parents and told them she got a new job. Then she emailed her boss at the marketing firm, thanking him for the opportunity and vacating her current position. That night, she went to the bar to quit and was met with rounds of drinks from the owner, who had no hard feelings.

***

When Monday rolled around, Shosh woke up early and was getting ready when there was a knock at the door. When she opened it, there was a package on the tattered welcome mat with a letter reading "Dress for the job you want, not the job you have, - Royce" with smiley faces and poop emojis drawn all over it. Shosh opened the pink box, bound with purple leather straps and inside were a variety of outfits, all colorful and stylish, similar to the types of clothing Royce wore frequently in her videos. Shosh laid out some clothes from the box, showered, and finished getting ready, putting on a pair of orange tennis shoes from the gift box, along with a blue plaid skirt and white dress shirt. She had seen Royce wear a similar outfit, which she playfully referred to as "Catholic school chic."

On her way to Royce's building, Shosh received a fair amount of odd looks from other professionals riding the subway into Manhattan. She looked like a teenager and felt ridiculous, but she was willing to do whatever Royce wanted if it meant her debt would be wiped out completely in a matter of months. *What's a few months of looking like an idiot compared to a debt-free lifetime?* she asked herself.

At Royce's building, she rode the elevator all the way up, staring at her reflection in the doors while waiting to reach the penthouse. When the doors opened, the first thing Shosh noticed was an odd smell, like the scent of burnt rubber or something, filling the air. As she stepped off the elevator she looked around for Royce. The penthouse was a mess. She had seen Royce's upload on Saturday night; the group of people she had over had wrecked the place more than she imagined. The camera only caught a small glimpse of the mayhem in the penthouse and in no way reflected the actual amount of mess that was thrown all over. Shosh walked into the living room area and saw Royce lying on an inflatable pink flamingo, drinking coffee from a mug with Garfield on it saying "I don't do Mondays," and wearing a pair of pink Ray-Ban aviators.

"Oh my god, you're here, that's great. I missed you!" Royce sprung up and ran over to Shosh, hugging her hard. Coffee spilled on the floor behind Shosh, and she turned and looked around, confused.

"Where's Inge?"

"Oh, yeah, well, she had to take a trip back to *the motherland*, you know, like, fucking *Germany* or whatever, she'll be back in a few weeks, until then, it's just me, you, Garfield here, and like, this place, is that cool or what? We could have a *sleepover*."

Shosh stared at the girl. There was a faint look of sadness in her face, even with the massive aviators covering her eyes. "That's cool, for sure. Would you like me to clean this place up a bit before we get started on your lessons?"

"No way, you're dressed too cute for that, Inge hired like, some Vietnamese housecleaner a year or so ago, she's late as fuck all the time, but she'll be here soon, basically, you look adorable, I'm glad you got the clothes I sent you."

"Oh, thank you, that was really sweet of you to send them," Shosh said. "I didn't want to make another fashion faux pas like I did during our interview. So, what would you like me to do when we're done with school?"

"Well, there are a bunch of emails and comments to get to on my YouTube and Instagram. There's about three hundred Snaps I have to return to my followers, too, not to mention the DMs on Twitter and Insta, too. Wanna get started with those, then do class after lunchy?"

"Sure, whatever you like," Shosh said.

With that, the two sat down, put on some music, and went through Royce's social media accounts. They laughed at the variety of ridiculous messages sent by horny guys, most including pictures of their erect members of varying sizes. Royce told Shosh stories about guys she'd slept with, about which actors she knew had the biggest penises, the ones who didn't measure up. The fact that Royce was only fifteen as she described these encounters, often in detail, wasn't lost on Shosh.

Abda came by frequently, and Shosh learned that not only was Abda a fertility expert for Royce to showcase on social media, she also pulled double duty as Royce's personal wellness guru. Abda, it turns out, wasn't just a bubbly blond occasionally guesting in Royce's YouTube videos, but was, in fact, a licensed nutritionist, with her own practice on the Upper West Side. She was connected to Royce in the same way Shosh was, through Irwin Agencies, and was happy to share her message of wellness and health to Royce's enormous following. Abda was friendly, but protective of Royce when she was around, and often regarded Shosh with a careful eye. She was attractive, blond, tall with a tight, muscular body, befitting someone who ate nothing but beet root and worked out for a living. Royce often reflected on how she'd like to be as "fit" and "hot" as Abda but understood that because she spent so little time working out, it would be difficult to achieve the same results, so instead, the girl followed Abda's advice the best she could.

When it came to the actual tutoring and teaching portion of their day, Royce was a fairly remarkable student. She focused on the work, mostly in an effort to get it done so they could move onto "the fun shit" as she called it. Royce often impressed Shosh with her knowledge of history, and though she often interpreted things her own way, using common parlance instead of textbook-based terminology, Shosh found it refreshing to work with a student who seemed to have a passion for antiquity in a way no other student she'd met had.

***

The first week went on like this. Eventually, usually late in the evening, the Vietnamese housekeeper did appear, each day, to clean and make repairs when needed. The housekeeper didn't speak to Shosh, and only slightly acknowledged Royce, when greeted. While Royce was certainly annoying in the way that most teenagers, regardless of gender, are, she was also somewhat endearing in a neglected pet kind of way. Shosh pushed these thoughts out of her mind when she saw contract offers to promote items and appear in music videos and other things. Royce made more money than Shosh or any of her friends or family would ever make in their entire lives, and so Shosh tried to keep it in mind at all times that this was a girl who made money off the attention of others.

There were numerous offers from a variety of men, contracts from law firms for extended periods of Royce's time. The contracts called for her to meet these men at private airports all over New York and be flown off to exotic parts of the world to spend time as an influencer and experience their private estates or their privately owned resorts or spas or whatever. Shosh asked what, exactly, did Royce have to do for these men when she got to the locations and

Royce just shrugged and said "mostly posts from the places, whatever, nothing crazy."

The packages kept arriving on Shosh's doorstep. Each filled with five or six outfits. Royce, though she needed Shosh on-call 24/7, allowed her new employee one day off per week, typically a Friday. These days, Royce told her, were important for her own mental wellbeing and that she would typically go technology-free on these days. In the short amount of time Shosh had been with Royce, she never called her at a weird hour of the night, nor did she ever contact her on Fridays. She encouraged Shosh to "be her own woman on Fridays" and to "experience all that New York City has to offer." The fact that Shosh had been experiencing the sights and sounds of New York City for almost as long as Royce had been alive didn't matter. In Royce's fifteen short years on the planet, she had already amassed a variety of experiences that made Shosh's own seem childish in comparison.

Abda and Royce took the occasional appointment with women who spent a fortune for an hour of their time. Most of these appointments were set up through Irwin Agencies and involved women coming to Royce's apartment for one-on-one counseling or sessions with Abda where the two women would disappear into Royce's bedroom for an hour at a clip for a "healing panel" involving Abda's superfood-juice, followed by encouragement and words from Royce and then an "empowerment ritual," which was essentially a feminist/fertility take on chanting. Shosh was never allowed in the room during these sessions, but from time to time she found herself pressed to the door, eavesdropping, listening for any clue as to what "empowerment" meant to Royce and Abda. The room was silent, soundproofed, no doubt, but Shosh could sometimes make out the chanting as a low hum. She didn't think much of it after a while, and she felt that Abda and Royce, though they were charging a fortune for their time, were actually helping these women who showed up for these sessions. Many were repeat clients, some were one-offs, but they all left the apartment smiling and looking refreshed.

Shosh found herself oddly protective of Royce. Over the course of a few short weeks, she began looking at Royce as a friend, more than just a boss. Royce didn't act much like a boss, except when she had a tantrum of sorts, or a meltdown over what to wear for a particular video or selfie.

Still, things were off with her new job. Royce had a tendency to walk around nude, showing off her overly developed body whenever she could. Shosh, one morning, had entered the penthouse from the elevator and found the girl on the balcony, sans clothing, looking through the telescope. She seemed frantic most mornings, as though awakening from a nightmare and searching for some kind of escape. Mornings were confusing for Royce, as though she hadn't had much of a clue as to where she was, what she did the night before, or what she had to do, day-to-day. That fell under Shosh's job description, anyway.

Shosh inquired often about Inge, who was scheduled to return sometime the following month after being delayed due to family obligations in Germany. Shosh didn't pry any further, but she thought about the old woman often. Royce had commented that Inge was a "sweet kid" but couldn't "hang" anymore.

One night, Royce begged Shosh to stay late, and, having no reason to say no, as well as a contractual obligation to say yes, she did. They sat, watched *Mean Girls* (Royce's favorite movie), and talked about Shosh's high school experience. They ate pizza and relaxed and when Royce inquired about guys, Shosh changed the subject quickly. Royce often asked about Shosh's sex life, which always made her uncomfortable. She felt that maybe the child was trying to get a rise out of her, with all of her budding sexuality and comments about Shosh's private life.

"You never tell me anything juicy," Royce said, turning her attention back to the movie. "I always tell you everything, and you never give me anything back."

"I'm sorry, I just don't know that I should, you're --" Shosh started, then trailed off.

"What? Your *boss*?"

"No, you're a *kid*. It's awkward to talk about that stuff with a kid," Shosh admitted.

"Well, technically, as your boss, I could order you to tell me *everything*. I could order you to do whatever I want, right? It's in the contract."

Shosh thought about this. She supposed Royce was right. "I guess so, yeah."

Royce seemed annoyed. Shosh hadn't really seen her annoyed before. Something dark came over her face, the glow of the high definition TV casting light on the girl. "Maybe I should act more like a boss. I dunno. Inge did whatever I wanted, whenever I wanted, so, I dunno. I knew Inge's entire dating history, which wasn't much, but still, she gave me the juicy *deets*, you know?"

Shosh just sat there and stared at her. Royce's face relaxed, as though a revelation hit her.

"Shosh, stand up," Royce said, rising suddenly.

She did. Standing next to Royce, she felt pretty bad about herself. In her twenties and nowhere near as developed as this fifteen year old, it was almost unfair. Royce stood next to her, and grabbed her hand.

"What're you --?"

Without warning, Royce forced Shosh's hand onto her own breast. When Shosh recoiled in fright, Royce laughed. "Gotcha! Titty grabber!" Royce collapsed back onto the couch, laughing hysterically. Shosh just stood there, frozen, confused about what just happened.

"What the *fuck*?"

"That's the first time I heard you say the f word! Say it again!"

Shosh just stared at Royce, confused and disturbed. "Royce, please don't do that again, that was really inappropriate."

Royce stopped laughing. She stared at Shosh. "I'm sorry, Shosh. I just get carried away, sometimes, you know that. Sit down and watch the movie. Do you wanna order some ice cream or something?"

"Well, I mean, I could go get it if you like. I could use some fresh air anyway, if that's okay?"

"Yeah, yeah, fresh air, good thinking, Shosh, you're the best, I love that about you. Head to the shop on the corner, tell them it's on my account, they know the deal. I'd love some coconut-vanilla gelato. Is that cool? Get whatever you want, I don't care, anything."

Shosh grabbed one of Royce's hoodies and left the penthouse. While she walked down to the corner store, she thought about what had happened. *Royce was a disturbed young girl, taken advantage of repeatedly by so many people, she didn't really know how to act, right?* Shosh kept reasoning that because Royce had essentially grown up in front of a screen her entire life, and that eyes had been on her from the time she was twelve years old (possibly younger), that Royce didn't have a grasp on what was okay to do and what was unacceptable. Maybe this would be something they could work on together? Maybe make Royce a more rounded human being and not just an object of desire for creeps on the Internet?

When Shosh got to the corner store, she ordered the gelato, and when she told the clerk behind the counter who it was for, he threw in a few extra items from around the store, including snacks, a six pack of beer, and strawberries. "Please tell her Saul says hi," the clerk begged/asked Shosh as she left.

***

After two months of working for Royce, Inge still hadn't returned. When Shosh was at the apartment, Royce was as inappropriate as ever, but she hadn't touched (or rather, made Shosh touch *her*) since the incident previously. Royce's grades were good, steadily on the rise, and her ability to speak upon the natural and ancient wonders of the world came easily to her. She would often write detailed pieces, culled from hours of research, with almost in-depth, on-location accounts of historical events, like the eruption at Pompeii, or the sacking of Troy, or the destruction of Hiroshima.

Shosh loved listening to Royce read her material, as she often injected as much of herself into her work as possible. The girl was becoming a fairly remarkable performer in these moments together, and though Shosh had commented as much, Royce said that she didn't see much of a future in acting or performing of any kind, since everything she ever wanted she already had courtesy of YouTube, Instagram, and other social media outlets.

Shosh had a hard time keeping up with all of the messages Royce received. She also grew numb to the variety of nude photos the young girl received on a day-to-day basis, not only from men, but from women, as well. Over time, images of male and female sex organs became as regular to Shosh as grading Royce's essays and other work.

Royce and Shosh enjoyed their time together over those few months, with Shosh exposing Royce to things like transcendental meditation, which helped with Royce's attention deficit disorder. The girl wasn't diagnosed or anything, but Shosh recognized the signs, having seen it in hundreds of children during her teaching career. Royce didn't believe in traditional doctors or medication, instead she relied on "healing stones" and essential oils, things Shosh regarded as absolute nonsense. But with the vigor and health that Royce displayed day to day, it seemed to work for her, so Shosh kept her mouth shut.

The one area of health that Royce seemed deficient in was her breath. Shosh had noticed on more than one occasion that the girl's breath was like a freshly struck match, that sulfur-y egg-like scent, potent with burnt ozone. Royce chewed tons of gum and consumed mints like they were nothing. It worked for the most part, but every once in a while, mostly during their studies when Shosh was right next to the girl and Royce was focused on her work, the smell lingered. It didn't fit with Royce's image and health-guru lifestyle at all. The girl was remarkably clean, brushing and bathing multiple times a day, but for some reason, the offensive odor lingered in her mouth. Royce herself often smelled like fresh fruit, or sweet oils, so the breath thing really stuck out to those in close proximity.

Shosh also exposed Royce to "new" music like Fleetwood Mac, Air Supply, and more. The girl especially took to Fleetwood Mac and started incorporating a mix of their greatest hits into her daily routine. She wondered if she could ever get Stevie Nicks into one of her videos, but her ADD always diverted her focus to something else within a few minutes. Shosh got a kick out of Royce calling classic rock "new," because all Royce seemed to listen to was modern mumble-rap or soulful songstresses having "a moment."

***

One evening, at one of Royce's raucous parties, a young "influencer" made a pass at Shosh, telling her she looked like the oldest sister in a band called Haim and that he had to "know her" and "understand her light," which were things Shosh never imagined real humans ever said in person, only on YouTube or on Instagram, but nevertheless, here was such an instance. Shosh, more annoyed than flattered, rebuffed the young man's advances. He got upset and told her how he could take her to Taiwan or Taipei or Thailand whenever she wanted to go, and then he stormed off, disappearing into one of the clusters of colorfully attired guests in the apartment.

During the party, Shosh had lost track of Royce but eventually found her in a bathtub, smoking a joint and playing Fleetwood Mac on her iPhone for a group of kids all checking their Instagram and Twitter feeds. Royce, even though the bathtub had no water in it, stood, somehow soaking wet, and hugged Shosh. "They're loving this, Shosh, absolutely *loving* this!" the girl exclaimed, with Shosh spotting exactly zero evidence that anyone in the room was paying attention to Lindsey Buckingham's vocals.

Shosh had slipped into one of the guest rooms to change her clothes, the loudness of the party muffled. As she slid her top and then her jeans off, in the stillness and quiet of the room, she looked in the mirror at herself. In her examination, she discovered a gray hair. The first of what she would imagine to be many. Her father had gone gray when he was twenty-five, and her mother had been coloring her hair since she was in her early thirties, so Shosh knew the color of her luscious dark hair would begin vanishing soon. Just not *so* soon. And not while she was working for a child whose only job was to look cute and stylish.

In that moment of examination, Shosh suddenly felt eyes on her. She turned and saw nothing. The room was surprisingly empty and quiet, considering the party going on outside. Shosh often napped in this particular room while Royce was out at a photoshoot or interview or awards show. The cool, crisp air from the open sliding glass window washed over her body, and she shivered. She walked out onto the balcony overlooking the city. She felt brave, standing there in her mismatched panties and bra, her skin still cool from the wetness of the hug Royce gave her earlier. This guest room was on the opposite side of the main patio where the party was going on, so Shosh had at least a modicum of privacy away from everyone and everything.

The city sparkled around her, and Shosh thought back to her younger days of exploring it. Finding herself at bars with her friends way later than she ever expected, and the various fleeting romances she found. The kinds of things Royce would ask about, sexual experiences, Shosh's body, etc. She would sometimes catch Royce staring at her, sizing her up, Shosh often thought, and would half-jokingly call Royce a "creep," which always made the girl laugh.

Shosh started feeling self-conscious standing on the small balcony in her underwear, but she also felt a rush of freedom. She wondered if this was the freedom Royce often felt, traipsing around the apartment without wearing underwear and not ever giving a shit about who was looking. Shosh had asked Royce why she never wore anything under her clothes, and Royce said she wasn't ashamed of her body, to which Shosh replied "that's not the point, you're a young woman, society doesn't --" but Royce's attention had shifted by that point, so Shosh gave up.

Standing on the balcony, the cool air on her skin, Shosh felt unashamed of her body. She wasn't young anymore, not like Royce, and even with the discovery of a gray hair, she felt *good*. Working for Royce was maybe having a positive impact on her emotional and spiritual well-being, as well as the obvious positive impact on her debt. The gray hair was a natural thing, not due to stress or worry. Her mother often joked that her grays were caused by Shosh being a "little stinker," a term Shosh sometimes found herself using to refer to Royce, which always made the young influencer giggle.

Eventually, Shosh stepped back into the guest room and put on some spare clothes she had in a drawer. A pair of cutoff jeans, a hoodie with Elvis Costello's face, the words "Trust" in script next to his head. Royce had bought Shosh the hoodie after Shosh gave her a lesson on the importance of the two Elvises, Presley and Costello.

***

About a week after the party, Royce received an invitation from a Saudi oil magnate, inviting her aboard his yacht for a few days of sailing around off the coast of South America. The magnate, who was in his sixties, was worth more than a few small countries combined, and his yacht was the largest boat Shosh had seen to that point in her life, other than the Carnival cruise ships she sometimes spotted floating down the Hudson.

Royce demanded Shosh come on the trip, even though Shosh expressed exactly zero interest in tagging along. Royce said it would do her some good, so they flew to South America and boarded the magnate's yacht. He spoke in perfect English about the various features his ship had to offer, but Shosh was too enamored with the lodgings aboard to listen. The bedroom provided was bigger than her bedroom back home in New York, and it was across the hall from where Royce would be staying.

Shosh was curious about what Royce had to *do* to be on the boat, as there was no formal contract outside of a suitcase filled with cash that was handed off to the representative from Irwin Agencies, the same one who connected Shosh to Royce. He didn't seem to recognize her at first, but when Shosh reminded him of who she was, his brow furrowed and he gave her a knowing nod. He smiled and shook her hand, and told her how great a job she'd been doing. "And between you and me, the girl loves you," he said before Shosh and Royce boarded the boat.

Royce spent most of her time taking selfies and posting videos from the deck of the boat, with Shosh often nearby. The magnate had seemingly vanished, leaving the two ladies alone to enjoy the sun, the ship, and be catered to by the competent and attentive staff. Every morning there were iced coffees (*light and sweet for my girl, here*, Royce told the staff, in reference to Shosh) and a full breakfast of fresh fruit, yogurt, and more waiting for them in the dining room. Shosh inquired about where the magnate had gone, and the staff assured her he was still on board, but attending to business.

Shosh and Royce had some adventures when the yacht would dock for a few hours at various ports up and down the east coast of South America. Royce would indulge her followers with food from the locals, or some of the beautiful sights along the way. Shosh sometimes served as photographer, something she had gotten used to and pretty good at. Royce's social media presence didn't follow her to South America, and she often found herself anonymous among the crowds, whereas it was pretty difficult for her to leave the apartment in NYC.

The magnate had started appearing more often, typically with a few of his assistants, all female, with him at all times. Mostly he wanted to check in and see if Shosh and Royce needed anything, and asked Royce about how his account was with Irwin Agencies, something Royce assured him she knew nothing about. Shosh noted how the magnate's hand would often linger on Royce's shoulder, which the girl didn't seem to mind, but Shosh certainly did.

Shosh and Royce were more like sisters on this trip than ever before. She didn't want to ruin the trip with lessons for her charge, so she instead focused on their diving into local culture between meals and drinks on the yacht. Shosh had given up on trying to stop Royce from indulging in alcohol and the occasional drug, and the two often wrapped up each night on the yacht with a joint on the deck of the ship. Shosh was at first shocked to find her cares (or were they morals?) slipping away, but she chalked it up to the notion of freedom and spirit that Royce had been imparting to her in their time together.

"The past few months have been pretty sweet, right?" Royce asked one night on the boat.

"For sure. Your lessons have been coming along great, too," Shosh said. "You're an impressive kid, Royce."

"Thanks, babe. You're pretty impressive, too," Royce said, hugging Shosh. They finished the joint and flicked it into the ocean.

That night, Shosh lay in bed, unable to sleep. She worried it was something she ate keeping her up, the local food wreaking havoc on her system, maybe too much sun, something. She felt a little queasy, her heart racing, sweat soaking the sheets. Shosh had been sleeping nude on the boat, leaving her windows open for the fresh sea air, and the door to her cabin locked. She wasn't used to sleeping nude, but she found it necessary on the boat, considering how warm the nights could be and how the air conditioning had a tendency to click off on its own during the night.

As she lay there, she heard a rhythmic noise from outside her door. Rising slowly, she slipped on a pair of shorts and a tank top and entered the hallway. Checking, she couldn't see anyone, but she could still hear the noise. Muffled and rhythmic, the steady hum could still be heard. Shosh walked down the hallway and couldn't find any of the staff nearby, but she did pick up the faint machinery hum of the yacht's engine.

Walking back to her cabin, she heard the rhythmic noise again and turned to face where she realized it was coming from - Royce's cabin across the hall.

Stepping forward, Shosh braced her ear to the door and listened carefully. Still muffled, she could hear what she thought were voices, but nothing in English. She reached for the door handle and slowly turned it, realizing how Royce never seemed capable of locking a door, even at the apartment. Shosh slowly looked into the room, the sound growing louder.

Once in the room, which was nearly identical to her own, she looked toward the source of the sound: the bedroom. Inside, on the bed, in the darkness, something writhed and twitched in the moonlight. Shosh struggled to make out what it was through the small slit between the door and the frame, and as she crept closer, she felt her bare feet step into something wet and sticky. Pausing to look down, a sudden grunt startled her, and looking up again, she could barely make out Royce's face in the mass of what looked like flesh and moisture on the bed. The sound reminded Shosh of oatmeal, wet and mushy, being sloshed around in a bowl. The smell that hung in the air was musky and fragrant with fruit and flowers.

Taking a slow, sticky step closer to the slit in the door for a closer look, she tried to see in the dark, but could only make out

Royce's hair dangling over the side of the bed, a mass of flesh swarming her, seemingly devouring her.

Shosh's eyes adjusted in the darkness and her mind started piecing together what she watched the best it could - Royce on her back, seemingly pressed down by what could only be described as a massive tongue, or what she *thought* was a tongue, connected to a pair of shoulder blades. She thought she could make out hands gripping the bed, to the side of Royce's head, they looked elephant-like, massive and bunched with brown flesh. The only distinguishable feature was Royce's hair. She could just barely make out the girl's face in the mound of flesh retching and shaking on the bed.

Eventually, Royce's face emerged fully from beneath a sheet of thick meat. She looked sweaty, in a daze, her face slick with fluid. The girl gasped for air, chewing on something unseen. Her eyes were dark, a hazier shade of the normal bright gold-brown they usually were.

"More, I need more," Royce purred, thrusting herself into the mass. The flesh swarmed her face and in an instant, Royce was gone again, her hair dangling over the side of the bed.

Shosh, not knowing what to do, backed out of the room, her hands over her mouth. Her head suddenly erupted into the worst headache she'd ever experienced, and she found her way above deck, to a bathroom, hand braced on the wall of the slightly rocking vessel.

She sat on the toilet and felt her bowels begin to stir. Emptying the contents of the evening's dinner into the bowl, she replayed the images of Royce in her mind over and over again. Eventually, she cleaned herself up and stumbled back to her own room to lie down.

Shosh, in bed, listened for the sounds coming from Royce's room, but heard nothing. She was disoriented and confused, and she imagined that what she saw was impossible. *What was Royce doing? What was that?* As she thought, she felt the energy drain from her body and, eventually, she fell asleep.

She dreamed of Royce's body. Or at least, that's what it was at first. From images of the girl being attacked by that *thing*, to a flurry of sweaty flesh and mouths flickering open, tongues jutting out, teeth biting hard into brown flesh, blood emerging. Shosh awoke with a start, remembering the dream vividly. Flesh, sweat, teeth, and tongues, but no distinguishable features beyond that. The rhythmic sound of body on body contact. She found the sickness returned to her bowels at the thought, but she remained in bed until it passed and she fell back to sleep.

***

The following morning, Shosh was drinking coffee and looking out over the horizon as the ship glided silently. She stared at the wake behind the boat and watched the crew go about their business. She heard a yawn behind her and knew instantly that it was Royce.

"Hey girl," she said, hugging Shosh from behind. "Sleep okay?"

"Uh-huh."

"That's good. What's for breakfast?"

"Listen, I'm just gonna come out and say it … I saw you last night," Shosh said, a moment of hesitation in her voice.

Royce stared at her. There wasn't a hint of embarrassment on the young girl's face. Her cheeks didn't redden, in the way other teens Shosh had caught doing something they shouldn't have been doing during her time as a teacher had.

"Creeping on me while I sleep?" Royce finally asked, giggling and looking away, toward the water.

"Royce, you're a child, what I saw was rape," Shosh said, placing her coffee cup on a small round table. The word hung in the air between them. *Rape.* "We have to tell someone, what *was* that *thing*? You can tell me."

Royce laughed. "Rape? What're you talking about? I went to bed the same time you did last night, watched some Bella Thorne Netflix movie and fell asleep."

Shosh just stared at her. "I saw you, Royce, you can tell me if something happened."

Another laugh. "Shosh, you're a riot."

"I don't --"

Royce pressed a finger to Shosh's lips. "Let's go get some breakfast, babygirl!"

At breakfast, Shosh leaned against the deck rail of the boat. Royce put her head on her shoulder and leaned as well. The girl nuzzled into Shosh's shoulder as much as she possibly could. She loved the feeling of Royce snuggling up to her. Like a puppy getting comfy in your lap, a feeling of comfort and warmth flooded Shosh's body.

***

They spent the remainder of the trip together as much as possible. Shosh kept a close eye on Royce. For the most part, they didn't see much of the magnate the rest of their time on the boat, and the few times they did, he was on the phone, flanked by his assistants. The assistants didn't pay much attention to Shosh and Royce, and they were often on their phones, as well, speaking Farsi or occupied with their iPads.

That was part of the problem for Shosh. She didn't know if what she saw was real. By all evidence, it hadn't actually happened. Royce wasn't the kind of girl to lie about her sexual history. She had discussed things with Shosh that no teenage girl should know about, but Shosh's every thought contained the images of Royce in bed with *something* preying on her. Over time, the images became hazy, and Shosh started feeling that maybe Royce was right and that she dreamed the whole thing up.

The nightmares of flesh, mouths, and teeth kept coming back to her, though, and that was the worst part. The dreams weren't of a sexual nature anymore, but of rhythmic, sweaty *consumption*. Flesh and teeth and moisture, making her sick upon waking up from each nightmare. A deep sickness, in her bowels, as though her insides had been corrupted through her psyche's ability to obscure the events or illusion of what she saw that night.

***

Once they got back to New York, Shosh and Royce resumed their homeschooling, focusing on contemporary literature, something Royce showed little interest in. They often debated the merit of modern literature, talking at length about how social media is the new "great American novel," a point of view that Shosh at first considered silly, but as Royce made her points about the visuals matching up and creating beauty the way Kerouac's writing could, Shosh had to consider the young girl's point with greater weight. Royce understood that modern society was primarily visual, the shared instant gratification of liking a photo on Instagram replacing book clubs and literature circles.

Shosh eventually filed the incident on the boat away as fantasy, a dream brought on by her feeling sick that night. A fever dream of sorts, brought on by the heat, the rocking of the boat, and the food.

***

Whenever she was around Royce, as professional as their relationship was, there was still the needling of desire deep in Shosh's being. Over time, she tried to rationalize it as wanting to have that same free-spirited nature that this young girl already seemed to have, that her sexuality was a commodity of sorts, but that wasn't how Shosh was raised. Her parents instilled the notion that sex was meant to be special, that you only did *the deed* (that's what her dad called it) with someone who *meant* something to you. While there was plenty of time to explore this notion in college, Shosh only slept with two guys, one of which was her first real boyfriend, the other, a drunken encounter after a night of partying. Since then, Shosh had primarily focused her attention on work, which left little time for dating and sex. She never imagined herself with another woman, either, so the thoughts and images of Royce that flooded her brain at night confused her even more.

One afternoon, Shosh found her mind wandering, listening to Royce read Marc Antony's speech from *Julius Caesar*, act three, scene two. She thought about Royce's parents, and wondered where they were and if they knew about Royce's trips with rich men and women all over the world.

"Where are your parents?" Shosh asked, breaking Royce's concentration.

"What?"

"Your parents. I was just thinking that you never really talk about them. And you haven't mentioned them since your early videos on YouTube. I was looking at some of your older stuff the other day."

"God, that's embarrassing, I probably looked like a drowned rat, black, frizzy hair everywhere, a dumb guitar in my lap or some shit," Royce said, laughing.

Shosh smiled, thinking about Royce's early work, covering pop songs by Taylor Swift, Katy Perry, and others. "Your old stuff is cute, it's who you are."

"*You're* cute! Why do you ask about my folks? I text them and email them, but they know I'm busy doing my *thang*, so they don't visit or call too much."

"What do they think of your lifestyle, like, how do they feel about having a famous daughter?"

Royce's expression changed. A slight hint of sadness crawled its way across her face. "Fame to them is the movies, or like, a singer. They're not exactly social media-friendly. I didn't mention them too much in those older videos because they were pretty religious, and like, they really monitored me a lot, online and in school, very restrictive, you know?"

Shosh nodded.

"Social media, to them, was just a way to get into trouble, which of course, I did. I was bullied by kids in school. They shared an early video of me singing that Grimes song, you know the one. Where she sings about being attacked or whatever."

"I don't know that one," Shosh said, hanging on Royce's every word.

"Here," Royce said, opening Spotify.

The two listened to Grimes sing about being approached on a dark night and attacked by someone she didn't know was following her. Grimes' lyrics hung beautifully in the room, the sweet high pitch of her voice reverberating around, dancing through the corridors of the huge apartment. Shosh couldn't help but bob along to the song, despite knowing its dark origins.

"I loved that," Shosh said when the song ended. "I don't remember seeing that video on your YouTube."

"I deleted it. Once the kids in school found it, they ate me alive. I went home that night and took a bunch of pills, tried to kill myself. The kids in school said I was an 'attention whore' and that I couldn't sing, which of course, I couldn't, but I was just exploring, you know? I was trying to figure my shit out, I was just a *kid*."

"You're *still* just a kid, Royce," Shosh said.

"Yeah, but now I'm a kid with millions of dollars, that sorta' makes me an adult, I think," Royce said, the two of them laughing. "But yeah, I went home and took a bunch of NyQuil, which, I don't know, I thought it would kill me, but I remember waking up in the ambulance. I pissed myself. The only thing I remembered from being unconscious was like, an eclipse-looking thing. Like a sun blacked out by the moon or whatever."

"What do you mean?"

"I asked the doctors what it was, and they said it was just the neurons in my brain firing, my body fighting off the medicine I took," Royce said. "They didn't really know. Doctors, in my experience, know jack-dick about anything, by the way. My throat could be exploding and they'd say it was from a lack of vitamin D."

"What happened after you tried to kill yourself?"

"My parents home-schooled me. If you notice, I hadn't posted for like, a while between a couple videos. It was around that time I was home, recovering or whatever," Royce said. "The kids at school, some of them felt bad, but most didn't and still fuckin' bullied me and talked shit on my videos when I started uploading again."

"Haters gonna hate," Shosh said.

"Facts, baby doll," Royce said, high-fiving Shosh. "But whatever, they're a bunch of shitty upper middle class kids worried about acne, school dances, and Adderall, and I'm a successful, cool, famous chick living in New York City with my wifey Shoshana, going on boats with rich Arab guys whose names I don't know, and having parties with people who are exactly like me, but vape way more than me, so, who's laughing now?"

Shosh stared at Royce, noticing more of the sadness in her face. Royce leaned forward and kissed Shosh on the cheek.

"What was that for?"

"Because, you're just like, the best ever. No one ever listened to me tell that story, not even Inge, so, I appreciate you asking," Royce said. "Can we watch a movie?"

Shosh and Royce spent the rest of the night watching old John Hughes movies, which Royce hadn't seen before. When Molly Ringwald and Andrew McCarthy got together at the end of *Pretty in*

Pink, Royce cried. By the time they got to *Some Kind of Wonderful*, Royce had fallen asleep on Shosh's shoulder, which had become a normal occurrence. Shosh snuggled up to her and dozed off.

That night, Shosh's dreams were filled with images of the blacked-out sun, tendrils of white light swarming out from around it in a perfect circle. She heard Royce's voice in her head, whispers, detailing parts of the story she told her, over and over. *Whose names I don't know. But most didn't. Ate me alive. Attention whore.*

When Shosh woke up the next morning, on the couch, Royce was gone. She looked around the apartment and couldn't find the girl anywhere. In the kitchen, Shosh found a note letting her know that she had a podcast interview and had to head out early. She said to make herself comfortable, take a shower, and to "put on something cute," because Royce was taking her to lunch that afternoon.

Shosh followed her boss' orders and took a shower, using Royce's body wash, shampoo, and more. She hesitated when it came to using her loofa but used it anyway. Everything smelled sweet, candy-like, the way Royce always smelled. She went into the guest room, wrapped in a towel, and went through the drawers, going through the spare clothes she left at Royce's. She pulled out a pair of cutoff jean shorts and a tank top, but she couldn't find any of the underwear she left at Royce's. The bras and panties were all gone. Most of them were gifts from Royce, and certainly not cheap, so Shosh was curious where everything went. She searched the guest room top to bottom, but couldn't find them. She thought maybe the laundry people got her stuff mixed with Royce's, but when she checked Royce's drawers and closets, Shosh became overwhelmed by the sheer volume of couture on hand and gave up. Shosh was also surprised to see that Royce didn't seem to own a pair of underwear or any bras at all. Shosh wasn't used to not wearing undergarments, so the feel of denim on her bare skin felt alien to her. Thankfully, the tank top was more of a sleeveless t-shirt, and after checking herself in the mirror for longer than necessary, she determined that no one would be able to see any part of her body in the tank, bra or no bra.

At lunch, Royce talked about the interview and mentioned that she was asked to be a guest judge on *Project Runway*, a show she watched religiously. Shosh had never seen it before starting to work for Royce, but she had found it entertaining, and it made for mindless watching while she worked on lessons and material to cover with her student for the following weeks.

"Do you know what happened to the underwear I left in the guest room?" Shosh asked, sipping her iced tea.

"I threw them out, girl, they were so lame and some were super-ancient," Royce said, giggling.

"You should've told me, I went looking for them today and couldn't find any, plus, you bought most of them for me, so, they're not that old."

"I'm sorry, my darling, can you *ever* forgive me?" Royce playfully asked, batting her eyes and cracking Shosh up. "What do you want to do tonight?"

"Well, we have some material to cover, I'd like to get into some more poetry and --"

Royce rolled her eyes and started snoring dramatically. "Shosh, let's take a break from that shit, let's do something *fun* for once!"

This girl's entire life is fun, Shosh thought. "What would you like to do?"

"Let's go dancing! I know this great little hipster place, they serve watermelon water year-round, it's totally gross but I love the little red balls floating in the glass!"

"I'm not much of a dancer, Royce, but we can go if you want to," Shosh said.

"I refuse to believe you're not a good dancer, with those hips, you were born to shake that ass, and you know it!"

Shosh laughed. "If you could've seen me at the eighth grade dance, you wouldn't be saying that."

"I didn't even get to go to an eighth grade dance, so, I'd *love* to see that, without question," Royce said, laughing. "We'll head back to the apartment, put on some fun stuff, find some granny panties for you, tape those knockers down, and we'll go, sound good?"

"I don't wear granny panties," Shosh said, quietly.

"Not right now you don't," Royce laughed, putting her hand on Shosh's thigh. "You slut!"

Shosh slapped Royce's hand away and the two laughed. Shosh had, in some ways, gotten used to Royce's overly tactile way of teasing. While it made Shosh a little uncomfortable, she chalked it up to Royce being a bit awkward socially, and unable to recognize someone's personal space. This was sometimes a common trait among students who had a kind of developmental issue, and it wasn't the worst Shosh had ever seen. She had students with special needs who threw chairs and desks around the room, so an overly energetic teenager who would get touchy-feely in a weird way from time to time wasn't all that terrible. *Either way, inappropriate*, Shosh often thought, and was quick to correct Royce in one form or another.

The two spent the rest of the afternoon exploring book stores, getting iced coffees, and window shopping. Royce offered to buy Shosh everything that caught Shosh's attention, and the girl had to be talked out of it multiple times. Shosh came close to letting the girl buy her a first edition of *Jane Eyre*, but she couldn't let Royce do it. Royce seemed genuinely interested in the things Shosh loved, and it was this part of Royce's personality that Shosh loved about the girl. That inquisitiveness that appeared often, that thirst to understand and know Shosh that she couldn't find in others. It would be a lie to say that Shosh didn't often feel like Royce was becoming her closest friend, regardless of the age difference or employer-employee relationship. Shosh's own friends, who she had seen less of since starting this new job, were caught up in their own lives, getting engaged, having kids, moving to Long Island and buying houses that didn't seem to be worth the amount of money they all were paying.

***

At the apartment, Royce sprinted off into her room and demanded Shosh join her to try on outfits. The girl didn't always get the notion of privacy and certainly didn't see Shosh as a protective figure, more of a paid-for best friend. When Royce was in these hyper-energetic moods, Shosh often thought of the movie *The Toy*, where Richard Pryor is bought by a millionaire to entertain the rich man's young son. Royce's immaturity made it easy to write off her behavior, because it was evident to Shosh that the girl was possibly bipolar, with intense highs and extreme lows.

Shosh attempted to explain to Royce that it was inappropriate for her to watch the young girl try on outfits, but Royce would have none of that. Shosh didn't spend much time in Royce's room, so she didn't realize that Royce had purchased a four panel screen divider, decorated with cherry blossom trees. Shosh sat on Royce's bed, which was a mess, as the young girl dipped behind the divider and re-appeared numerous times in different outfits for their "big night out."

The thing that surprised Shosh the most about Royce's room was the *smell*. There was a light aroma that she couldn't put her finger on. Royce always smelled great, and was very hygienic (other than her breath), so for there to be a stale, almost musky-rust aroma hanging in the air in the girl's room was alarming. Dirty clothes are one thing, but the heavy scent just didn't make sense to Shosh.

After the sixth outfit, Shosh checked her watch, and noted that if they were going to be getting dinner before going to the club, they'd have to get moving. Royce finally settled on an oversized white sweatshirt, the word *Magic* written in thick black lettering.

"Alright, I'm gonna go put something on, and we can get moving," Shosh said, rushing out of the room.

Shosh went to the guest room and when she walked in, there was an outfit laid out for her on the bed. A pair of black jeans, a red blouse, and a black bra. No underwear. *Thank God there's a bra, at least,* she thought. She slipped the outfit on and it fit perfectly. When she exited the room, Royce was rolling a joint on the couch. When she saw Shosh in the outfit, her eyes went wide.

"Shosh, holy shit, you look hot. You're one thousand percent going to get laid tonight."

"First off, that's gross, second, thank you. When did you put this on the bed?"

"I dunno', when we got home, I guess. I figured it'd be cute and comfy for you."

"It is, so, thank you. Ready to go?"

"Lemme' roast this bone first, you devil," Royce said, sparking the joint. "You wanna hit this?"

Shosh shook her head.

"Such a narc. I've got more, just in case you change your mind. Let's motor."

***

With that, the two headed downstairs and got into an Uber. The driver lectured the two girls on how important it was to follow their dreams, and Royce agreed with him, talking about how she never gave up on her fantasies of being a famous painter, and now she was. Shosh tried to hide her laughter at Royce's ability to bullshit with the guy, but he ate it up, believing every story and every take on color theory that Royce threw at him. Eventually, they arrived at the bar, Inanna, and went inside.

Wildly different than what Shosh imagined, the bar was filled with young people, bearded hipsters, girls feigning interest in the band playing a cover of "It's Only Natural" by Crowded House, most drinking brightly colored cocktails and speaking in hushed tones. Royce looked at home in the space, slipping into a corner booth and looking at the crowd of people around them. There was a small plaque that read "reserved" at their table, and when Shosh gestured to it, Royce stated "Only the best for my girl," and smiled.

A waitress came over and Royce ordered two watermelon waters, as well as a few small plates of food. The food that arrived was all stuff Shosh had never tried before, so, nervously, she sampled each one. Royce laughed, watching Shosh's face as she reacted to the foods, studying whether Shosh loved or hated whatever she was slipping into her mouth. Shosh ended up enjoying only one of the plates, a bowl of Indian-inspired meats and rice, which seemed to be the most familiar dish of them all. Royce refused to explain the dishes, insisting that Shosh "explore by taste only" and not be "influenced by names or labels."

Royce and Shosh spent the time eating, drinking watermelon water, which tasted way worse than Royce described, and talking about life. At a certain point, a wicker Chianti bottle showed up on the table as a gift from the owner of the establishment. About an hour into their dinner, the band wrapped up, and a DJ took over, playing songs from his MacBook. Royce's eyes lit up when the synth-pop song that had been droning on for the past five minutes shifted to a slower, rhythmic jam.

"Holy shit, I love this song, dance with me, Shosh, come on!"

The two had been drinking from the Chianti bottle for a while, and Shosh didn't put up much of a fight. She stood up, and the two took to the dance floor. They weren't the only ones, and soon even more people crowded around them. Shosh's entire body felt warm, a heady mix of whatever they were drinking and the sweet scent of Royce's shampoo filling her nostrils every time her long, dark hair whipped into Shosh's face.

As they danced, Shosh felt hands sliding around her waist. Turning her head slightly, she caught the handsome face of a guy she spotted earlier, standing at the bar with a friend. The friend had his arms around Royce, and they were pressed together tightly about two feet away. Shosh felt the handsome guy's hands begin roaming all over her, stopping at her waist and gripping her by the hips. Shosh turned and kissed him, the two locked together for a long time before Royce and the guy's friend shuffled over to them.

Shosh, in a state of overheated excitement, whatever was in the chianti bottle rushing to her head, turned and found herself kissing the friend. The handsome guy smiled and turned Shosh's face back to himself, kissing her again. *That's hot* said someone behind Shosh.

Another set of hands found their way to Shosh's hips, and she felt pressed between two people, both tall and strong. One set of lips found their way to the back of her neck, while the handsome guy's face pressed to her own, kissing her deeply.

Shosh turned, and found herself kissing the friend again. A hand slipped into the front of her jeans, working its way down. Shosh continued kissing the friend, finally disengaging and turning back to the handsome guy. She opened her eyes and let out a sigh of pleasure into his ear. She felt more kissing on her neck and turned again to kiss the friend. When she opened her eyes mid-kiss, she was shocked to see the friend standing behind whoever she was kissing.

Leaning back, she saw Royce, her face contorted in pleasure, arms wrapped around Shosh's waist. Shosh looked down and saw that it was, in fact, Royce's hand down the front of her jeans. She screamed and pulled away from the two figures, disappearing through the crowd, which resembled a blur of flesh, bathed in red light, faces barely visible. The only face that had any clarity was Royce's, and her eyes seemed to glow faintly yellow in the red light of the club.

Shosh smashed her way through the reddish hellscape and into the ladies' room. In the bathroom, sweaty and confused, she wiped her face with a wet paper towel and shook the cobwebs loose. A pounding at the door startled her and when she opened it, Royce was standing there, confused.

"What's going on, are you okay?"

"What the fuck, Royce? What were you doing?"

"Having a good time with two hot guys, what's the deal?"

"You know what the *deal* is, you were kissing me and … and … *touching* me," Shosh stammered, her body shaking.

"Shosh, I was at the bar when you were having fun with them on the dancefloor," Royce said. "Are you okay? You're all sweaty."

Royce reached for Shosh's forehead, but Shosh slapped her hand away. "Don't fucking touch me!"

"Shosh, I don't know why you're doing this, we were having a good time, just chill out."

"I want to go home right now," Shosh said.

"Okay, no problem, go meet me outside, I'll call the Uber."

***

Shosh stood outside the club, shivering and queasy. She replayed the incident over and over in her mind, and she couldn't shake the image of kissing Royce. *Was it Royce's hand that was touching her? Was it one of the guys? How long had she been waiting on the sidewalk? Where was Royce?*

Shosh took her phone out and called Royce. No answer. She texted her, and waited. Nothing. Frustrated, she started walking in the direction of Royce's apartment. Eventually, she hailed a cab and upon arriving at the Balaam, she used the penthouse code given to her by Inge so long ago, and went up to the apartment. Once there, she noticed how dark and empty the place was. Flipping on the lights, she walked through the apartment, looking for Royce. The girl was nowhere to be found.

Shosh made her way to the guest room and sat on the bed. She shivered, the cool air whipping through the apartment. She walked to the window and closed it, disrobing and heading into the guest bathroom along the way. She sat in the tub, the shower raining down on her, and eventually, sat longer, letting the room fill with steam. As she slipped on a pair of pink sweatpants and a t-shirt, Shosh lay in bed, the darkness and quiet of the apartment washing over her.

***

In her dreams, Shosh made love to the handsome guy from the club, then his friend, all while Royce stood nearby, watching. Shosh was turned on by the thought of another person watching her have sex with first one and then two men, but when the two men turned *into* Royce, the slurping and melding of flesh, teeth and hair, Shosh awoke, screaming.

"You okay?"

Shosh turned and found Royce lying in bed next to her, rubbing her eyes, waking up. "What-*why're* you here?"

"You were in here when I got home, Shosh, I wanted to snuggle and sleep, I hope that's okay ..."

"Royce, I - - I don't know what happened tonight, but I'm not feeling great and --"

"Shosh, it's okay, just snuggle up with me and fall asleep, we'll have breakfast in the morning and we can relax, okay? I'm sorry you're not feeling good," Royce said, her voice soothing and comforting Shosh's frazzled nerves.

Shosh pulled the blankets back over her, pushed her body closer to Royce's, and after a while the warmth of the two of them together lulled her back to sleep. She didn't have any nightmares; instead, she saw the blacked-out sun, the tendrils, the white swirls around it. It, too, was calming, in the same way Royce's words were, and there was a contentment filling Shosh's entire being while she slept that night.

***

The next morning, Shosh studied herself in the mirror, noting more gray hairs. She chalked it up to stress, but then she reflected on how relatively stress-free her life had been recently, outside of the bizarre nightmares or blackouts or whatever they were. She thought that maybe constant exposure to a "free spirit" like Royce was having a negative effect on her wellbeing, but she realized that, if this were, in fact, the case, then truly it was *Shosh* who was the problem, having had such an insulated life prior to meeting Royce.

She showered and got dressed, finding a fresh pair of jeans, brand new underwear, a bra, and top waiting for her when she stepped out of the shower and into the guest room. *That kid moves quick*, she thought, imagining Royce darting in and out of the guest room to lay out the clothes.

As she dressed, she heard what sounded like an exhale coming from the closet. Deep and slow, air escaping, providing relief to whoever let it out. The first thought that ran through Shosh's head was that Royce was watching her. She felt anger and betrayal welling up inside her, but she controlled it, measuring her movements and emotions as she slowly crept toward the closet.

"Hello?" Shosh opened the closet and peered inside. Nothing there. She moved some of the clothes around, but again, found nothing.

***

"You should take a few days, Shosh, I can manage without you, I'm just shooting the *Project Runway* thing, and the company will take care of getting me there and back," Royce told Shosh after Shosh informed her that she felt she was either getting sick or was feeling overworked or overly tired. Royce surprised her in that she felt that she was possibly overworked. The girl admitted that she knew working with her was a handful, and that she was amazed Inge lasted as long as she did, and was happy with everything Shosh had done for her to that point.

Shosh was particularly moved when Royce admitted that she felt like the two were sisters. Shosh, an only child, had always wanted a sister, and in many ways, she found one in Royce. The recent nightmares that had been plaguing her were the only issues that had arisen between the two. Shosh thanked Royce for understanding that she needed some time, and told her that if she needed her, just call or text and she'd be there.

As Shosh left the apartment that afternoon, she thought she caught a hint of heartache in Royce's face. The same look had been there when Royce talked about her suicide attempt, and Shosh felt terrible about leaving the girl, but she knew she was tougher than she looked, even in that moment, with her looking like the saddest girl that ever lived.

Even with all the strangeness that had been happening between the two of them, Shosh still felt protective and had love in her heart for the kid. What started as glorified babysitting had turned into a relationship that bordered on sisterhood, regardless of their age difference. Shosh looked at Royce like a little sister, and even with the incident on the boat and the trouble at the club in her mind, Shosh hoped that some time away from the kid would help get her head on straight and allow her to do a better job. There wasn't much time left on her contract, and she wanted to make sure she finished strong, so there was no doubt in the company's mind that she had done a good job and earned her loan repayment.

Would I miss her? Shosh thought, during her trip on the Long Island Rail Road to visit her parents. *Would she miss me?*

Would going back to her normal life as a bartender or teacher or whatever be exciting after living the high life with Royce? Maybe she'd be able to keep the job after the repayment happened, considering how much Royce seemed to like her. *That kid loves me,* she thought, flicking through Royce's Instagram, reviewing pictures of the two of them on the boat and at other functions. In one picture, there was a smudge, and thinking it was on her phone screen, Shosh rubbed it, then licked her finger and rubbed it, but it remained. The smudge was over her own face in a picture she had seen earlier, perfectly clear. She wondered how an image could blur from one swipe of her phone then chalked it up to bad service as the LIRR darted through various Long Island towns.

***

After arriving at her parents' split-level ranch situated in one of Long Island's many cookie-cutter suburban paradises, Shosh sat at the dinner table with her father, a tall, handsome sixty-something who didn't quite understand what Shosh did for a living since starting to work for Royce. Shosh's mother, dramatically shorter than the father, big-hipped and lovely, told her friends and other family members that Shosh was a personal assistant to an actress, which was perfectly fine with Shosh. Her parents didn't really understand social media or the power it held over people, so, to explain who Royce was and explain how she has millions of people hanging on her every thought and word would've made her parents' heads spin.

"Kiddo, either way, we're proud of you and we're happy you're home," her dad said, pouring himself a glass of Scotch. He offered some to Shosh, and she toasted with him, smiling.

"Is that girl going to be in anything we can go see?" her mom asked, bringing over a bowl of assorted nuts.

"Nah, mom, she's more of a stage actress and artist, so, lots of off-Broadway stuff, I guess you could say," Shosh said, popping a Brazil nut in her mouth.

"You always steal all the Brazil nuts, leave some for me this time," her dad said, laughing.

Shosh's mom sat down next to her, and started playing with her daughter's hair. "Sweetie, look at you going gray so early," she said, her sweet voice masking her surprise as best she could.

"I know, ma', crazy right? Just kinda' started one day, more and more every morning, it seems," Shosh said, with a shrug.

"That's how it happens, kiddo. Your mother's been dyeing her hair for thirty years, so, you get it from her," dad said.

"I have not!"

Shosh couldn't help but laugh at her parents. She always admired how in love they seemed, no matter what happened. They did the best they could, raising Shosh in a good school district, while also sending her to Temple to learn the extensive history of the Jewish religion. Shosh didn't enjoy her religious studies much, but she appreciated that her parents wanted her to be in touch with her roots. Her dad toyed with the idea of being a rabbi in his youth, but when the opportunity to work for a local aerospace firm that was a primary economic provider and job creator on Long Island presented itself, Shosh's dad went to work and retired with a monstrous pension. Her mother worked part-time as a school secretary and clerk, so, money was never an issue. Shosh was lucky to be raised on Long Island, with two great parents, in a great town, but she also realized that she'd never be able to afford that same kind of life. That kind of life was no longer attainable, traded instead for the debt that forced her to work for a YouTube personality and led to early-onset gray hair.

"I think I'm gonna hit the hay," Shosh said, kissing her dad on his cheek, then, the same for her mom, before heading upstairs to bed. Her room looked largely how she left it, walls adorned with pictures of various boy bands, actors, and more. A *Dawson's Creek* poster hung over her bed, a red-taped heart around Joshua Jackson's youthful face. Shosh was, in fact, a Pacey-kind of girl, and she smiled to herself thinking of her teenage years obsessing about her crush.

She felt herself growing more tired and checked her phone.

Nothing from Royce.

Not that she had expected to hear from the girl. She knew she was busy with the *Project Runway* filming. Shosh was still a little bummed that the girl hadn't sent her a meme or message or anything. Usually, when they were apart, Shosh had a deluge of messages from Royce, with every little thought or desire that went through the girl's head. Shosh glanced out the window, at the moon, and felt more tired. Slowly, she began drifting off to sleep, and the moon, in the blurriness of her tired eyes, began to become milky in the dark sky, tendrils and swirls emerging from it, extending outward.

***

Shosh's eyes opened, but she couldn't move. The sky outside was red, the moon completely black. Instantly, she knew she was dreaming, but unlike most of her dreams, she was still in her room at her folks'. She tried to sit up and failed, her body completely locked in place. Shosh had never suffered from sleep paralysis before, so for it to suddenly hit her made no sense.

"Mom?" Shosh called, voice cracking. The sound wasn't her own, it sounded deeper, more guttural. Her own voice confused her.

Her eyes darted around, and in the corner, she saw a figure. Dark. Tall and thin. No discernible features, other than what looked like protrusions from its back, thick, heavy-looking, heavier than its body, an impossible difference between the two. On a normal person, the protrusions would weigh them down, whereas this being, this *figure*, swayed in the red light, effortlessly, gracefully, moving to a low hum somewhere in the room. The hum sounded almost like words: *ahhhst-as-as-sta-lay-dee-eve-st*

"Please …"

The figure moved, rather, *glided* toward Shosh. Its feet never touched the ground, and a tail, tracing the floor behind it, maintained only the slightest connection to the carpet in the bedroom. Shosh's eyes went wide as it moved closer. She tried to move again, but simply could not. The figure, now standing directly next to Shosh, stared at her. At this proximity, Shosh could make out eyes that looked like two black coals, light red cracks in them. No pupils, no definition. Cracks with red light coming from within. The words in the air seemed to take form:

Lady-ening-sta-

Shosh's body was filled with an intense feeling of dread. Every atom in her screamed to run from the room. Her fingers and toes twitched with adrenaline. The figure placed one three-pronged claw on her thigh. Its hand connected with her bare leg, radiating warmth, and almost immediately Shosh's body exploded with pain. The figure floated, with no sound, over her, staring directly into her eyes. Tears streamed from Shosh's face, and her throaty gurgles couldn't register anything louder than a harsh whisper.

The figure lowered on top of Shosh, and began tracing its claws all over her body. Shosh began twitching, crying, and screaming, but nothing came out. Her mind burned with the desire to push this thing off her and sprint from the room, screaming, but the paralysis had somehow gotten worse. Her toes could no longer wiggle, and her hands merely gripped the bedding tighter. The figure removed Shosh's clothing, and as Shosh began to tremor with adrenaline and fear, the entire room went black.

Eventually, Shosh saw the moon outside the window. It had returned to normal. Her face was streaked with tears, and a light numbness pulsed through her body. Her clothes were strewn on the floor, and she was nude. There were scratches on her thighs. A three-fingered hand print. She grabbed her phone and took a picture of the mark, but when she checked the photo, the print wasn't there. There was a tremendous soreness between her legs, running from her sex and up to her behind. She moved slowly, carefully, finding every movement painful, and looked in the full-length mirror.

In the mirror, after she flipped on the light, Shosh saw trails of blood from between the crack of her backside. Panic washed over her and when she turned to face the mirror, she saw bruises and hand prints all over her body. Another trail of blood led from the impossibly tender spot between her legs, down her right leg to her ankle. The panic began to fade and in its place, anger festered, with a healthy dash of confusion. She took multiple photos of her body in the mirror, and in each picture, there was no evidence of what she was seeing with her own eyes.

Shosh sat on the bed, slowly. The soreness radiated through her. Her mind raced, confused. The dream was awful, for sure, but the reality of what was happening to her body was far worse. A nightmare she could rationalize, like on the boat, but this, the blood, the bruises and the pain, with nothing visual to back it up. *Was she starting to lose her mind? Isn't it common knowledge that if one wonders if they're going crazy, then that automatically means they aren't?* The basic premise is that crazy people don't know they're crazy, they just believe they're sane. Shosh had thought multiple times through her life that she was crazy, and thus took that to be an indicator that she was, in fact, sane.

But this was different. She was seeing things that weren't there. *Feeling* them, too. She didn't know what to do about the pain. The discomfort of her every move was a sharp reminder of what had happened to her in the nightmare. What the figure did as she lay frozen was real enough that she woke up frightened, but to know that it was apparently *real* in every sense, was far worse.

***

The next morning, Shosh took a walk around her old neighborhood, thinking that the soreness would somehow wear off with a light jaunt. She didn't know if going to a doctor would be a good idea, and the bleeding had stopped somewhere between her sitting on the bed in shock and her shower that morning. The soreness and pain remained. It was Sunday, and the doctors' offices in her home town weren't open anyway. She thought about going to an emergency clinic or to the hospital, but they'd have her fixed for a straitjacket before she finished her story, so, she let the incident fester in her mind while she walked and decompressed. Every step resulted in a dull soreness that served as a reminder of the figure, the coal-black eyes with red cracks. The figure said nothing during their interaction, which may have been a blessing because Shosh couldn't imagine what its voice would sound like.

The bruises on her thighs and the rest of her body began to fade throughout the day. By lunch time, which she had with her parents on the back deck of the house, they had all but vanished. Bruises typically stayed with Shosh, her pale flesh remaining purple, then that awful yellow-black as they started to disappear. But these bruises, they didn't linger. The tenderness remained, though. Shosh's parents noticed how tired she seemed, and expressed concern a few times, but she assured them it was the quiet of the suburbs and that she wasn't used to it any longer, after living in the city for so long.

"City life will kill ya, kiddo," Dad told her, taking a bite of his bologna and cheese sandwich.

"The city's for the birds, sweetie, you should move back home, take some time to find a nice teaching job out here," Mom said. This was probably the eight thousandth time Shosh had heard her mom say this very particular combination of words, and each time, Shosh rolled her eyes and sometimes mouthed the last piece of the statement along with her mother. *Nice teaching job out here.*

Shosh would be returning to the city as soon as she could. As angry and upset as she was about the nightmare and the happening, she was missing the hectic vibe of being around Royce. She still hadn't heard from the girl, and she even thought about texting her the images of the bruises and more, but when they weren't there, she decided against it. That would just be her sending semi-nude photos to her boss, and that obviously was a terrible idea.

***

The Long Island Rail Road shuttled Shosh back into the city Sunday night, and when she got to her apartment there was an uneasy feeling. She crept around, checking every corner, and turning on every light, and even though the apartment was tiny and it would've been almost impossible for anyone to be hiding there, Shosh was very careful.

"You're losing it, kid," Shosh said to herself once all the lights were on and she was plopped on the couch. Her phone buzzed. Checking it, it was Royce, welcoming her back to "the city that never weeps," which Shosh was confused by but wrote off as Royce genuinely not knowing the phrase "the city that never sleeps."

Shosh turned on Netflix, took some Advil to dull the soreness that still lingered between her legs, and fell asleep on the couch watching a rerun of *Orange is the New Black*.

***

Royce had never smiled wider in all the time Shosh knew her. The kid was exploding with happiness at her return and Shosh realized that she had never had anyone react that way to her arrival or return ever before. She was both touched by the sincerity of Royce's missing her, and slightly annoyed that she hadn't heard from her during the few days she was away.

"Babygirl!" Royce exclaimed, nearly tackling Shosh as she stepped into the girl's apartment, which somehow seemed larger than it did before. Shosh seemed to notice a hallway that she didn't remember previously, a room at the end, orange light beaming from beneath the door.

"How was the taping?"

"*Project Runway* was fun, I ended up getting a fuckload of clothes for free, which is cool. I also got the number of one of the contestants, who I thought was gay, but turns out is just *very* into fashion. We're going to hang out this weekend, I think," Royce said, nearly tripping over her own words, she was going so fast.

Royce took Shosh's hand and guided her to the couch. They sat, cross-legged, across from each other. Royce refused to let Shosh's hand go. The girl's skin was soft, cool, comforting. Shosh missed that. Royce was wearing a Christmas sweater, even though the holiday was still months away. There were small LED lights twinkling on and off, which was distracting to Shosh at first, but after some time, seemed perfectly normal. "How are your parents? Still old?"

Shosh laughed, "They're old*er*, that's for sure. They're good, though. Thank you for asking. Did I miss anything else? Any word from Inge?"

Royce shook her head. "No way, Jose. I think she's staying in the mother country permanently. Which means, and, I was going to wait to mention this to you, maybe over dinner tomorrow, but I've been thinking."

Shosh stared at Royce. She had a feeling she knew what was coming, and she wouldn't know how to react to it once the girl made the proposal. There was excitement in Shosh's stomach, but also terror at the thought of being with Royce any longer than she needed. A job was a job, and her debt was practically gone, but still, the idea of being bound to this bizarre child made her anxious.

"I want to make an honest woman out of you, Shoshana," Royce started. She never called Shosh by her full name, so to hear the girl say it was truly strange. "I wanna put a ring on it. I want you to be my girl forever and a day, you know?"

Shosh smiled. The way Royce was talking to her made her blush, but also was weirdly inappropriate, even though she was kidding. "Royce, I --"

"Would you be interested in staying with me? I know I'm cray-cray, I know I'm annoying, I know that I'm just a dipshit teenager, but I'm someone who *needs* you. I've never felt that way before, Shosh, I've never *needed* anyone, but you, I *need* you. You're literally like an arm, or a heart or something, and I'm just the rest of the body. That sounded weird, didn't it?" The girl spoke quickly, her nerves and anxiousness getting the better of her. "That's why I didn't bother you during your trip to your parents, I was like, figuring my feelings out. I love you, Shosh, you're like my mom, my best friend, and my girlfriend all rolled into one Jewish person."

Shosh couldn't help but laugh at the girl. Royce thought about what she just said and laughed, too. They cackled in the apartment, and Shosh's eyes started tearing up. Nobody ever expressed their "need" for her before. She knew that Royce was a needy kid, but the reality was, any assistant could do what Shosh did for her. But she also knew that the opportunity to be Royce's assistant/teacher/friend was something that wouldn't come around again. Not in this lifetime. Boat trips with rich Middle-Eastern oil magnates, parties, expensive dinners, etc., often paid for by Royce's social media influence. This came around rarely, so Shosh felt the desire to stay with Royce, intoxicated with the potential future of leisure she could have with the girl.

"Is it okay if I think about it?"

Royce's smile faded. She nodded. "Yes, absolutely. Very prudent, m'dear. Take a day or two to think about it." The girl seemed genuinely hurt but did her best to hide it.

Shosh felt bad, as though she stabbed the girl in the heart. She knew that she'd probably end up taking the job, but she wanted to be thorough and check every box and every avenue before accepting.

"You okay?" Shosh asked, putting her hand on Royce's thigh.

Royce nodded. "Totes. Let's order a pizza or ten and watch *Mean Girls*."

***

Back at her apartment, her stomach full of pizza and head full of Tina Fey jokes, Shosh felt listless. The size disparity between her own meager apartment and Royce's palatial one was never lost on her. At her hand-me-down kitchen table, she started jotting down the pros and cons of staying with Royce. The pros easily outweighed the cons, but Shosh very consciously made note of her increased stress, bad dreams, and physical changes. The gray hair, the bleeding. She looked up causes for waking up bleeding from between the legs online, and found a few very real causes for it, one of which being basic hormonal changes, which Shosh tried to convince herself was the cause. It didn't explain the nightmares or the sleep paralysis, which she still hadn't told anyone about, and wasn't sure she ever would.

That night, Shosh dreamed of the boat. The tangle of flesh, meat, and teeth on the bed. Royce's face, her hair. The sweat and the smell that hung in the air. These images shifted into the black sky, the only source of light, the tendrilled moon, which resembled a blazing ball of hot light, not the sun, something larger, something more ancient and discordant. Shosh stood, in her dream, on the edge of a cliff in the heart of New York City. An impossible geography, the cliff resembling the street, with everything before it torn from the ground, as though a giant being had scooped the street up and tossed it away. Water pipes erupted, flowing into a dark abyss below her. The chill of the night made the tiny hairs on Shosh's arms stand up, and she realized that, not unlike her usual dreams of being nude and in high school, she was nude and standing in what would normally be a busy section of city.

Yet there was nothing around. No other people. No cars. Businesses were lit up, but empty. There was no sound. No honking of car horns, no sirens, nothing. The stillness and eerie calm of an empty New York City street wasn't lost on Shosh, and instead of dwelling on it, she cast her gaze skyward, at the ancient orb glowing, hanging, as though it was placed there by something much larger. A glowing sphere of a Christmas ornament, dangling for Shosh in the night sky. She weaved, standing alone on the precipice of the cliff. She took a tentative step forward and fell off, her body twisting and spiraling to whatever waited beyond the darkness.

***

She woke up on the floor of her bedroom. She hadn't fallen out of bed since she was a child, and yet, here she was, twisted in her sheets, face down on the floor. Shosh wondered where the stress was coming from, because even though the demands on her time with Royce were plentiful, at the end of the day, this job was a breeze compared to others she'd had. In the corner of the room, Shosh thought she saw the figure from her nightmare. She saw a flicker of light, and when she raised her head for a better look, there was nothing there. The familiar sulfur smell of a struck match hung in the air, confusing her even more. She stood up and looked around the room. Nothing out of the ordinary.

Hours later, Shosh sat at a small bistro in Tribeca, waiting for Royce. When the girl arrived, she was wearing a hoodie, heavy jacket, and jeans, her entire body covered, except her face. The hood of her jacket was fur-lined and framed her face perfectly. She had a pair of Ray-Bans on, and she looked very out of place at the trendy spot.

"You in disguise?" Shosh asked, chuckling.

"I'm *literally* freezing today. I think it's the cleanse Abda has me doing. I'm shitting my brains out. and I am just frozen solid. If I wasn't being paid to promote this shit, I wouldn't do it. Anyway, I'm sorry, enough about my icicle ass. What's good, babygirl? Did you decide to stay with me and make me the happiest girl on Earth?"

Shosh couldn't help but laugh at Royce's almost-frantic explanation and question. The girl was almost shivering, even bundled up. "I'm curious if you knew a good doctor. I've been having some issues lately, and I've been worried about finding someone discreet."

"Holy fuck, are you preggo? Do you need it scraped out of you? What happened? Who's the lucky almost-dad-to-be? Does he know? Is it too late for a scrape job?"

"Stop the clock, kiddo, no. I've just been having these … dreams, I guess? Nightmares, really. Scary shit, lots of darkness and ugliness. I can't really describe them," Shosh said, taking a sip of coffee, which was cooling down rapidly.

"Nightmares? Jeez, Shosh, I'm so sorry. I read once that our nightmares are tied to anxieties. I think I read that on Instagram, actually," Royce said, her voice lower, suddenly caring. "Of course I know someone. I'll text them right now."

Royce took her phone out and in an instant, Shosh had an appointment that afternoon. "Shosh, he's amazing. He's a shrink. He can prescribe pills. He'll do whatever you need. Teaches at NYU, I think. I don't remember. Some fancy school. You're all set and it's all taken care of."

Shosh smiled. She was amazed by the girl. Another check in the positive column: this girl could get things done at the drop of a hat. "Thank you, Royce."

"Don't mention it, babygirl. Just get your head on straight so you can keep working with me. I can't have you going off your rocker," Royce said, smiling, and taking Shosh's hand from across the table.

***

At the doctor's office later, Shosh sat on a large leather couch opposite Dr. Sunderland. He was in his fifties, handsome, his bald head encircled with clouds of wispy white hair, the last of what, according to the photos around the office, had been a proud mane at one time, from the looks of it, in the seventies.

Sunderland was Royce's go-to therapist, and so he was very familiar with Shosh, and knew quite a bit about her already, which, at first, was disquieting, but ended up being a time-saver.

"You had these nightmares while at your parents' house?" he asked, staring into Shosh's eyes. Shosh had difficulty keeping her eyes on his, as many people do. Eye contact wasn't a normal thing for her.

"Yes, sir," Shosh said, turning her gaze to the window, at a dove perched on the metallic gold railing. It pecked at a small mound of fur dangling lazily over the edge of the railing.

"Your debt is practically wiped out. Your job seems to be going okay, right? What stressors do you have outside of your time with Royce? A boyfriend or girlfriend?"

Shosh shook her head. "Nothing like that. My entire life sorta' revolves around my work. Has for years. Not much time for a social life. But even then, work isn't that difficult. You know Royce. Her life is essentially extended playtime."

Sunderland smiled. "Sure, but demands on one's time, in this case, *Royce's* time, as well as her *attention*, affects you, as her handler and teacher. What about your time with Royce do you find the most stressful? Are there aspects that are more influencing or stressing than others?"

"There was a moment when we were on a boat, not long ago, I thought I saw something. But I think I was hallucinating," Shosh said.

"Hallucinations? Were you on any drugs or did you drink anything that night?"

"No drugs, but a couple drinks. Nothing too crazy," Shosh lied, hiding the fact they smoked pot earlier that evening.

"What did you see?"

Shosh hesitated. Then, she realized she needed to be honest in order to make strides, so, she described the mass of flesh. Royce's face. The smell in the air. The feeling in her stomach. The doctor's stone-face reassured Shosh that he wasn't judging her, that he was listening to her insane ramblings. His eyebrows arched when she mentioned the figure in her bedroom at her parents' house.

"Would it surprise you to know that Royce is sexually active?"

Shosh shook her head.

"What if I told you she was a virgin? That she uses her sexuality and the innate desires of others to manipulate and maneuver in her chosen career or, her *field*?"

"She's a virgin?" Shosh asked, confused.

"It doesn't matter, my point is, I think what you saw on the boat was a combination of things. I think there was an element of being inebriated, for sure, but also that you had some form of food poisoning. Combined with possible sea sickness, and your stress from work, that's a lot for the human mind to unpack."

"But it seemed real, the smells, the sounds --" Shosh began.

"The human mind is a powerful thing. There have been instances of people being able to smell certain things from childhood that helps to reassure them, cookies baking in the oven, for example, during times of extreme stress, as a coping mechanism," Sunderland said.

"What about the thing in my parents' house?"

"You've never seen anything like that before there? I'm not saying your parents' house is haunted or anything, I don't believe in that stuff, but, again, that could be a stressor from childhood rearing its ugly head. You ever see that thing before?"

Shosh shook her head. Dr. Sunderland stared at her. His eyes pierced through her, and she diverted her gaze again. "You have trouble maintaining eye contact, Shoshana, do you know that?"

She nodded. The dove outside was gone, and so was the fur-covered mass it was playing with. "I've never been good at it."

"Shosh, the vaginal bleeding, the soreness, I think was all brought on by what we would've called hysteria back in the day. It's an old term, but it's tied to stress and a feeling of being overworked. You've got a lot on your plate, including whether or not you're going to stay with Royce," he said. "It's all connected."

Shosh nodded. "So, I'm going cuckoo bananas?"

"In clinical terms, yes," he said, breaking the tension with a laugh. "It's a surprisingly common thing. You hear often about stress taking its toll on people. The gray hairs, the bleeding, the soreness, it's your body's way of telling you that you're under stress. I'm going to prescribe something. It's a natural supplement from a root found in Iraq. I think it'll help with the nightmares and the tension you're feeling."

***

Shosh filled the prescription and started taking the pills immediately. That night, she texted Royce, and thanked her for making the appointment, and Royce responded with a .gif of a duck falling off a log into water, which Shosh didn't understand, but realized probably meant that Royce was high or with friends.

That night, Shosh dreamt of nothing and it was an incredibly welcomed development. The following weeks were largely the same, Shosh working with Royce on her studies, going with her to movie premieres, and helping her film "wellness" videos of Royce espousing the wisdom of a healthy lifestyle, all the while devouring pizza, cheeseburgers, and other foods she spoke out against in her videos. The only real development was that Shosh decided to stay with Royce, and accepted a position working with the girl where Irwin Agencies provided nearly double what she was making as a teacher, while also completely wiping out Shosh's entire debt.

Shosh got rid of her apartment and moved in full-time with Royce, taking the guest room and making it her own personal space. Royce's studies had gotten better, and Shosh's lessons involved trips to libraries, museums and more, enhancing her lessons and bringing the world alive for the girl. Dr. Sunderland and Shosh continued their sessions, and Shosh felt legitimate growth in their time together, feeling her stress and frustrations slipping away with each session. Shosh had never put much stock in therapy before, but she was amazed at Sunderland's ability to get to the heart of the issue, not to mention the medication that worked to rid her of her nightmares and fears with no impact on Shosh's everyday life in any other way.

The two had settled into an almost domestic lifestyle. Mornings were for studies, quick posts on social media, then lunches were for planning, then whatever event at night, followed by relaxing and planning the next day, depending on what time they got home. Shosh had almost taken on the role of den mother to Royce and had started dressing more like the girl. Shosh's friends had all but vanished, and her entire life started revolving around Royce and their life together. Royce never failed to tell Shosh how much she loved her and often referred to her as "wifey."

Royce and Abda still held their wellness sessions, but they'd become few and far between. Shosh didn't pay much attention to Abda when she was around, because the sessions didn't last very long and it was pretty common by that point. Abda and Shosh made smalltalk from time to time, nothing more, and Abda would often compliment Shosh's work with Royce, letting her know that the girl seemed more "centered" or "focused" on her work than ever before. She credited Shosh a lot, and was incredibly flattering, but beyond the surface-style discussion, Shosh never got more out of the woman.

Shosh's comfort with Royce had grown, and she found herself enjoying not wearing underwear, the same way the girl often did. There was a certain level of freedom she found in just being herself, and enjoying the feeling of couture on her flesh. Royce and Shosh often tried on outfits together, and Shosh was no longer disturbed by being nude around the girl. They tried on outfits, shared clothes and more, and none of it bothered Shosh any longer. When Royce kissed Shosh on the mouth, a quick peck in a changing room in a small boutique in Harlem, Shosh found herself not pushing the girl away, but was still left a little uncomfortable by the occurrence. It was after Shosh complimented Royce on a particular outfit so Shosh thought it was the girl's way of saying thanks. It wasn't uncommon for Royce to peck Shosh on the cheek, so, one on the lips amidst thousands on her cheeks wasn't a huge deal.

***

In the apartment one night, Shosh rested on the couch while Royce recorded a video at the kitchen table. She was discussing Shosh and how important "her girl" was to her entire operation. She talked about how Shosh had been with her almost an entire year and that she was so thankful to have her in her life, and that she was as close to in love with her as she had ever been with anyone. Shosh smiled, listening, thinking what the girl was saying was sweet, and when Royce closed out her video and put her phone down, Shosh rose from the couch to thank her, turned to the kitchen and saw nothing, Royce was gone.

"Royce?" Shosh walked into the kitchen, thinking maybe the girl was hiding, but she couldn't find her. She checked Royce's phone, unlocking it with a six-digit passcode, and checked the girl's social media. The video she just recorded was posted, and timestamped, so it happened, but somehow, Royce slipped out of the room at an impossible speed.

Suddenly, the front door to the apartment opened, and Royce walked in, carrying two pizza boxes. "Tonight, my love, we feast on the souls of our vanquished enemies!"

Shosh laughed, "Where'd you go? You were just here."

"Just here? You were asleep on the couch, I dipped out to grab dinner. It's nine, babygirl," Royce said. Shosh checked her watch. It was, indeed, nine at night. When she checked the phone seconds earlier, it was only seven forty-five. How did so much time just vanish in a few seconds?

"I think I need to sit down," Shosh said, bracing herself on the kitchen counter. She suddenly felt dizzy, confused, and the last thing she saw before she collapsed was Royce's face, her eyes dark, cracks of red where her beautiful eyes once were. Shosh screamed as she lost consciousness.

***

When Shosh's eyes opened, she was in a dark room. The only light was from the nearby windows, courtesy of the moon, and when she tried to move, she couldn't. She was on a bed, and a window was nearby, overlooking the city. The view indicated she was still in Royce's apartment, but not in a room she had ever been in before. She deduced that the view was of a part of the city she had never seen from any of the windows in the apartment, and then she remembered the hallway she never saw before, when she came back to the apartment after her trip home to Long Island.

"Royce?" her voice was weak, and her throat dry.

She couldn't move her fingers or toes, it was as if her body was completely frozen. Her eyes darted around, tears forming in the corners. She closed her eyes and tried to talk herself awake, thinking she was having another nightmare, but she wasn't. In the darkness, Shosh heard the sound of bare feet on the tiled floor. She could only barely make out movement at the foot of the bed, her eyes couldn't quite focus. The tears obscured her vision, and her eyes burned.

As her eyes adjusted, she noted there were other figures in the room, just out of view. The faint scent of sulfur hung in the air. Shosh felt weight on the bed, the memory foam mattress compressing, as though a heavy person was sitting next to her. Shosh opened her eyes and saw a shadowy figure, slight of frame, slender, seated next to her. She immediately recognized the figure as Royce, in the nude, her back to Shosh.

"Royce?"

Royce extended her hand, without looking, and placed her finger over Shosh's mouth, whispering "Shhhhhh, babygirl."

Royce turned to face Shosh, and when she saw the girl's eyes, she tried to scream, but couldn't. Her throat was drained of all moisture, and the croak that came out in place of her scream crumbled in the air, sounding brittle and weak. Royce smiled. From her back emerged the same protrusions as the figure at Shosh's parents' house, heavy, boney structures, impossible in their connection to a figure so slight, and yet, there they were. Black blood oozed from Royce's back, spilling onto Shosh's thighs and body. She felt the cool muck dripping onto her body, but still couldn't move.

Shosh looked toward the other figures in the room, but couldn't make them out. Some were clothed, some weren't, but all started to chant something barely perceptible. Shosh's eyes continued to well up with tears, and she refocused her gaze on Royce. When her eyes locked with the two coals, cracks of red light beaming from the dark spheres, Shosh closed her eyes. She opened her mouth and began muttering the phrases Sunderland taught her.

Royce's mouth cut off Shosh, mid-sentence. Disgusted, Shosh did her best to recoil, trying to push against Royce, but the young girl was strong and the paralysis was perfect. She maintained her grasp on her and pulled her closer. "Don't fight it, Shosh. Stop, I know you want to. Don't you wanna make it with me?"

Shosh watched as Royce's body began melting. She was confused at first, then realized it was like on the boat. Royce's face remained perfect, other than her otherworldly eyes, and her flesh, slick with sweat and moisture, began gliding, like an oil slick, all over Shosh. She nearly began to retch at the flesh crawling all over her, the feeling of skin on skin not like anything she ever felt. She began to feel her body waking up, the numbness fading away, the cool air of the open windows washing over the bits of her flesh that were exposed and not engulfed by Royce's impossible body.

Sta-ast-ast-

Shosh pushed against Royce and finally scrambled free, her body sparking to life enough to move, the numbness vanishing in waves. She screamed and ran to the window, bracing herself against it. Royce stalked toward her.

"Shosh, come here. I need to taste you, please, I *need* it."

Shosh glanced out the window, at the New York City skyline, then at Royce, whose body began to reconstitute itself in the moonlight. Shosh looked at her own body, bruises and marks everywhere. The cool air felt alien on her after being covered in Royce's slick, wet skin.

In Shosh's mind, she saw images of the tendrilled moon. Royce had crept closer, walking slowly, her arms outstretched, pleading. The figures around the room continued chanting, the sound rising, becoming almost deafening. "Shosh, listen to me …"

Eveni-- Shosh heard in her head. Royce's voice? No, something else. Something throatier. Shosh climbed onto the windowsill, filled with terror. *Astart--* She didn't understand what was in her mind. What this word was, where it was coming from. The chanting had grown louder, more rhythmic. Shosh lifted her foot and braced her hands on either side of the window, half-in, half-out. A dove flew past the window, catching Shosh's attention. In that moment, Royce was on her, her skin melting, sliding up Shosh's left hand, then her entire arm, engulfing her.

Asta-- Shosh heard again, her mind racing, her body fighting, fists, elbows and kicks flying everywhere as she tried to get away from Royce, and push herself further out the window. She knew she couldn't survive the fall. That didn't matter to her. What mattered was not being consumed by whatever this thing was that Royce had become, or, had *always* been.

Astarte. The humming grew and the figures stepped closer. A look of pure ecstasy was plastered on Royce's face, drooling and distant. Shosh felt pins and needles run through the parts of her body that were being consumed by Royce, and she screamed, her voice returning slowly, still craggly and broken, but almost there. Shosh pushed herself more out of the window, but she felt Royce's grip tighten. She dangled outside, the back of her head smacking into the cement and glass of the building, the New York City skyline, at night, upside down, spread before her like a reflection in a river.

Royce let out a soft moan. Shosh felt her body lifting up, slowly, and realized that Royce was pulling her back into the apartment, through the window she pushed herself from. Before Royce's flesh could cover Shosh's right arm, Shosh's mind raced to pull with all her might from the girl. As they struggled, Shosh grabbed a small horse lamp from a table beside the window. Tearing it free, she began stabbing at Royce's fleshy sacks and they erupted with cold, dark blood, splattering and twinkling in the moonlight.

"Shosh, no!" Royce screamed, the lamp exploding glass all over the fleshy coverings. Shosh slipped from Royce's grasp, and spiraled, nude, out the window, toward the hard pavement below.

***

When the police set up their crime scene tape and started gathering evidence, everything seemed pretty cut-and-dry. Shoshana, under stress from work, and her dwindling personal life, flung herself from the window in the apartment. Royce, who was genuinely devastated to lose her best friend, posted multiple photos and videos of her and Shosh to Instagram and other outlets, often with flowery notes about their friendship and their love. Shosh's family received a large sum of money from Irwin Agencies, and her parents didn't make any inquiries.

THE MONITORS

"This place we're going, what's it called again?" asked Martin, adjusting his sunglasses as the small sampan cut through the water toward a tiny, twelve-mile-long island in the waters of southeast Asia, not far from the northern coast of Australia. Martin was already sunburnt from the week spent island-hopping around the greater Sunda Island chain, and was starting to feel tired from the similarity of the scenery, place to place, island to island, the same experiences with the same locals, for what seemed longer than a week. Suffice to say, Martin's boredom was mounting.

"Gili Motang," said Laurie. More tanned than Martin thanks to her Italian ancestry, Laurie was also infinitely more excited to spend more time island-hopping before returning home and getting ready to head back to college. Laurie, with Martin, Kevin, Dale, and Ruby had planned this trip for months after deciding that they needed "one last adventure" before their senior year kicked off. A backpacking, island-hopping trip around Southeast Asia was booked, and the five friends enjoyed time in the sun and surf and a variety of exotic food and drink.

"Supposedly volcanic, according to this," Dale said, reading his guidebook. He had kept extensive notes on the different spots the gang had visited, including his favorite foods, drinks, and lodgings. The group had saved plenty of money by booking early and had, with Dale's guidance, mapped out their day-to-day routines as cheaply and efficiently as possible. Dale going into accounting after college clearly made sense to everyone.

Kevin and Ruby snuggled at the back of the sampan, asleep. The previous night, they kept Martin awake with their constant lovemaking, since they had adjoining rooms separated by a cheap wooden door at the tiny beachfront hotel Dale had booked for them. Kevin was, by far, the most in-shape in the group, having run nearly a hundred obstacle course-style races, and having spent more time in the gym than in the classroom back at school. Ruby, his new girlfriend, didn't know everyone all that well, but fit in nicely, and was certainly welcomed by Laurie, who, otherwise, would have been the only other woman on the trip. The two got along great, and Ruby's sarcasm was well received by everyone except Martin, who was often on the receiving end of her razor-sharp barbs.

"Looks tiny," Martin said, looking at the island. The sampan slowed and pulled up to the beach, the clear blue water carrying them listlessly onto the sand.

"Barely a dozen miles, Marty," Dale said, hopping out of the boat, helping the captain with the bags. Dale had made a deal for the captain to return in two days to pick the gang up, unless otherwise called. Dale had a satellite phone, a Christmas gift from his parents, who knew their baby boy was going to a foreign country for the first time and wanted to be able to get in touch with him whenever they wanted to. Martin was quick to tease Dale about his calls to his parents, but when Martin was nearly knocked unconscious while surfing three days earlier, the satellite phone came in handy when calling for help, so the ball-busting ceased.

"We could probably set up camp in there," Laurie said, pointing at a small cave near the edge of the beach. The sand stretched about thirty feet from the mouth of the dark opening, leading to the water. It would make for an easy pickup two days from now, and it gave them plenty of beachfront property to enjoy the sights, the surf, and more.

"This okay?" Dale asked the captain. "Two days?"

The captain nodded, speaking very little English, and said "Yeah, two days, see you then."

Dale and Kevin finished unloading the bags from the boat and helped push the sampan back into the ocean. Ruby and Martin started gathering some wood from the small jungle outcropping about forty yards from their campsite while Laurie began creating a firepit. Dale and Kevin explored the cave, which stretched deep into the cliffside of the island. After walking about thirty yards without seeing anything troubling, they began setting up tents and sleeping bags and unpacking other material. Once they had the campsite set up, Kevin dug his surfboard into the dirt and started waxing it while Dale made notations in his guidebook.

Laurie, Martin, and Ruby had gotten the fire going, using the gear they brought with them, including a hatchet, multitool, and knife. Cutting the branches and logs down to size made them easier to spark. Ruby's hatchet was a last-minute addition to their material, and barely made it through customs, but after some explaining and sweet-talking, they let her keep it. The knife, since it was plastic and could be disassembled, made it through easily, its parts scattered in different pieces of Martin's luggage.

Kevin and Dale emerged from the cave, packages of food in their arms. Once the water got boiling, the gang recapped their trip to this point. Martin's "near-death experience," as he referred to it, was the highlight, and made everyone laugh. It was typical Martin, clumsy while surfing and nearly splitting his skull open in the process.

"Thank God for the sat-phone," Kevin said, laughing.

"What was your favorite part of the trip, Laurie?" Ruby asked.

"Getting to spend time with you guys, obviously. This is going to be a busy year, so, taking the time to really enjoy each other's company is huge, you know?" Laurie seemed a little sad while she said this. "Who knows how much time we'll have to get together once we graduate, we'll all be working and starting our lives."

"Is little Laurie gonna miss us?" Martin asked, playfully shoving her.

"I'll miss you guys, that's for sure," Kevin admitted, staring at the fire. He finished his protein bar and took a sip of water. "School sucks, but the real world is worse. We better get together at least once a month, otherwise, what's the point?"

"If we're all in the same area, I'm down with that," Dale said. "The company I'm interning for has an office in Tampa, I might have to go there if they offer me a gig after graduation."

"Tampa, huh? Mommy and daddy gonna' be cool with you being so far from Resting Hollow?" Martin teased, cracking Laurie up in the process.

"Yeah, yeah, yeah," Dale said, rolling his eyes.

"Marty's just jealous his parents desperately want him to leave Resting Hollow, Dale, so, you're very lucky," Ruby said, throwing a piece of cornbread at Martin.

The gang cleaned up their dinner, and sat watching the water for a while before deciding to call it a night. Kevin and Ruby stayed out later than everyone else, watching the waves, the reflection of the sky in the water, and the soothing crash of the ocean against the cliff nearby.

***

The next morning, Laurie exited the cave and noticed multiple sets of tracks around the campfire. Numerous pairs of small, maybe 7-inch-long prints with five toes were scattered all over their campsite from the night before. Massive lines in the sand followed the tracks, some in circles, some in zigzags all around the area.

"The hell is that?"

Laurie jumped when she heard Martin's voice. She turned and slugged him in the chest, right on his sunburn. She mentioned the prints and how there were so many all over the place, including quite a few that led into the cave. Martin admitted he hadn't seen anything inside the cave when they were heading to bed the night before. Laurie said she didn't either, and when the rest of the group awoke, they said the same.

"I heard some shuffling late last night, but I just assumed it was one of you guys taking a leak," Ruby said.

Confused, they decided to continue with their day, surfing and enjoying the area. Ruby, Kevin, and Dale hiked up the cliff, cutting through the jungle, and on their trip discovered more sets of prints, some bigger than the ones on the beach. Ruby snapped a few pictures with her phone, and Dale doodled a quick picture of them in his guidebook.

At the top of the cliff, Kevin stood on the edge and looked down at the crashing water below.

"You think it's deep enough that if I jumped I'd be okay?"

"Absolutely not, dude," Dale said, looking down.

Kevin continued staring down. He looked at Ruby, who mouthed *don't even think about.*

With that, Kevin smiled and jumped off the cliff. Dale and Ruby both screamed, and it was truly unknown whose pitch was higher. Kevin's body seemed to hang in the air forever before slamming into the water below.

"Kevin!" Ruby screamed, dropping down and leaning over the edge of the cliff.

For longer than Ruby and Dale were comfortable with, Kevin didn't emerge from the water, until finally, he popped up, spitting water and waving to them from below.

"It's amazing, you have to do it! Fastest way back down the cliff!"

Ruby laughed and rolled her eyes. She looked at Dale. "You game?"

"I have my book and you have your phone, it's probably not a good idea," Dale said, looking down at Kevin swimming around.

Ruby rolled her eyes. "Dale, live a little."

With that, she tossed Dale her phone and jumped off the ledge, splashing hard to the water below. Dale remained at the top watching the two of them, he turned and headed back into the jungle, on his way back to the campsite.

***

As Dale walked through the jungle, he spotted more of the prints from the campsite. Kneeling down and examining them more closely, he picked up a light scent that reminded him of the time Kevin left a slice of pizza under the bed in their dorm. Meatball and onion, rotten to the core. Gagging a bit, Dale stood up and tracked the footprints east and west. It appeared that the tracks were moving from the campsite toward the small beach below the cliff, near where the gang had set up camp.

In the distance, behind him, Dale heard what sounded like a low rumble. Turning, he saw nothing, and swiped at the various mosquitos and flies that had been biting at his neck all day during his trek up the cliff. The rumble got louder, and the more he listened, Dale realized it was more of a hiss.

At first the hiss sounded like an air pump, like the kind used to fill balloons, bounce houses, and other childhood distractions, but as he listened, it sounded sharper, more naturalistic, and slightly staccato.

Dale looked around, the sound getting louder. He started walking toward the cave and the campsite, but still had about fifty yards of jungle between him and the relative comfort of the camp. He turned and followed the tracks along the ground for a little while, until suddenly, the hissing grew loud again. Looking around, he saw nothing. The jungle didn't even sway from the light breeze in the air. Suddenly, he felt a sting at his ankle. Looking down, he smashed the mosquito, resulting in a smear of blood. He wiped the remnants of the bug on his shorts, and scratched the bite absently with his other foot.

Taking a sip of water, the hissing picked up again. Out of the corner of his eye, he saw movement from the bushes to his left, but by then, it was too late. He felt the clamping of jaws around his ankle, the one the mosquito just nipped.

Screaming, Dale felt his legs go out from under him, and without warning, he was swarmed by three more enormous, dark, reptilian creatures. They hissed and made a light "barking" sound in between taking bites of Dale's body. He felt jaws snap down on his legs, arms, and the left side of his ribs. Struggling to his feet, he started running, his limbs roaring in agony. As fast as he moved, the creatures kept pace.

Dale reached a thicket of trees and began climbing, but as he started to pull himself up, he felt the jaws clamp around his entire foot. The creature pulled him down from the tree and the reptiles swarmed him again, this time clamping hard on his neck, thighs, and chest. Dale screamed for the last time as his neck was torn open, blood spurting everywhere. He twitched, confused, scared and cold, his body going numb and his vision blurry.

***

Laurie, at the cave's entrance, stood up, hearing what she thought was a scream from the jungle. She looked around, and walked toward the wall of deep, tropical greenery. Martin emerged from the foliage; arms laden with coconuts. Laurie took one and looked at him, confused.

"Fresh coconut milk, straight from the coconut. Pretty cool, right? I thought maybe we could catch some fresh fish, use some of the coconut milk to help season it? Have a cool, local dinner here, instead of protein bars and stuff from cans?"

"Sure, sounds good," Laurie said, preoccupied with the sound from the jungle. "Did you hear something when you were in there?"

"The jungle? I thought I heard a monkey or something, like the ones we saw in Indonesia at the zoo, you know? I remember reading in Dale's guidebook that they have a relative that's native to here. Why? What'd you hear?"

Martin had sat down on a fallen log and produced his survival knife and a rock to knock a hole in one of the coconuts, and seemed focused on that, so Laurie just shrugged and shook her head. "I guess that's it, I dunno', sounded like a scream."

"A scream? Aren't Kevin, Dale, and Ruby dicking around on the cliff?"

"True," Laurie said. "Can I help you with those?"

"I'm good. This is more tedious than difficult. Maybe nab us a fish or two? That'll be the hard part."

"Sure, leave the hard part to the woman, that checks out," Laurie said, rolling her eyes, faking being offended.

"You know me, Laurie, always leave the hard work to the ladies," Martin said, laughing.

The truth was, Laurie was a damn good fisherman. She had packed her travel rod with her when she knew they'd be island-hopping, in the hopes of getting to actually use the skills she learned with her dad, uncles, and grandfather growing up fishing in the various streams and lakes of upstate New York. Her family had summered in Montauk, and she had been shark fishing since she was nine years old. At twelve, she won a junior trophy and from that point forward, she considered herself an angler. College had an impact on Laurie's ability to go fishing, but any chance she got to get out to a body of water, she took the opportunity. So far on the trip, she hadn't gotten to flex her fishing muscles, but today was the day.

By the time Kevin and Ruby returned from the cliff, clothes half-dried from their walk in the jungle, Laurie had caught half a dozen parrotfish and one rabbitfish. Martin had prepared a sauce of coconut milk, salt, seaweed, and a dash of sugar. The concoction wasn't as sweet as he hoped it would be, but in the end, it turned out fine. While Martin prepared dinner, Kevin looked in the caves for Dale, who everyone assumed slipped into the campsite for a nap before dinner, from the hot walk through the jungle.

"He's not there," Kevin said, emerging from the cave.

"Well, where could he be?" Ruby asked, drinking from half a coconut.

"Maybe calling home?" Laurie asked, adding more wood to the fire.

"His loss, dinner's gonna' be awesome," Martin said, adding more sugar to the sauce after tasting it. He was glad he brought some small packets of salt, pepper, sugar, and more on the trip. Adding them to canned meals helped him stomach the repetition of camping food.

"Smells great, bud," Kevin said, sipping from one of the coconuts. "Great idea, by the way."

"Sometimes I have good ideas," Martin said, smiling.

***

As evening turned to night, the group started worrying more about Dale. They decided to partner up and head opposite ways along the coast, through the jungle. Ruby and Kevin went east through the jungle, while Martin and Laurie went west. Exploring different parts while keeping their eyes and ears open for any hint of where Dale disappeared to.

"I'm more annoyed than worried about the guy, to be honest."

"Because he missed your fancy dinner?" Laurie asked, playfully.

"Technically, *your* fancy dinner, too. You were the founder of the feast, after all," Martin said. "No, I'm annoyed that we have to spend the night looking for the guy when we should be relaxing around the campfire."

"I get that, but what if he's hurt?"

"Then why isn't he calling for help?"

"Maybe he's unconscious?"

"He better be," Martin said, pulling back a thicket of vines revealing a small, empty area of jungle, with a thick canopy of trees and vines dangling, the tips of the vines glowing yellow from some kind of floral bud. "Check this out."

Laurie walked over and looked into the small area. "Wow, that's beautiful. It's chilly in there, too."

Martin walked inside and Laurie followed. The ground was softer, covered in vines and moss. As they explored, they examined the glowing buds. "If Dale was here, he'd know what these were,"

Martin said, examining the buds. The green in the area seemed to glow beneath the yellow light. Everything was lush. A deep green, moss had covered every rock, and every inch of bark on the trees. There was a faint, sweet smell in the air, like freshly cut grass mixed with lavender.

"I can't get over how much cooler it is in here than outside," Laurie said, sitting down and leaning against a moss-covered rock.

Martin walked over and sat next to her. "Too bad we didn't find this place first, we could've set up camp here."

Laurie rested her head on Martin's shoulder. "Kinda' cool we found it now, though."

"No pun intended, right?"

She smiled. She raised her head to meet his and the two kissed. After a few minutes, they parted. Martin, confused, stared at Laurie. "Where did that come from?"

She shrugged. "It's beautiful here. I dunno', just got caught up, I guess."

"I'm all for getting caught up," he said, leaning in for another kiss.

A rustle in the vines behind them caught Laurie's attention. She leaned away from Martin and looked around. "Did you --?"

"Yes, I did," Martin finished her thought. "It was behind us," he whispered. "Slowly."

Carefully, they both stood up and looked around. They heard the rustling. There was a hiss, and Laurie's eyes darted all around them. Martin gripped her hand tightly and they stood, back-to-back, looking in every direction. The air suddenly shifted from the faint sweetness of the flower buds to something that resembled old meat or the smell of rust.

The reptiles erupted from the covering all around them. Five at first, then more, surrounding and cutting off potentially all avenues of escape for Laurie and Martin. Martin screamed and pressed himself closer to Laurie, who wasn't much calmer than him, but she remained focused on trying to find an exit. The two shifted, slowly spinning, both eyeing up the creatures around them. More seemed to emerge from the jungle. There were around fifteen of them now.

"We need to get the fuck out of here," Martin whispered, his voice shaking.

"Look over there, by the rocks closest to the tree line. If we can scramble up those rocks and jump into the jungle, we could make a break for it, maybe," Laurie whispered, steadying herself the best she could, both to calm Martin down, and also to convince herself that the idea was a good one.

"What are these things? Giant lizards?"

"I think they're Komodo dragons," she said, quietly, inching their way toward the rocky area near the tree line.

Martin watched as the largest of the dragons slowly stalked through the crowd of smaller ones. Eyeballing it and trying to wrap his head around how big it was, Martin figured it to be around twenty feet long. He immediately thought of being swallowed whole by the creature, and his body trembled at the thought of those massive jaws clamping down on him. Martin suddenly felt the urge to pee.

"Now's our chance, stay close," Laurie whispered before the two of them broke for the rocks. The closest Komodos snapped their jaws at them as they ran, and Martin felt the scrape of one of their teeth nick his foot. He shouted, thinking it was the end, but continued sprinting. When they reached the rocks, the two of them scrambled up and leapt into the jungle, landing hard on rocky ground.

The Komodos moved swiftly, following them. Laurie, ahead of Martin, looked back only once and saw him, at full sprint, trailed by ten of the creatures. They hissed and barked and snapped at his heels, but he remained just out of reach. Laurie navigated the jungle as best she could, retracing their steps back to the camp.

As they tore through the jungle, branches, leaves, and vines whipping their bodies, Laurie felt a rush of exhilaration, her body pumping adrenaline like she never felt before. Her breathing was deep and measured, as though all of her time camping and being in the wilderness had trained her for this very moment.

Eventually, Laurie and Martin worked their way back to the beach, both shouting for Kevin and Ruby. Once to the mouth of the cave, Laurie paused and looked around. The Komodos hadn't broken through the jungle yet. Martin stood behind her, trying to catch his breath, sweating hard.

"You okay?" she asked.

Martin shook his head. He sat down on the rocks leading into the cave. Even in the dark, Laurie could see the bite on his leg. It wasn't large, maybe about four inches, but she couldn't tell how deep it was. In the moonlight, Martin's blood looked black.

"Martin, you're gonna' be okay, alright? One of them bit you --"

"I know, I know, I felt it while we were running. Fucker took a chunk out of me," he said, between catching his breath. "Where the fuck are Kevin and Ruby?"

Laurie looked around. "I don't know. Stay here. I'm gonna' go grab the first aid kit in my tent. If those things come back, shout."

Martin nodded. He watched as Laurie disappeared into the darkness of the cave.

***

Kevin and Ruby made their way through the jungle, pausing to look for Dale wherever they saw an opening or outcropping in the jungle. When they got closer to the water, they found a small beach, where they took a break to soak in the sights. They sat down together, enjoying the waves crashing onto the sand and the rocks, about thirty yards off shore. Eventually, Ruby rested her head on Kevin's shoulder and started to fall asleep. About twenty minutes later, Kevin followed suit, the waves, the cool breeze, the warm air lulling him into a deep slumber.

Kevin's eyes shot open. He tried to lift his head to look around, but couldn't. His mind was cloudy, the periphery of his vision blurry. He felt disoriented and confused, unable to make out anything other than what was directly in front of him.

He could make out the stars clearly, white pinpricks of light against a dark blanket of sky. He tried to lift his head for a look at Ruby, but he couldn't. Thinking that maybe he was dreaming, Kevin did everything he could to look down at his chest, thinking Ruby might be lying on him, and his muscles might be asleep, but he couldn't see her, as much as he stretched and struggled against his own paralysis.

He was racked with sickness, his stomach churning, muscles tired. It felt like he ran three Spartan Races in a row, and his stomach was spasming, rippling with queasiness. Kevin was able to lift his arms and legs a tiny bit, but felt as though his body was heavily weighted down, as though an extra eighty pounds had been injected into him somehow, like his veins were filled with lead.

A groan caught his attention. Kevin darted his eyes in the direction he thought it came from, his immediate left, but again couldn't see anything. He tried to speak, opening his mouth as much as he could, but it would only budge a few centimeters. He felt a shift, as though a rope tied around his ankle had tugged him downward, toward the water. He remembered the beach they were on was pretty small, but even so, high tide wouldn't be able to tug on his body in such a violent, jerky way.

"Hu-hullo? Ru-ru-?" he attempted, but nothing could come out. "Hel--"

He felt saliva building up in the back of his throat, and swallowed hard. It had become remarkably difficult for him to do so. His throat had become as paralyzed as his body. His eyes continued darting around, frantically. Kevin realized he was no longer asleep, that this wasn't a nightmare, that something had gone wrong, something had caused him to become paralyzed, and something was tugging on his leg.

His eyes were watering, and fear had completely consumed him. He tried to scream, but it came out as a light gurgle, the spit he was unable to swallow dancing around on the back of his tongue. The force on his legs increased and he was pulled, slowly, with steady breaks in movement, downward, toward the water. Once he was within ten feet of the ocean, he suddenly found himself face down after being flipped over with a quick burst of movement in the wet sand. His head was positioned at an angle, and he finally saw Ruby.

Or at least, what used to be Ruby.

Even in the darkness, he could see that her lower half was missing. Her entrails were sprawled on the sand, and her eyes were wide open, along with her mouth. She looked like she was screaming, but her face was locked and there was no sound coming from her.

As Kevin was pulled into the water, he tried with all his might to move. His muscular frame had betrayed him when he needed it most. The numbness persisted. His body grew weary as the water began washing over him. As he sank beneath the waves, he tried screaming again, but nothing came out. His body twisted in the weightlessness of the water and Kevin finally saw what had been pulling him all this time. A ten-foot Komodo dragon, sinking with him beneath the waves, its mouth locked on his right leg.

***

Laurie pulled back the flap of her tent and slipped inside. She quickly found her first aid kit and started her way back to the entrance of the cave and Martin. She worried about him. His wound seeped dark blood, and she didn't know if anything in her kit would help him much. She grabbed a backpack, checked it, noted how much food and water was left, and headed back.

Once there, she saw that Martin was leaning against the cave wall. His breathing was shallow and slow, but steady. Laurie popped open the first aid kit and began cleaning Martin's wound. He watched as she poured antiseptic on, then wiped it with a cloth rag, which she tossed into the fire pit afterward. She returned to him and began dressing the wound, tying it tightly. As they sat, she shared a bottle of water with him, and continued to stoke the fire. The Komodo dragons were nowhere to be found, and they sat, quiet, and watched.

"Where the fuck *is* everyone?" Martin asked, his voice tired.

"I don't know, Martin, I wish I could tell you," she said, eyes on the jungle. She heard the occasional bark of the dragons, and sometimes a hiss, but never saw movement in the tree line.

"The boat will be here tomorrow morning," he started. "If they're not here, what do we do?"

"We wait, I guess."

"Wait? With those things running around? No thanks," he said, chuckling.

Laurie chuckled, too. "Maybe we leave without 'em? Leave a note saying we peaced out back to the mainland?"

Martin laughed and nodded. His vision was starting to get blurry, but other than that and the heavy waves of exhaustion washing over his body, he felt fine. "Laurie, do you have the knife or anything?"

She nodded and pulled the knife out of the bag. *A lot of good it'll do if that big one gets close,* she thought. She envisioned a million scenarios where she had to defend herself against the Komodos using this tiny survival knife, but in every single scenario, Laurie met her demise. As Martin fell asleep, Laurie stayed awake, watching the jungle.

Watching for movement.

***

The next morning, Martin awoke with Laurie standing over him, blocking out the sun. He looked up at her, groggy and confused, and noticed she had a large stick in her hands. He thought she looked like Donatello, the purple-masked Ninja Turtle who used a staff to fight evil ninjas. He smiled at the thought, but when he looked toward the shore, at what Laurie was looking at, his smile faded.

Along the beach, between them and the water, where the boat would be picking them up, were half a dozen Komodo dragons. In the morning light, he could see their coloring better, dark green, almost black or gray, their pinkish-red tongues flittering out of their mouths from time to time.

"Laurie --" Martin began.

"Stay quiet. They haven't made a move yet. Been like this for a while now. Just stay quiet," Laurie hissed.

Martin, terrified, felt his eyes welling up with tears. He swallowed hard and pushed them back, bracing himself against the wall of the cave. He began rising slowly, doing his best to stand on his damaged leg. He looked down and noticed that he had bled through his bandaging. He noticed the knife on Laurie's belt and took it out, holding it in an attempt to remain on defense.

"When is the boat coming?"

"I don't know," she whispered, eyes locked on the dragons.

"We won't get past them. There's too many," Martin whispered.

"I know, just relax, it'll be fine," she lied. He knew she was lying. He always did. Laurie was typically very honest with her friends, but when she did tell a lie, they could all see through her.

"Maybe if we start a fire? Scare them off?"

"They'd be on us pretty quickly, wouldn't they? Plus, there are more, in the trees. It's not just these ones blocking the beach. There are more, lots more," she said. Her voice quaked. She was exhausted. Her body was tense. Remaining on guard had put her close to mental and physical exhaustion.

He stared at the dragons. He prayed that beyond them, in the distance, the boat would be arriving any minute. "The boat has to come soon, it *has* to …"

With that, one of the Komodo dragons started closing the distance between them. It stood next to the fire pit, its tail swishing back and forth in the sand.

Martin braced himself against the wall, knife at the ready. Laurie did, too, the sharpened, business end of the staff pointed in the Komodo's direction.

It stepped closer. The others, along the waterline, started following.

Laurie knew instinctively that it was now or never. She knew that she and Martin would have to do their best to fend them off, until they could find higher ground, or a place the Komodos couldn't reach them. Martin looked weak, pale, from blood loss, no doubt. His wound hadn't closed at all, and he was sweating profusely.

"This is it," she said, gripping the staff tightly.

Laurie charged at the Komodo dragon, moving swiftly and purposefully, swiping at it with the stick. Martin followed suit, staying at her back, watching the sides and the rear. She swiped with the pointed end of the spear at the dragon, who hissed and snapped at her as she attacked. She screamed obscenities, a rainbow of off-color remarks, and the Komodo dragon stammered back, closer to the water where it came from, and Martin smiled, thinking the creature's feelings were hurt by Laurie's coarse language.

Laurie kicked a stick toward Martin and nodded at it. He reached down and grabbed it, holding it like a club in one hand, and the knife in the other. Two other Komodos swept in from the sides and Martin swung at them, bringing the club down on one of their snouts, sending them backward. The other snapped at his legs, and he jabbed with the knife, missing narrowly as the dragon slipped backward, its tail whipping in a manic frenzy.

A smaller Komodo dragon, one that hadn't made a move yet, charged Laurie, and with impossible reflexes, she spun the spear around and stabbed the blade through its body, pinning it to the sand. It hissed, scrambled and twitched a moment before it finally died. The other five dragons backed away, closer to the water. Laurie reached down and pulled the spear from the sand, noting the Komodo's blood dripping from the tip. She took some in her finger and wiped it on her face, eyes wide, rage the only thing keeping her sharp.

"Laurie … look," Martin pointed off toward the water, and when Laurie turned, she expected to see the larger dragon emerging, but instead, saw the boat off in the distance. She smiled, but then movement in the tree line caught her attention.

She turned, Martin's eyes still on the boat and saw the big one breaking through the trees, stalking slowly on its huge legs toward them. The Komodos between them and the water scattered wider, forcing Martin and Laurie to re-focus their attention every few seconds as the dragons shifted to different positions around them.

The boat was still about a hundred and fifty yards off shore, and the beasts were closing the distance. Laurie knew her spear would essentially be useless against the big one, so she prayed that the boat would get to them before the big one did. Another dragon crept closer and Martin bludgeoned it, hard, forcing it back. Hissing wildly, it drooled everywhere, and Martin thought he broke the beast's jaw with his attack, but wasn't certain. Attempting to finish the job, Martin crept closer and stabbed the beast in the side of the head, killing it, but when he tried to remove the knife, another Komodo moved in, biting him on the wrist. Laurie spun and stabbed the biting Komodo in the stomach, and it broke free, tearing her spear in half, taking the pointed end, still buried in its belly, into the jungle, screaming and hissing its way into the green darkness.

The big one still closed in. Laurie and Martin were about seventy feet from it now. Laurie's mind raced, imagining the creature swallowing them whole, but in reality, knew that they'd be bitten first, then ripped to shreds by the smaller dragons long before the big one could make its move. Laurie felt a pang of terror surge through her body, her adrenaline leaving her cold. Martin shook, holding his wrist, which was bleeding way more than it should, and they stepped further back, the warm ocean water slapping into their feet, and eventually, the backs of their legs.

"Martin, can you swim? Do you think you can swim?"

He gave her a half-hearted thumbs up and with that, the two spun and dove into the water, swimming quickly toward the boat. Martin turned, doing his best to track the Komodos, but couldn't see anything, the water beating him, and his consciousness draining slowly from his wounds. The saltwater burned at his open injuries, but he kept swimming, with Laurie a few feet in front of him.

"Don't look back, Martin, just keep going!"

After a few moments that seemed like hours, Laurie was pulling Martin into the boat. The big one stood, poised at the edge of the water, its massive tongue flicking through the air, staring at them. The smaller Komodos had entered the water, but without a ladder, they'd be unable to get on. The boat pilot had a rifle slung over his shoulder, and helped Laurie carry Martin aboard. He started the engine and the boat shot off, putting tremendous distance between them and the Komodo dragons waiting on shore.

Laurie knelt next to Martin, whose breathing was getting more and more shallow.

"You look so tan," he said, weakly.

She held him for a long time, the boat surging through the water, the pilot asking what happened to the others. Laurie just sat, holding Martin, until he took his last breath and closed his eyes, head on her shoulder.

ELEVATOR OF THE DEAD

By the time Henry had left the office, the news had started reporting that the dead were rising from their graves. He hadn't been paying attention to the news, of course, because he was on a deadline. Mr. Mitchell, the firm's ranking partner would be furious if Henry didn't get his report written up before the morning, so Henry, being a recent hire to the firm's pool of legal assistants, had to burn the midnight oil to get the report done. So what if he stayed two hours past his normal quitting time? His wife would understand. What's two extra hours taking care of their six-month-old without him?

A lot, he thought, pressing the "Door Close" button in the elevator. He saw that there were two other floors lit up, so he wasn't the only one staying after hours in the Capri Building, located in the business district of Manhattan, referred to as "Silicon Alley" by those trying to make tech development in New York a thing. The Capri was an older building, but nice enough. Henry's firm primarily did contract and licensing law, nothing exciting, no murder cases or juicy divorces, just the humdrum day-in-day-out boredom of rich guys bringing on the latest software company's whizzbang tech to streamline efficiency or whatever the latest buzzword was.

Henry was worried about leaving his wife alone with their kid for a couple extra hours. When he texted her to let her know that he needed to stay late, she responded with a thumbs-up emoji and a smiley face, but he knew her smiley face emojis were often loaded with subtext, depending on which she used. This one, the traditional smiley face, meant that she was distracted and rushing, meaning the kid was being a pain. As cute and fun as their baby girl was, more often than not, Henry missed being able to relax at home with his wife after work, smoke a little pot, have sex, and fall asleep watching re-runs of *Seinfeld*. The kid interrupted that. Henry didn't know that the end of the world would interrupt even more.

The elevator stopped on the tenth floor and a young woman, hair graying down the center of her head, tiny, wearing a black and white pantsuit, stepped on. Her suit jacket had shoulder pads, and Henry wondered if the jacket was a hand-me-down, because didn't those go out of style in the nineties? He smiled and nodded, and she did so as well. She had a briefcase, the initials "TS" monogrammed in gold.

One more stop before the lobby, the fifth floor. Henry slipped a piece of gum in his mouth, and thought of offering a piece to the woman, but worried about offending her, so fought the urge. He was hoping he'd be able to catch the subway home, zipping over to Brooklyn in a fifteen- or twenty-minute ride that would go by uneventfully. He took his phone out and didn't have service, which wasn't unusual in the elevator, thinking maybe his wife texted him, but nothing.

On the fifth floor, two people stumbled into the elevator. Two men, one holding the other up. Behind them, in the quick glimpse Henry caught down the corridor, three figures lurched toward the elevator, a buzz of sound around them like bees. The lights were off, lit instead by the emergency red flashers of the hallway. No sirens, though. No fire alarm.

In the commotion, the tiny woman was barreled over by the two men, the one who was helping the other slamming his hand against the "Door Close" button frantically. He was screaming something in Spanish, Henry couldn't understand it, but he tried to see over the man's shoulders as the doors closed. Once they did, the man who was shouting in Spanish pressed the buttons for the top floors of the building, and once the elevator started moving, he slammed on the alarm button, stopping the elevator instantly.

The lights in the elevator clicked over to red, and Henry looked around, confused. The woman was still on the ground, shouting at the two men who came bursting in, and Henry tried to help her up, but when he offered his hand, she pushed it away, pulling herself up on the rail inside the elevator instead. Henry took a good look at the man who had hit the elevator's alarm buttons. He was in coveralls, and his name tag said "Tony." He was young, big, maybe two-eighty of solid muscle. The arms of his coveralls were tattered, and even in the red light, Henry could make out a scratch beneath the tear in his sleeves.

"Hey, you're bleeding," Henry said, putting his hand on Tony's shoulder.

Tony paused and looked. He was breathing heavily and had a far-away look in his eyes. He was sweaty and appeared confused, as though the wheels were spinning quickly but without a direction in mind. As though thoughts were happening all at once, an information overload.

"Habla inglés?" the woman asked, brushing herself off.

"A little," the large man said, wiping his brow. "He needs help. Hurt bad."

Henry knelt down and looked at the man lying in a lump at their feet. The elevator, though large enough to support a capacity of ten people, suddenly felt tiny with only four. Henry looked the man over, but didn't move him. He could see scratches and tears in the man's face, along with what looked like ... bite marks?

"What happened?" Henry asked, confused. He checked the breathing of the man on the floor. Deep. Steady. He was still alive, despite the scratches of varying depth, and the bites. "Did something *bite* him?"

"In the lobby, many of them," Tony said.

"Many of *what*?" the woman shouted. She was in Tony's face and seething.

"No se," he said, quietly.

"Listen, let's calm down a bit, my name is Henry, I'm a legal assistant at —"

"Who gives a shit? We need to get out of here!" she screamed.

"Me llamo Tony," Tony said. Henry smiled and gestured to Tony's name tag and they both chuckled.

"Nice to meet you, Tony. You work in this building? I haven't seen you before," Henry said, reaching into his messenger bag for some hand sanitizer in the hopes of cleaning Tony's wound.

"This my first week," Tony said, sheepishly.

"Helluva first week, Tonto," she said. Tony looked away from her, embarrassment on his face.

"What's your name?" Henry asked her.

"Tina," she said, rolling her eyes, sighing.

"Nice to meet you. We may have to move him, will you help me?"

"I'm not *touching* that fuckin' guy, are you kidding?"

Henry squeezed some sanitizer onto Tony's shoulder, and instructed him to rub it into the injury. He handed Tony a handkerchief to dress the wound, and Tony did so while Henry turned to Tina.

"I know you're upset, but something's going on. This guy is hurt, *bad*. He's bleeding like crazy, and Tony's arm is hurt. You and I are all he's got," Henry said, locking eyes with Tina.

"If we're all he's got, then this guy is fucked," she said, angrily.

Henry rolled his eyes. "Fine, thanks for nothing."

He knelt down again and rolled the man onto his back. For the first time, he saw the extent of the wounds. Deep cuts and bites ran along the left side of his face and neck, his suit, once a classic eighties drape (courtesy of Alan Flusser), now ripped to shreds and drenched in the man's blood.

The red emergency lighting of the elevator made examining the wounds difficult, and Henry decided that no amount of hand sanitizer or cloth dressing could help the man. For a second, he wondered why Tony tried helping him, seeing how mangled he was, but then realized that Tony was just doing his best in a tough situation.

"What bit him? Other *people?*" Tina asked, to no one in particular.

"Los muertos," Tony said, quietly. He was clutching a small gold crucifix around his neck and praying softly in his native tongue.

"Los muertos? The fucking dead? Shut up, amigo, por fay-vor," Tina said, shoving Tony.

"That's enough!" Henry said, stepping between her and Tony. "What's your problem? Other than being the bitch in your office, what else do you bring to the table?"

"Fuck you guys," she said, taking a seat in the corner of the elevator, and producing a bottle of water from her bag. "Shouldn't the emergency personnel or whatever have called over the speaker?"

"Not if shit's hitting the fan all over the city. A couple people stuck in an elevator wouldn't be a high priority," Henry said, looking at the ceiling of the elevator. He was looking for the emergency exit, and found its outline. "We need to know what's going on out there. Anyone have reception?"

Everyone checked their phones. Nothing. Henry knelt down and pulled the injured man's phone out of his coat pocket. He, too, had no service. Henry played with the man's phone a moment, but couldn't unlock it, since it was passcode protected.

"We can use our phones' internal radios to check for news. I've never used mine before, but if we all turn our phones off to conserve the batteries, we can at least have an idea of what's going on, if whatever's going on is all over the place, or just here, we'll know," Henry said.

"I'm not turning my phone off, fuck that," Tina said.

Tony turned his phone off and tucked it in his pocket. Henry turned the injured man's phone off, too, just in case. He handed it to Tony, who pocketed it. Henry dialed in the radio on his phone, struggling to find it for a few minutes, but it crackled to life. Henry looked at Tony, happy that it actually worked, but Tony's eyes were locked on the phone itself. Henry used the touch screen to search the FM radio band, only getting static.

Eventually, they landed on a Spanish-speaking station. Tony put his hand on Henry's shoulder urging him to stop. The words coming out of the phone didn't make much sense to Henry or Tina, but Tony listened intently, his eyes going wide, mouth agape at various points. The announcer, who spoke in a deep, steady voice, only spoke a few recognizable words to Henry, but the main one that stuck out to him was "los muertos." *The dead.*

"Tony, what's he saying?" Henry whispered. Tony shushed him and continued listening.

After twenty more seconds of listening to the message, it started repeating itself and they all realized they were listening to a pre-recorded loop. Tony slumped to the floor, head in his hands. He looked at the man in the center of the elevator, still breathing, but barely holding on. Tony traced his hand along his own injury, and began to cry.

"What'd they say?" Henry said, kneeling down and placing a reassuring hand on Tony's shoulder.

"El fin del mundo," Tony whispered, his eyes swollen with tears. "The end of the world."

"What?" Tina shouted. "What'd he say? End of the world? Bullshit!"

Henry waved her away. "What else did they say, Tony? Take your time."

"We don't have time to waste, talking to this asshole, we need to get *out* of here!" she screamed, looking around, a wave of claustrophobia hitting her, hard.

Henry stood up and tried putting his hand on her shoulder, attempting to reassure her the way he was trying to reassure Tony, but she slapped his hand away. "Don't fucking touch me!"

"Look, just try and remain calm. We're going to get out of here, but we need more information. Just relax, we're going to get out of here. We can go up through the ceiling exit if we need to. Just chill the fuck out."

Henry wasn't suited for this. Tina was in a panic, and Tony was broken. The man on the floor was dying. Henry never had any kind of crisis training. He got his bachelor's in English and writing, for Christ's sake, and even with that useless degree, he barely got the job as a legal assistant after collecting unemployment for four months, having been fired from his job at a social media firm during a round of cutbacks. What about his wife? What about their baby? Henry felt an immense amount of guilt hit him, thinking that he wasn't a good husband or father for not thinking about them the entire time they'd been separated. He felt upset thinking that they were alone, and if this was, in fact, the end of the world, the "fin del mundo," as Tony put it, then Henry had in fact, been a terrible husband and father for not thinking solely about his family.

"I want to know where we are," Henry said. "Tony, I'm going to go through the ceiling of the elevator and see if we're lined up with a floor or between floors or whatever, can you spot me?"

"Yes," Tony said, rising. He wiped his tears away with a massive hand, smeared with blood, either his own, or from the man on the floor.

With help from Tony, Henry was able to push open the emergency hatch above them and pull himself up onto the roof of the elevator. He looked around the shaft and was surprised at how warm it was inside. The stale smell of oil and grease filled his nostrils, and the entire shaft was bathed in the same red as the elevator car itself. He looked toward where the door would be and noticed they were between floors eight and nine.

"We went up a few floors, eight and nine to be exact," Henry shouted down to the others in the elevator car. "I think maybe we try for nine."

"The eighth floor has the maintenance elevator," Tony shouted. "Takes us outside, to the alley behind the building. Could try that?"

Henry dropped back down into the car. He looked at the man on the floor, then at Tony's shoulder. "What else did the radio say? About los muertos?"

"He say that they rise. From the grave. People who get bit or scratch from them, when they die, they come back," Tony said, carefully.

"So *you're* fucked," Tina said, the stress of the situation making her laugh.

Henry looked at Tony's wound. It was still bleeding. He didn't know how to dress a wound, and had no idea if the hand sanitizer would work, but it was all he had. Henry had started practically bathing in the stuff when his daughter came along. The thought of bringing Manhattan germs home to his wife and kid was unacceptable.

"You're gonna' be okay, I promise," Henry said, nodding to Tony.

Tony, smiling, nodded too.

"You shouldn't lie to him," Tina said. "Even *I* know that."

"So what's the move? Those things, the ones that attacked him," Henry gestured to the man on the floor. "They were on the fifth floor. That means they could be all over either floor eight or nine by now, who knows?"

"Or they might not be there at all. I say the maintenance elevator is our best bet," Tina said, pulling a cigarette from her purse and lighting it.

"Really?" Tony asked, rolling his eyes.

"Got a problem, Tonto?"

Tony shook his head. Henry thought about the choice. It seemed obvious, the maintenance elevator would take them outside, but who knew what was waiting for them? Maybe it really *was* the end of the world and the dead were rising from their graves all over. Maybe it was a localized thing, only a few city blocks or something? Wouldn't the military be mobilized and be able to handle this situation pretty quickly? Firepower and weapons able to overwhelm a bunch of shambling dead people? Were they shambling? Were they really dead? Henry's mind raced.

"Tony, help me pry these doors open, we're going for the maintenance elevator," Henry said. Tony helped him pull the doors apart, which wasn't very difficult, and when they did, the second set of doors leading to the eighth floor was the only thing between them and the corridor leading to the maintenance elevator, which Tony said was across an office of cubicles, a large row wide open in between to allow the delivery of supplies and other goods.

Tony placed his ear to the door, and held his hand up for quiet. Henry and Tina looked around, confused. "You hear that?"

"Hear what?" Tina asked, shoving Tony out of the way and putting her own ear to the door.

"A sound. Like a buzzing, like flies or something, listen close," Tony said.

"I don't hear shit, let's go, let's get this open," Tina said, pulling on the doors. Even with her tiny frame, she was able to push the doors open herself, and with her head down, she didn't notice half a dozen hands slipping through the door until one of them grabbed her by the hair and started pulling.

"No! No, God, no!" she screamed. Henry grabbed her hands, Tony, too, and they started pulling her back into the elevator car. Eventually, the doors wedged halfway open and those in the car could see what was on the other side. About ten office workers. Eyes glowing a faint yellow. In various stages of death, some damaged more than others, chunks of flesh missing, bite marks and scratches all over them.

Tina roared, her voice cutting through the rhythmic buzzing of the creatures pulling at her. More hands appeared through the small opening in the elevator. They grabbed her face, her shoulders, whatever they could. Her jacket was pulled off, shoulder pads going with it. Somehow, Tina was even smaller than initially thought, and as she was pulled through the tiny opening, Henry's eyes locked with hers and noted the pleading. All hostility and anger that had been in her eyes had vanished, and in its place, desperation.

Tony held on longer than Henry did, once Henry realized it was to no avail. The creatures were on her, the dead tearing her flesh, pulling her arms from the sockets and tearing her from the elevator car. Her tiny frame didn't help her. To pull Henry, Tony, or the guy on the floor through would've been difficult, even for five or ten of these creatures, but to pull Tina through, no problem at all. Her screams were cut off by one of the creatures biting out her tongue, which was the last thing Henry saw before he turned to vomit. Tony slid the doors closed, then closed the doors of the car, as well.

For a moment, the gravity of what had just happened hung in the air. Tina was gone. Henry wiped his mouth, leaned against the wall and suddenly felt that the elevator was bigger.

"We go to the ninth floor, hope for the best, maybe take the steps down to the eighth floor, take the maintenance elevator to the back alley. What do you think?"

Tony nodded. "What about him?"

Henry looked at the man. In all the commotion, they didn't know if he was still breathing or not. Henry leaned down and listened. His breathing had become slower, deeper. "We could carry him with us, I go through the roof of the car, you hold him up, I pull him through, we carry him together to the stairwell on the ninth floor."

And so they went. Tony helped Henry up through the emergency exit on the ceiling of the elevator car. Once he was through, he started pulling the doors to the ninth floor open. He looked into the office and noticed it was empty. The rows of cubicles were bathed in red light, like everything else, and Henry couldn't pick up even the slightest hint of movement on the floor. He couldn't tell what kind of business it was, but the rows of cubicles and large, glass-walled offices were filled with trinkets: photos, toys, and more, their owners nowhere to be found. Henry was thankful it was after-hours in the building for the first time that evening.

"Okay, lift him up," Henry whispered to Tony. He watched as Tony, at first, struggled with the injured man, slinging his left arm over his shoulder and hoisting him to his feet. Tony wrapped his arms around the man's lower waist area and lifted carefully. The man slumped, but Henry reached through the emergency opening and did his best to keep him propped up to keep the strain off Tony, who was doing the heavy lifting.

Henry wrapped his arms under the man's and started hoisting him up. Tony, still in the car, pushed the man's legs up and through the opening, and in a few seconds, the man was on his back, on top of the elevator.

"Everything okay?" Tony asked.

Henry paused and checked the injured man's breathing. Nothing. Henry stood up and looked down to Tony. Without warning, the injured man's eyes bolted open, a soft yellow glow replacing his pupils and cornea. He rose slowly, and started toward Henry, a low grunting emerging from his mouth, the first noise he'd made since stumbling into the elevator car what seemed like ages ago.

Henry backed to the edge of the car, and looked around desperately for something with which to fend the man off. The man stumbled slowly toward Henry, and Tony, who was directly under the opening in the car, shouted for Henry to keep moving, and to stay away from the injured man, along with smatterings of Spanish.

As the injured man closed in on Henry, he stepped directly into the hole in the roof of the car and fell through, slamming his face on the lip of the opening.

The reanimated man fell directly on top of Tony, who screamed. They struggled for a while and Henry, poised on the edge of the opening into the car, could only watch as the injured man sunk his teeth into Tony's throat. Tony's screams became deafening, his eyes meeting Henry's, even as Tony pushed the injured man off himself. Henry, confused, looked around desperately, but couldn't figure out what to do, and as Tony screamed and fought the man in the car, Henry slipped onto the ninth floor, hoping to open the door and get Tony out of the car.

As he slid down, he opened the rest of the shaft doors, then started pulling on the car's doors. They wouldn't budge. Henry listened as Tony's screaming eventually died out, and then slumped against the elevator car's doors. He felt a pang of guilt, and frustration, knowing that there wasn't anything he could do. He felt different than when Tina was pulled apart. She was nasty. Tony wasn't. He was a genuinely good soul, and Henry wept for him as he would a close friend, even though they only knew each other for a short while.

As Henry sat there, leaning against the elevator car's doors, they slid open and he fell backward. With the doors open, he dropped back into the elevator car and looked around at the bloody carnage inside. The injured man's legs were broken and he was attempting to crawl over the body of Tony, who lied between himself and Henry.

Henry stood up and looked at the injured man, at his glowing yellow eyes, and grabbed Tina's pocketbook, as well as his own messenger bag, and started climbing back out of the elevator and onto the ninth floor.

Once he was clear of the car, Henry turned around and saw Tony's body twitching back to life. He guessed that turning into one of those things had to do with how quickly one passed away, and because Tony died almost instantly, he was reanimated almost instantly. Either way, Henry started walking toward the maintenance elevator, having swiped Tony's keys first. Henry was at least smart enough to know that he'd need maintenance or janitorial keys to get the elevator to work.

Meeting the massive metal doors of the maintenance elevator, Henry put the keys in, turned them, and waited. Once the elevator arrived, he wondered why it still worked when their own elevator was locked in place. He figured it was an emergency-type thing for the Fire Department or cops, so they could get in and out of the building quickly, but either way, he didn't care, he was happy that the elevator worked and wasn't full of those things.

Henry got inside, turned the key, and pressed the button for the bottom floor, which was supposed to open into the back alley of the building. The maintenance elevator moved slower than the regular one he was stuck in moments earlier, but Henry used the time to see if he had service. Thankfully, he did, and saw that he had multiple texts from his wife, asking if he was okay and what was going on. He texted her back, telling her he was alright and would be trying to get home as soon as possible. He told her loved her, and sent a heart emoji.

She responded back with one as well.

Henry smiled when he saw it. He knew she always meant the heart emoji. Even when she was stressed out, overtired, or overworked, the heart emoji was the most sincere one in her book, and Henry took solace knowing that she was okay, and that their baby was okay.

As the maintenance elevator doors opened, Henry heard a familiar buzz, not unlike the eighth floor where Tina met her demise. The doors opened slowly, and spread before Henry were thirty or so of the creatures, crowded together in the alley, shuffling and moving almost in unison, their yellow eyes glowing brightly in the darkness.

KELLY, WATCH THE STARS

On her thirtieth birthday two years ago, Kelly received her fifth intrauterine insemination, or IUI as her doctors called it, and like the previous four, the results were a failure. By the time Kelly turned thirty-one, she and her husband were divorced, and her dreams of starting a family were tossed out the window. Her therapist extolled the virtues of using the time after her divorce to discover her true path or true self, but that's not what Kelly did.

Instead, Kelly focused on the cause of her infertility, which was, essentially, what resulted in her failing marriage and was a chief architect of her shattered self-image as a woman. Her husband was always supportive, but the stress and cost of the IUI treatments became too much, and when Kelly pressed him to try again, he knew he couldn't stay and that he had fallen out of love with her in the process.

Kelly's doctors determined that the massive amount of scarring on her womb was the primary cause of her infertility.

She had been a success in every facet of her life, from high school to college to meeting the perfect guy to having the perfect home, Kelly inspired envy in her friends and even some of her family. She saw her own imperfections when she looked in the mirror, but she was often complimented and told how beautiful she was by those around her, especially by her husband who all but worshipped her. Kelly took care of herself when not working and enjoyed time with her husband and friends whenever possible. She had a perfectly normal life. Her inability to have a child and to lose so much as a result of her infertility pushed her to the edge.

Kelly was never defined by her femininity, by her ability to have children, but it was something she *wanted*. Something she felt would've made her whole. The experience of parenthood, of creating and nurturing life, was something Kelly desperately wanted to experience. It was the ultimate challenge, motherhood. And Kelly wasn't one to shy away from a challenge. She wanted to experience the incredible connection and bond between a mother and child that she had read so much about and heard about from her friends so often.

At first, both Kelly and her husband argued about the scarring, that the significantly high amount and nature of it indicated to her doctors that Kelly had once had a child or some kind of botched abortive surgery, but this wasn't the case. Kelly would've remembered life gestating in her body and eventually being delivered. Her husband didn't believe her, and because he felt betrayed by what he thought were Kelly's lies, along with the mounting pressure and stress of the IUI treatments, he decided to leave.

After her divorce was final, Kelly became obsessed with hypnosis. There was nothing in her waking mind to indicate any memory of previously having a child or some kind of surgery that resulted in her barrenness. While her friends tried to get her out of the house for brunch or "ladies' night" or whatever they had planned, Kelly would spend her time at a hypnotist who specialized in past-life regression, undergoing sessions to look back at her past and see if some kind of hidden cause for the scarring on her womb lurked in the recesses of her mind.

It was during her third session with the hypnotist that images of a bright, green-lit, sterile-looking room filled her mind. While still under hypnosis, Kelly discussed figures darting around the room, staring at her, with almond-shaped eyes that led to slits in the corners of their heads. Figures whose eyes were so black, they resembled the vast, cloudy darkness of the ocean at night. Kelly recalled how she saw her own reflection in their eyes as they opened her body and examined her insides, all while she remained awake.

In the reflection, she thought her body resembled the frogs she used to dissect in science class. Pinned open with its insides, reeking of formaldehyde, displayed for all the world to see.

The figures were smaller, like children, some a few inches taller than another, but remarkably similar. To tell them apart would be difficult.

Kelly lay on what could be described as an operating table, being poked and prodded all over her body by these tiny figures who never uttered a word, who just moved about the room with purpose, sometimes tools in hand, other times carrying pieces of equipment that Kelly couldn't place. They were nude, their bodies smooth and sexless, and their fingers were long and slender. They reminded Kelly of breadsticks. The taller ones rarely touched any of the equipment and seemed to function more in an observational capacity.

Kelly's body was completely motionless on the table, and she, too, was nude. As the session continued, Kelly remembered the figures removing her insides and placing them across her body, and she could feel the warm wetness of her intestines, stomach, lungs and more being shifted and moved so the figures could access her easier.

The figures took their time examining her body, using tools and devices in a variety of ways and a variety of places to gauge a response, most of it painful, all of it uninvited.

She recalled how the table shifted, almost on its own axis, rotating and positioning to meet the needs of the figures examining her. She remembers her legs pulling apart on their own, and the figures inserting a variety of tools inside her.

When Kelly emerged from hypnosis, she had a feeling that it was during these procedures that her womb was ruined by the figures. On one occasion after a session, she doubled over in intense pain, a ball of fire searing in her gut. The hypnotist told her that he had never seen a patient have a reaction to his therapy in such a way before, and Kelly was anxious to return to his office the following week for another session.

Over time, with the help of the hypnotist, Kelly determined that she had to have been around the age of fourteen when this was going on. The reflection in the figures' eyes was her only key to getting a visual of herself while under hypnosis.

The room was clean and empty other than the cold table she was lying on, her naked body, a nearby floating assortment of tools, conical, almost like a cornucopia, its mouth filled with metallic, jagged horrors.

As the sessions progressed, she found herself withdrawing from her friends, family, and work. Her job as a middle school social studies teacher was never fulfilling anyway, and the kids in her class, as sweet and well behaved as they often were, only served as reminders of what she could never have. The structure of work itself, the environment of the school, the seemingly endless stream of birth announcements from her co-workers, and the constant rotation of maternity leaves resulted in Kelly taking time off to do the only thing she thought about when she wasn't being hypnotized every week: finding those responsible for what happened to her.

She knew this was a lofty goal and that it probably wouldn't even be possible, but she did her research and joined a variety of groups that she would've once thought insane. Reddit groups that talked about abduction were her first stop, and these gave her an insight into various individuals who shared stark similarities of their stories with her own. Eventually, Kelly found a group online dedicated to women who had mysterious infertility issues. Many of the women cited alien abduction, curses, and other seemingly insane reasons for their abnormal infertility problems.

While reading and commenting on others' posts, Kelly found herself reading accounts of individuals who had successfully made contact with these beings. She never referred to the creatures in her hypnosis state as "aliens," because that would've been too absurd, even though that's most likely what they were. To Kelly they were always "beings" or "figures" or "those fuckers."

As she read accounts from across the decades, there seemed to be one commonality: seclusion. This was always the criticism of abduction cases; there weren't often individuals in major metropolitan cities who found themselves abducted by creatures from beyond the stars. Kelly herself always believed these stories to be nonsense, but that was until she started retracing her steps and thinking about where she was around the time she would've been abducted.

Her family had a house outside of Resting Hollow in upstate New York. The town itself was small and secluded, nestled at the base of a sizable mountain range, and along the Hudson River. Her family's home stood in the woods about forty-five minutes outside of town, and Kelly, her little brother, and her parents would often vacation there to go fishing, hiking, and to relax, usually in the summer after school wrapped up for the year.

Speaking to the hypnotist, Kelly was curious about the concept of "lost time," the sensation most abductees report upon returning to reality and Earth. Kelly felt that, should she be able to account for a potential loss in time she could better narrow her search into where she was and exactly how old she might have been at the time she was taken. Sessions continued, and Kelly relived the events of the abduction over and over until eventually new images, fleeting at first, then taking firmer hold, began to bleed into the sessions.

In the memory, Kelly was exploring the woods with her dad, who was walking about thirty feet ahead of her. It was summer, and the sun was beating down on them, peeking through the thick canopy of trees above. Her father, who had just gotten back from town for food and supplies to go fishing the following morning, wanted to show Kelly a nearby stream that had been dammed off naturally by "beavers, squirrels, whatever likes to build dams," he said.

Kelly remembered sweating profusely while they walked. Her dad forged ahead, and she fell behind even more until eventually, her father was out of sight. Dizzy, tired, and with no water around, Kelly took a seat on a fallen tree and tried to focus. The light above began to swell, and as it did, a low hum filled her ears. She looked around, trying to see if maybe one of their neighbors was zipping around on his four-wheeler or something, but there was nothing. The leaves around her began to rustle and float off the ground, as if wind swirled around her, but she didn't feel anything. The heat became unbearable, and she toppled over, dropping to the dirt and leaves at her feet.

The next memory that revealed itself involved Kelly floating down a corridor, flanked by two of the beings. She had been stripped of her shorts, t-shirt, and sneakers, and when she looked around, the corridor seemed to swell and vibrate around her, membranous, almost alive. At the end of the slick tunnel was the room she remembered from her previous sessions.

When she woke up on the hypnotist's couch, she rubbed her eyes and looked around. Determining she was actually fifteen, Kelly's anger raged more than in previous sessions. When he asked, Kelly told the hypnotist that she began to feel rage at the notion of her young self being abused by these creatures. Fifteen years old and tortured by these monsters was too much for her to wrap her head around, and Kelly erupted into a fit of trembling ferocity and tears.

After taking a few minutes in the bathroom, splashing cold water on her face, Kelly found herself at a nearby bar where she pounded multiple Manhattans and thought about what to do.

She called her parents and asked if they remembered that summer, and they didn't, other than her dad recounting his version of events the day she "ran off into the woods" when they were going to look at the beaver dam.

Her parents had still been frequenting the cabin, and she asked if they'd let her stay there a few days. They, of course, agreed. They felt that she, having quit her teaching job, needed "time to relax" and "to get herself together," so when Kelly showed up on their doorstep for the keys to the cabin, they told her they loved her and that they hoped she'd be able to clear her head in the fresh mountain air.

Once there, Kelly spent about a week walking the wooded path the best she could from memory. Her weekly hypnosis and therapy appointments were cancelled, as she deemed potential contact with the beings who hurt her was more important and far more therapeutic than decades of psychoanalysis or hypnotism.

Her hypnotist wished her luck and told her he'd be there, should she wish to resume their sessions.

She spent her nights watching the skies, hoping and praying that she'd see something. Any sign to indicate that something hid up there, watching her, or waiting. A couple of times, on the clearer nights, she was able to see satellites passing by, and once she even saw a shooting star, but there was no sign of the beings who stole her innocence and took away the one thing she and her ex-husband had wanted from their life together, along with the love and happiness they once felt for each other.

As one week became two, and eventually three, Kelly found her daily routine turned into waking up, making coffee, showering, researching how to get in touch with the beings, and walking through the woods, alone, with no water or provisions of any kind, in an effort to best simulate the day she and her dad were in the woods.

She had brought nothing with her that time, and the creatures seemed to want her. The heat was like she remembered, oppressive and sticky, like walking into a room whose windows were sealed shut as spring turned into summer, the air stale and thick. During her trips into the woods, she was able to find the very same fallen tree from her youth to take a rest. She'd sit, silently praying and hoping she'd be taken again, staring up at the canopy of green above her.

Her parents and friends would check in with her, even though she had long detached herself from the idea of maintaining social norms. Kelly explained to her friends that she was at the cabin to "find herself," and her friends, all Facebook moms who lived for mimosas and talking about reality TV, thought she was an amazing free spirit dedicating herself to growth of consciousness, or whatever Instagram was telling her friends was a cool and evolved concept that week.

Kelly's parents, however, were worried and weren't afraid to tell her so. They gave her weeks to "find herself," but in the end, that time just seemed to force her deeper into her "neurosis," as her mom said. It was during a particularly heated discussion with her mom that Kelly finally admitted that she wasn't finding what she was looking for at the cabin and would be returning to her apartment soon. Her mom said "be careful" and "don't get lost" like when Kelly was a kid. Frustrated and annoyed at herself for admitting her failure to her mother, Kelly hung up.

That night, she went for her usual solitary trek into the woods. When she arrived at the same rough area where she took a rest all those years prior, she leaned against a tree and took a swig from her water bottle. She used her phone as a flashlight and looked into the woods, not seeing much of anything. Any possible fear of the unknown dark had long-vanished.

In that darkness, in those woods, Kelly found herself in a way she didn't expect. Would the creatures simply re-appear and take her away? Would she be operated on again, torn to shreds and re-assembled in some sadistic, wide-awake dissection project? To take inventory and think upon her life, the life she had led with her husband, their attempts at procreation. Kelly found the futility of it exhausting. All that time wasted observing ovulation schedules and planning sexual encounters instead of enjoying the touch and taste of the flesh as it should be. Kelly vowed to herself that she would never put a schedule to her sexual conquests. She would enjoy her partners, every part of them, without thought of the creatures, her infertility, or her ex-husband.

The horror of what happened to her as a young teenager had repercussions she was never prepared for, and it had ruined her life in the process.

While leaning against the tree, she wondered what to do next. She had tried shining a flashlight into the sky. She had tried smoke signals. She had tried multicolored, battery-operated flashing Halloween and Christmas lights. Anything she could imagine would catch the attention of the beings from the sky. Nothing worked. They probably would never work. Kelly was alone in the woods, with her thoughts and her future wide open in front of her.

If nothing else, this realization, this connection with her personal self, was enough for her. Her hypnotist would deem this a "breakthrough," no doubt, and Kelly smiled to herself, imagining a world free of concern over her past, the future wide open before her.

At first, she didn't notice the rustling of leaves around her. The wind that began to kick up. She was lost in her thoughts, and these things were invisible to her. When the light exploded from above her, shaking the canopy of leaves, Kelly's eyes went wide. The light enveloped her and she began floating upward, toward the light.

There was no fear. No anxiousness. Kelly's flight or fight instinct never kicked in. Her life was essentially lost, and on a primal level, without hesitation, she accepted what was to come.

For the first time in a long while, something had gone according to plan for Kelly. She smiled as she ascended into the canopy, then higher, floating above the forest. She looked down and saw the cabin not far from where she was. She looked over toward Resting Hollow, the lights of the town twinkling in the night. When she looked skyward, all she saw was sharp illumination.

Bathed in the light of the ship, which hummed ever louder as she floated ever closer, Kelly shut her eyes and waited.

***

When Kelly reopened her eyes, she was in the green room from her sessions. She was nude and lying on the same table she had remembered while under hypnosis. This time, though, there were no beings or tools.

She was alone.

Kelly rose and explored the space, running her hands along the smooth, curved walls. That was something she didn't realize from her sessions, the room was circular. The ground felt cold, almost spongey, and when she sunk into it at first, she was nervous she would slip through completely, but after about half an inch she was able to gain her footing and continue exploring.

Why are you here?

Kelly didn't know where the voice was coming from. She looked around, trying to find one of the beings, but she was still alone.

"You took something from me," Kelly said. She was struggling to keep her calm.

You want it back?

Kelly nodded. "Yes, I do. And I want to know why you did this to me."

You're hearing us in your head. There aren't many of us left. We needed your tissue to try to find a cure. We failed. There aren't many of us left.

"I don't give a shit how many of you there are. You didn't have the right to take what you took from me," Kelly said, her voice rising.

Please, we didn't mean to --

"Fuck you. I'm glad there aren't many of you left, if that's the truth," she said. "You've taken everything from me. You've taken so much from so many. Who do you think you are to do that? Do you even remember me? Because I remember you, you fuck."

For a long while there was nothing. Kelly stood at the center of the room, nude and seething, her body tense. Sweat beaded on her chest and upper lip. Her heart pounded, and the rage and anger within seemingly oozed through her pores.

Maybe you're right. Lie on the table. When you awaken, you'll be in the same spot where we found you.

Kelly climbed back on the table. As she drifted off to sleep, she dreamed of the beings, this time, the room pure white, the beings moving quickly, no tools, no examination, just a blur of motion.

When she opened her eyes, she was in the woods. It was morning, and she was still nude. She looked down at her stomach and saw a small incision, already scarred over, remarkably faded but noticeable to her, a slight imperfection just above her belly button.

Sometime later, after multiple therapy sessions and time spent reconnecting with her friends, Kelly was getting a checkup from her doctor in anticipation of the upcoming school year and her new job. Kelly even found herself dating again, having met a mechanic from Resting Hollow who seemed a little slow, but who was genuinely a sweet and caring guy.

He believed every word of Kelly's story, and loved her even more for it.

While reviewing her bloodwork, the doctor casually said "congratulations, everything seems fine so far."

When she asked what he meant, the doctor informed Kelly that she was five weeks pregnant.

FULL UNDERSTANDING

Glenallen Montgomery sat alone on his porch, a cigarette dangling from his mouth. He watched the early morning sky break as the sun, peeking through the mountains in the distance, began to rise. He enjoyed coffee and wore his favorite robe, a gift from his brother for his fiftieth birthday.

Glenallen retired early, having made multiple investments in technology and cashing in on the dot com bubble, and then on large tech firms, so there was no job to rush off to.

He had been a mailman before retiring, and vacating his job early affected his pension, but the money he made from his investments was more than enough to make up for it. He enjoyed his days as a postal worker, rising early, delivering the mail, staying in shape, and getting fresh air. Even in winter, he enjoyed bundling up and being prompt with his deliveries.

He never married, nor did he have any children, and Glenallen remained a solitary creature out of both habit and necessity. In his free time, he vacationed, visited the library, and spent time investing, a little here, a little there at first. Over time he recouped every penny, and his investments soon ballooned to more than a thousand percent. To say that Glenallen was well-off was an understatement. By the time he turned thirty, Glenallen already had a ritzy house in the Palisades section of Resting Hollow, an area marked with million-dollar homes and wide, expansive estates. He found himself in one of the latter, with a massive yard, a sizable pool, a tennis court, and more. Most of the estates in the area had these amenities, and Glenallen, in the summer, found himself swimming and whacking tennis balls frequently, with the help of a tennis machine.

He had what could be called "friends," but not many. They often showed up for get-togethers at his home, at Christmas time, in the summer, etc. At the same time, Glenallen found that he couldn't relate to them. He couldn't move beyond the surface connections that often tied them together - co-workers, neighbors, etc. People from Resting Hollow were friendly enough, undoubtedly, but Glenallen found he had little in common with the everyday folk around him.

Mostly because he knew *everything.*

From a very young age, Glenallen felt he was different. When his test scores were off the charts in elementary school, he was teased by his classmates and was studied by graduate students at the local university.

In high school, tired of the attention he received for his academic achievements, Glenallen decided he would start getting questions wrong on tests, often resulting in grades of 98 or even, his lowest, a 95. The son of a single mother, and having never met his father, Glenallen and his brother were often very competitive with grades, but in the end, it didn't matter because Glenallen always brought home perfect or near-perfect scores while his brother often found himself with low 90s and high 80s, excellent grades, but significantly lower and less impressive than Glenallen.

In college, Glenallen studied liberal arts and earned his degree free of charge, due to academic scholarships. He was accepted into a variety of master's and doctoral programs, but he declined the offers and joined the post office where he worked happily until his retirement.

Glenallen can tell you anything you want to know about the world. His knowledge is all-encompassing and varied and ranges from the macro level to the tiniest bit of minutiae. The knowledge didn't just appear in his head one day, either. As a child, in his mother's arms, he could understand completely what she was saying; however, he didn't quite understand the concept of language. What began as images and notions dancing around his fragile, still-forming baby-mind, soon formed into worldly, true absolutes. His mother's words began to have actual meaning to him. Television suddenly made sense. Glenallen spoke his first words at two months old.

Over time, Glenallen found himself unable to connect to most people around him. His withdrawal from social norms resulted in more testing, but he didn't show any signs of social disconnection outside of his inability to truly care about the rigors of day-to-day life. Operating almost like a human computer, focused on completing his daily routine of breakfast, school, home, dinner, television, bed, Glenallen found himself bored with the tedium of his life. As a retired individual, he found this same boredom creeping in more and more every day.

The tedium of never being able to learn anything new. The horror of never discovering. Knowing how every mechanical, natural, and emotional thing operated. Understanding what is wrong with a problem by being able to think through every single possible outcome. Looking at an anthill and being able to map the entire network under the ground.

Glenallen often found himself teetering on the edge of sanity, day to day, staring into an abyss filled with everything: complex math equations, weather patterns, technological discovery, baseball percentages, trends in oil prices, governmental oversight, local government policy, fast food developments, movie production filming schedules and locations, how to calculate the "sweet spot" of a baseball after every pitch, the correct lanes to drive in based on time of day, faster and safer flight patterns, the number of kernals in every bag of popcorn, the rate at which the leaning tower of Pisa was sinking into the Earth, by the second, where Amelia Earhart is, what happened at Area 51, the truth about who killed Kennedy, the best place to get pizza in the entire world, the cure for cancer, what happened to the original Paul McCartney.

Over time, and after observing and connecting to all of these concepts, every day, his entire life, he learned how not to fall into madness, how to create a catalogue of what he called "super-sanity" that would allow him to know all things, correctly predict the paths of every conversation, and more. By fully immersing himself, moment to moment, in what was immediately around him, Glenallen developed a sphere of influence where he was able to function in a sane manner, second to second, without anyone knowing the depths of his understanding. Telling others the things he knew wouldn't make his life any easier, so he didn't bother.

This day, however, would be different.

Glenallen, after accessing what many refer to as the "dark web," has decided that this day would be his last. With no more hills to conquer and no mysteries remaining in the world, Glenallen had hired a man named Tom to come to his home and shoot him in the back of the head this morning. Tom had already been paid twenty thousand dollars to perform his task and had already sent a text message to Glenallen informing him that he is, in fact, on his way.

Glenallen thought about the world. He thought about how the bullet will tear into the back of his skull, burrowing through and hopefully out his forehead. Tom mentioned that he utilizes a silencer, which helped to slow the bullet down, while also remaining relatively quiet. Glenallen knew this, of course, but appreciated Tom's explanation nonetheless. Glenallen understood that the bullet would exit at an angle that would place it in the wooden fence around the pool if he kept his head level in the way it currently was. The sun was rising, the sky burning orange, purple, and gray. Glenallen's favorite mix of color.

The door to the backyard opened. Glenallen smiled and closed his eyes. Soon, all of the knowledge in the world would be lost. He would cease to exist. Cease to know. As footsteps grew heavier behind him, Glenallen thought back to his mother staring at him as a baby.

Her smile and eyes and how they implied that the entire world was his to conquer. In many ways, he did. The world knelt at his feet with the knowledge he held. He could have done anything with all the knowledge of the world. In the end, he wanted only simple things. A home. Time to do what he pleased. A bullet to the back of the head.

Death has always been a mystery to many. Glenallen, who knew everything there ever was to know in the world, knew that death was the only possible hill to conquer. Faith and religion were not concepts that went unknown to him, but the vagaries of life after death were things that Glenallen's knowledge didn't connect to. What truly waited on the other side of the veil was the only mystery to which Glenallen aspired.

As Tom raised the silenced pistol to the back of Glenallen's head, his finger taught on the trigger, Glenallen took a deep breath. As he exhaled, he took one last look at the sun and the burning sky. Orange, purple, and gray.

GREEN GOSPEL

The entire world had finally gone green. Plastic was outlawed and effectively eliminated. The sea turtles stopped choking on straws. The oceans were cleansed of plastic, courtesy of a coalition of actors, activists, musicians, and tech evangelists.

The self-righteous took credit for these events. At first, small groups of environmentalists, many of them crunchy, angry, and dreadlocked, appeared on a variety of news programs, espousing that it was they who had finally gotten their message across to those in power in a way that mattered and thus, saved the world. This led to politicians and others assuming credit. Eventually the idea of who was responsible for saving the world became a meme to those following the events. Images of hippies and actors and other left-minded individuals assuming credit became commonplace, with no one able to truly trace where the first action came from.

Nobody realized that it was the planet itself who was to blame for the slow-creep of sudden green-minded consciousness that rooted deep within the public over the course of a couple decades. The sudden "green gospel" as many referred to it took hold over time, due to centuries of planetary neglect and abuse. Earth itself had finally developed a way to combat the one scourge that could end all life as we knew it - humanity. At first it was subtle, ideas emanating from the beautiful, unspoiled regions of the planet, mind manipulation and influence masked as "inspiration" for the weak-minded and those with a focus on their social media presence, in addition to their carbon footprint.

As mankind retreated from fossil fuels and the reliance on unethical products, countries and economies began to collapse, only to be absorbed by a free movement of people, a roving band of like-minded individuals who found themselves functioning as traders and convoys traveling from place to place spreading the gospel of the green utopia. At first, many saw these roving bands as your run-of-the-mill hippies until they sat and listened, wide-eyed, at the impossible truth of the world's struggle with humanity. The green utopian movement grew over time, until entire nations fell under its spell. The spell and gospel of the world itself.

Decades passed. Pharmaceutical companies were the last to fall. Their stranglehold on individuals suffering from a variety of maladies made them indispensable for a time until the green gospel produced what was hailed as a miracle serum that dealt with a variety of issues. Many believed this serum to be created from hemp, sunflower seeds, and other "alternative" sources, but it was truly mined from deep within the Earth's surface, an until-now untapped vein of green fluid with restorative properties unheard of since prehistoric times.

It had emerged from a blue hole in Bolivia, as disciples of the green gospel bathed and celebrated the untouched splendor of the deep, blue pool of water.

As this ultimate "natural" cure spread due to its apparent effectiveness, many weaned themselves off the medicines they required to live. The miracle didn't work for everyone, but in most cases, many found themselves living a life free of big pharma, a life unspoiled by chemicals and side effects.

Many retreated from the large cities, which had become overcrowded since the beginning of the 21st century. Taking to the countryside for smaller homes with greater land, people began working in their gardens, planting trees, and nurturing the environment more. As major corporations fell and banks began to follow, people found themselves readjusting to the concept of a barter system, while also re-establishing natural means of production for basic products like bread, salves, and more. It wasn't hard.

As time progressed, the green gospel spread further. The utopia dreamed about by so many had become true. People began sleeping in mud piles to further increase their connection to the Earth. Many stopped bathing, allowing the dust of civilization and the planet to cake their bodies. Others bathed in natural springs, lakes, and mountain streams. Clean, drinkable water was provided across the globe by those who believed in the green utopia. Crops were planted. Alternative, planet-friendly means of transportation were created, both out of ingenuity and necessity. The bees came back.

Man would emerge each morning, from mud pits and huts, caked in the filth and muck of their new utopia, and take to the fields and gardens to develop the land and cultivate a variety of sustainable crops. Meat was still consumed, but in sustainable quantities. Man and animal alike became free-range.

Many of the true believers of the green utopia would rise from mud-caked beds along the coastal regions of the east to greet the sun. The planet, in its new existence, began to heal, as people's lifespans grew shorter, and the world resumed a more primitive, natural lifestyle. Men, women, and children wore tattered clothing, some going almost threadbare before replacing their attire. Resources were maximized. The air became cleaner. Mankind had given control of its destiny back to planet Earth, and planet Earth was finally saved.

THE SUGAR BOWL

With the bowl's top off, I knew it was time to strike.

Darting quickly, I somehow avoided the gaze of the elderly couple who owned the bowl, and the house that contained the sugar bowl, as well as the other foods and items contained within. I only had a base understanding of the concept of ownership, but I know enough to realize that these two wrinkly creatures often left sweet fruit out in cold metallic bowls on the counter, rotting in the sun and the air. I often found myself getting to taste delicacies I never fathomed, feasting on beads of fruit-sugars as bananas, apples, and other treats went uneaten.

Today was different. After getting a small taste of leftover white granules that the old man accidentally spilled on the counter while refilling the colorful ornate bowl, I knew I found my new favorite treat. When my legs dipped into the shaky white powder, I scanned the area. The intoxicatingly sweet aroma of the sugar made every part of my body quiver in anticipation. As my eyes darted around at the mountain of magic I was standing on, the old woman placed the top back on the bowl, thrusting me into complete darkness.

It didn't matter to me. I had what I wanted. Tasting the delicacy beneath my feet, I entered a realm of ecstasy few could ever attain. The enzymes in my body began to pulse, and when I glanced back to my feet, I felt my digestive juices begin to splurge outward, all over the sugar under my body. The trembling mountain of white softened a bit, and I started sinking into it, tasting it more with my feet. As the sweetness digested, I dipped my proboscis into the heavenly nectar and began drinking it. The taste sent me over the edge, and more digestive enzymes erupted from within, every inch of my body craving the taste and feel of the liquified magic.

I felt the entire bowl suddenly begin to move. Scared, I started fluttering around in the dark, slamming into the walls and the lid. My powerful wings flapping hard, I landed in the pile again, and my body involuntarily erupted with digestive fluid. I instinctively began to suck up the digested fluids, even though one of my wings might have been damaged.

The bowl eventually stopped moving, and I was able to regain my footing inside, my legs sinking deeper into the white crystalline delight at my feet.

I wasn't able to escape the bowl, so it hit me that all I could do was eat. I spewed my digestive enzymes repeatedly all over the mountain, slurping more and more up as it became ready to eat. I felt my body surging, as if alive for the first time in my short life. The rush of energy I felt was new and vibrated from deep within my core. The sweet fluid that came from the enzymes turned my mind into pure discovery and imagery. The only instinct remaining in me was pure, unbridled gluttony.

The white mountain belonged to me. And I, to the white mountain.

I felt my mass beginning to increase, the walls seemingly closing in around me. I was drinking the sweetness at a greater pace. Even though I had fully satiated myself on the nectar, all I wanted was more. It was as if my system couldn't function without it, and without it, I knew I would die, and thus the taste, energy, and desire for more only increased.

My body felt as though it had been hooked up to that glowing electric thing hanging on the back porch. The column of blue-white light my brothers and sisters become entranced with as they soar to their painful electric deaths.

My enzymes were becoming thinner, so, after a while, even though my mind didn't want it, I had to take a break. I found myself huddled against the curved wall of the bowl, twitching my wings and rubbing my legs together to keep the taste of sticky love at the forefront of my desires.

After some time, I began to eat again. The pure decadence of the heaven that alluded me my entire life was the delicious mistress I never knew existed and never knew I wanted.

My body increased in size until eventually, after days of eating, I felt my wings pressing against the top of the bowl. My feet were touching the bottom of the clay bowl, sending cold chills through my warm, energized body. The mountain had thinned in the center of the bowl to the point where I stood, surrounded by small hills of the white deliciousness.

Eventually, I was pressed against the bottom of the bowl, my body too large to maneuver. I slurped at the scraps of enzymatic fluid remaining at the bottom and missed flying. My wings twitched, barely able to move inside the bowl, and I mourned the freedom of the open air of the elderly couple's home.

As my eyes darted around the inside of the bowl, and my proboscis slurped up the last of the liquified enzymatic deliciousness nearest my head, I felt life and energy slowly twitch away from my body.

PANELS

Mack had been assigned a large territory in Resting Hollow called The Palisades, which was predominantly mansions with huge, sun-drenched yards. Some traditional Victorian-style homes scattered the area, most owned by older families who didn't sell when the developers came through. He had, for the most part, been successful in this region in the past, but today was different. The solar company he worked for usually operated off of leads, calling people who filled out surveys online about green energy, but today a client called Mack's company directly and *wanted* to sign up. Because the home fell under Mack's territory, the call went to him, and he knew he wouldn't need to do much persuading to get the homeowners to buy since they were motivated from the get-go.

The home was one of those old Victorians, painted purple, with green awnings. Mack hadn't seen a house in the area quite so vibrant as this one, but he appreciated the personality. Three stories, with a wrought-iron fence bordering the property. He examined the roof from the street and noticed it had some severe angles that might make installing the solar panels difficult, but that wouldn't deter him.

As he walked to the front door he noticed movement in an upstairs window but couldn't quite make out what it was. He heard the shuffling and moving of furniture inside the house, and when he knocked, he noticed the home fell eerily silent. There was a warm breeze in the distance, and Mack turned to look at the mountains that lined the valley. When he turned back to the door, it was open, and inside stood a tall man wearing a black suit jacket.

"You must be from the solar company," the man said, extending his hand to Mack.

Mack entered, nodding to Mr. Kingston as he moved into the parlor of the home. "This place is great, lots of personality." Mack looked at the decor of the home. To call it Gothic would be an understatement. Skulls, black velvet, paintings, and more littered the space. Mack ran his finger along one of the skulls and couldn't figure out if it was porcelain or real. For the first time, Mack noticed the curtains were closed, though it was a beautiful, sunny summer day outside.

"Thank you. My daughter's the one who decorated. Care for some water?"

"No. Thanks, Mr. Kingston. I noticed your roof earlier," Mack began. He heard a creek of the floorboards above him and glanced up.

"My daughter. She's upstairs doing some schoolwork," Kingston said.

Mack felt Kingston inch closer behind him, the hair on his neck stood up. He noticed a smell of rust when the man stepped closer. He saw other oddities scattered around the room. A strange, glowing, blue-white piece of rock under a glass dome; a stuffed cat, in a perpetual state of what could be either meowing or shrieking; yellowed photos of men and women in period attire around different locations in Resting Hollow. Mack recognized the town square, the church, and other spots in town.

"Our family has ties far back in this town, one of the reasons we couldn't part with this place when the developers came calling so many years ago," Kingston explained.

Mack noticed that Kingston was extraordinarily pale, his veins visible beneath his temples, blue and sprawling.

"So, in your message you mentioned that you wanted to go for a full setup, I think ten panels should do it."

"Whatever you think would work best," Kingston replied, inching closer to Mack.

Mack looked to the stairs. He felt uneasy and was filled with a sudden urge to leave. He walked to the windows and slid back the curtain a bit. Kingston backed a few feet away. "You definitely get a lot of sunlight here, so, I can see ten panels working, for sure."

He didn't notice it before, or maybe it was from sliding the curtains back, but Mack suddenly picked up the smell of barbecue. "Smells like someone's cooking on the grill," Mack said with a chuckle. "Let's take a look at that roof. I have a ladder in the truck."

Mack went to the front door, but Kingston cut him off. "Let's take a seat in the kitchen and discuss details. Whatever you have to do, I'll sign off on, young man, I like the cut of your jib. I don't know much about solar illumination."

"Mr. Kingston, you can't be much older than me, and we have to take a look at the roof to make sure the panels can be supported. Anything in the attic? Bats in the belfry?"

Kingston laughed. Mack did, too. "Come. We'll go out the back door, through the kitchen."

Mack followed Kingston into the kitchen but paused when he saw that the door leading to the back yard was nailed shut. He turned slowly and watched as Kingston stepped toward him, seemingly floating, albeit, with rapidity of a snail. "Mr. Kingston, let me help you with this door."

Mack produced a hammer and crowbar from his bag, keeping them close after numerous encounters with stubborn attic doors and roof accesses in town, and for a moment, they formed a makeshift cross. Kingston hissed and launched himself backward, colliding with the wall. Mack, confused, began to remove the nails, and by the time Kingston was on his feet, Mack had popped the nails out of the door and was halfway into the back yard. He walked around in the afternoon sun, the shadow of the home cast large and looming. Mack looked at the roof, then at Kingston who stood, mouth open, drooling in the doorway.

"You should come see, Mr. Kingston, I'll explain the process a bit," Mack called to him.

"That's quite alright, my boy, I'll wait here," Kingston was rubbing his hands together and smiling, waiting for Mack to come closer. While Mack was staring at the roof of the house and taking measurements, he noticed a young girl in the upstairs window. Pale, dark hair like Kingston, but beautiful, a look of concern on her face. Mack waved. "You must've spotted my daughter, Valentine."

"Pretty girl," Mack said, smiling. He walked back toward the kitchen door, and Kingston's eyes went wide with anticipation before finally, he lunged at Mack. Catching his foot on a patch of mud, Mack slipped and landed on his ass, sprawling in the muck. He heard a horrifying scream and turned to see Kingston, having dove over him, caught in the sun. He was on fire, and writhing around in the mud, trying to put the flames out. "My god, Mr. Kingston!"

Mack rose and ran into the house and began filling a large metal bowl with water. He ran back outside and threw the water on the still-writhing Kingston. When the fire wouldn't go out, Kingston's screams began to die, and his body turned to ash, scattering in the warm wind. Mack stood on the back porch of the home, watching what used to be Kingston blow off into the afternoon sky.

Mack stood, dumbfounded, and looked around. In the doorway, Valentine stood, barefoot, her lavendar dress wrinkled and scattered with flowers, both real and in the print on the fabric.

"Is he dead?"

Mack shrugged. "I – uhh, I guess?"

She smiled. Stepping toward Mack, he reached for her, expecting her to erupt into flames once the light hit her. "No, wait, don't!"

Instead, she grabbed the crowbar from his bag and began to break off the shackles around her slender left ankle. Once it was off, she stepped into the sun, smiling, the sun dancing on her face, and through her dark hair.

In the light, she looked elemental. Something not quite human. Her skin almost radiated gray, veins of purple energy pulsing beneath her flesh. She was beautiful.

Valentine walked over to Mack, kissed him on the cheek, and in a blinding flash of purple-white light, soared into the sky.

Mack again stood, dumbfounded by what just transpired. He looked around, closed the back door to the home, gathered his tools, and walked to his car.

SUPPORT

Rabbi Herskovitz had been hosting the support group for things that went bump in the night for nearly forty years. Over time, some faces left the group, but a few remained, steady and returning, week to week, drinking the free coffee, eating the free donuts and kugel (the rabbi's own recipe), and telling stories about their various cultures and troubles and the difficulties facing their lives.

Herskovitz always looked forward to hearing the latest saga facing the vampire contingent. Their numbers began to diminish in the mid-1980's, at the start of the AIDS crisis. The virus had a devastating effect on the blood-suckers. Around that time, the vampires began building blood banks for obvious reasons. They used these fronts not only to provide services to those who needed blood transfusions, but also to satisfy their own thirst. A vampire need only enter a bank owned by one of the various vampire families and present a special card that, to humans, looked like a blank white credit card. In reality, the card had text on it that was invisible to human eyes but perfectly visible in bright purple coloring to anyone whose eyes were adjusted to the vampire spectrum.

In the 1970s, when Herskovitz assumed control of the group, replacing his mentor, Rabbi Fischman, there was a resurgence in demonology and the practice of the dark arts. Demonic entities were never Herskovitz' favorite clientele in the group, mostly because they had a tendency to smell like sulfur, and the basement they met in week to week didn't have any windows, but also because they seemed so arrogant. One of the vampires, Ted the cabbie, often noted that when a demon was in attendance, they always seemed to be judging everyone in the group, looking down on them, because they were more ancient and obviously "smarter" than anyone in the group. Herskovitz never thought of anyone in the group therapy sessions as "evil," just that they needed to be *heard*, regardless of whatever they were up to.

The demons also preferred to show up disguised as little girls in white dresses, which Herskovitz thought was creepy.

The various figures in the group would talk about their week-to-week struggles, and Herskovitz would listen, often offering advice on how to center oneself and avoid minor annoyances, which, as anyone in therapy knows, is easier said than done. The few werewolves remaining in town often came in human form and always missed the full moon sessions. Herskovitz encouraged them to join the group while in their more feral forms but understood that, more often than not, the wolves had little or no control over their actions when the full moon was out.

The ghosts were the most regular in the group, showing up to typically reflect on their lives as living beings and to discuss how the living had no idea what was going on in the world or how to handle anything. Herskovitz listened to hundreds of stories about ghosts trying to communicate with the living only to be met with screams and confusion and often the arrival of a priest to "cleanse" the house of them. The ghosts took this as the ultimate offense and often left their former domiciles under protest, the arrival of the priest or holy figure signaling that the ghost truly didn't "belong" there anymore.

Herskovitz met his wife at one of these therapy sessions.

Kitty O'Doyle, who lived in Manhattan during the days of the civil war, and who eventually found herself killed during a fight at the dockside bar where she waited tables when two union soldiers erupted into a fight over tobacco preference. While Kitty was, in fact, a ghost, she had been expelled from the bar she haunted when the new owners took it over in the 80s and turned it into a lively and colorful gay bar called The Pec Deck.

Kitty was and always will be beautiful.

Herskovitz didn't know if it would be frowned upon to ask out one of his group attendees. While Judaism meant that he was to go out into the world, find a wife, and have many children, Herskovitz hadn't met the right woman, and yet, Kitty was sitting right in front of him. It was Ted the vampire who encouraged him to ask her out, and when Kitty said yes, her eyes lit up and Herskovitz' cheeks turned red. He didn't know what ghosts wanted to do on dates, so they ended up going for a walk. Kitty used most of her energy to make herself visible to others as they walked; otherwise, it would have looked like Herskovitz was talking to himself. At the end of the date, Kitty felt something she hadn't felt in more than a hundred years - a connection.

They were married six months later, and while the prospect of having a bunch of children wouldn't materialize, Herskovitz was happy. Kitty stopped coming to the group therapy sessions since she found somewhere to belong, and Herskovitz felt lucky, having the most beautiful woman he'd ever seen waiting for him at home each night, making old fashioned dishes for dinner and always legitimately happy to see him.

To call them a cute couple would be an understatement.

The group therapy members often found solace in one-another and frequently reflected on the sad state of the world. The vampires, most of which had been in the United States since the 1800s, observed political and social changes with great scrutiny, whereas the demons only cared about the deplorable nature of humanity. The ghosts just seemed annoyed at humans for missing things that seemed so important. Little moments of beauty that went by a millions times a day, unseen by most human eyes.

Over the years, a kaleidoscope of creatures and spirits discussed the changing world around them. All mourned the places they left behind. Most felt like leaves in the wind, floating from one place and time to another.

THE ARBORIST

Cleo had always been the outdoorsy type. When she went to college to study forestry, she never imagined she'd find a job so quickly after graduation, let alone at the nature preserve outside the Palisades section of Resting Hollow, her hometown. The arboretum was named after a local minuteman, one of the founders of the village, Bayard Milton, and it attracted thousands of visitors every year. With plenty of social, political, educational, and artistic offerings, the Milton Arboretum served the town of Resting Hollow well, bringing in a lot of tourism every fall and summer, notably for its picturesque views of the mountains, the Hudson River, and the foliage.

Cleo practically grew up in the Milton Arboretum, surrounded by the deep forest of beech trees, Eastern white pines, larches, and sycamores. Cleo felt at home deep in the woods. The canopy of trees above her allowed her time to think, and the smell of pine always made her feel comfortable.

As a child she spent countless hours walking alone in the woods, often thinking herself silly for hearing what she would later dub the "siren's call" of the forest, as though she was beckoned out into the woods by some unseen force.

Now, as a fully-bloomed arborist, it was her job to protect the very things she grew up adoring. Resting Hollow didn't have any issues with deforestation; the entire town supported the thriving abundance of nature that encircled and gave the town its splendor, and the Native American tribes in the region regarded the areas scattered throughout the valley and mountains as holy in many respects. It was a miracle the white man had, too. Cleo had frequent conversations with the Native American elders from the tribe in the area, discussing the spiritual connection she felt to the forest. Cleo's parents, co-workers, and friends thought Cleo was a nut in the best way possible. Her dad often referred to her as his "little juniper," which made Cleo smile.

"If you heed the call of the forest, it's important to remember to hold onto one's self," the local Chief told her one evening, after a lecture on botany at the arboretum's nature center.

"What do you mean?"

The Chief thought a moment. He was a kind man, always willing to donate his time to the arboretum in support of Cleo's proposed lectures and projects. "The forest can promise you many things. Not all of them can be delivered."

At night, in bed, Cleo dreamed of the woods. She dreamed of being nude, walking among the trees in a thick fog, moss and moist leaves beneath her feet, her hands grazing bark and branch.

In these dreams, she always ended up in the same place, at the base of a massive cluster of beech trees, their branches stretched wide and high into the sky, blocking out the sun. There was no such cluster in the Milton Arboretum, and she never saw anything like it in her travels.

Once at the base, Cleo's feet would often become entangled in the roots, and she'd find herself sinking into the dirt. It didn't scare her; she usually smiled at the thought of becoming "one" with the tree, the world turning red around her, a thick, blood-soaked canvas of trees, grass, roots and dirt.

She enjoyed the feeling of the roots, vines, and branches slithering all over her body, scratching her skin, marking her all over.

It was when she started waking up with marks on her body, marks that she once only dreamed of, that she began to worry.

One afternoon, while Cleo wrote up a report about a potential fungal infection in one of the pines along the shore of the river, Cleo heard the voice she'd been hearing since she was a child.

No real words were ever said, but Cleo understood them perfectly.

Walk among us.

Where are you?

Be here.

Where do you belong?

In the woods, the voices often quieted down, almost to a whisper, but Cleo found that the farther she was from the Milton Arboretum and the sheer volume of trees there, the louder the voices became, sounding as though spoken directly next to her ear.

On a late afternoon, while studying the infected pine, Cleo thought she heard the whisper ask for help. She found herself replying "I am, that's what I'm trying to do," to no one in particular.

Thankfully, her office and lab were typically empty. She was the senior arborist, so if she wanted privacy, whether someone was there or not, she got it. She usually preferred to be left alone to study her findings in peace.

The voice was clear enough that it would be impossible to simply ignore, desperate and pleading.

She stepped outside of her office, then out, into the evening air, and listened for any sound of people. Kids, teenagers mostly, would sometimes sneak into the arboretum, drink, get high, fool around. All things Cleo did when she was a teen. Only she always made sure to clean up whatever mess she left behind. Kids today didn't seem to do that.

When Cleo went to bed that night, she had the same dream as the night before. And the night before that. Over and over, the intoxication of letting herself be pulled underground by the roots and vines. The aroma of the woods. The clean, crisp air. The feel of the ground and moss beneath her feet. The next morning while in the shower she noticed again the thin scratches on her feet, calves, and thighs.

At work that day she collected more samples of the infected tree, the wind blowing behind her and carrying the smell of the woods.

The whispers persisted, but she ignored them, focused on her work.

She couldn't ignore the scratches on her legs and feet. When she returned to the lab and completed her studies for the day, she decided to check the security camera footage from the night before. They revealed nothing out of the ordinary. She didn't see her naked self walking the grounds under some kind of ridiculous arboreal siren's song.

She laughed at the thought.

That night she slept, and again the dream came to her. This time it was different. She wasn't nude. She was wearing what she wore to bed. She walked into the woods and found the cluster of trees. They seemed to pulse with an internal energy that Cleo never felt in the dreams before.

Almost like the thumping of heavy bass, the pulse seemed to blast through her body, chills soaring up the back of her neck, the tiny hairs standing on end. She swallowed hard, her body rocked by the sensation emanating from the woods.

As she stepped closer, she noticed the crimson light glowing from within a tangle of vines and roots at the base of the cluster, the infected tree among them. She ran her hands along the fungus on the tree, noting how thick it had become.

You are welcome here, child.

Cleo turned, expecting to find the source of the voice behind her, but she found nothing. She wasn't sure if she was dreaming any longer, and instead found herself becoming queasy, the pulsing becoming rhythmic, drawing her closer to the cluster of undulating, glowing vines at her feet.

As she pulled the vines and roots apart with her bare hands, she felt the moss beneath her feet begin to shift, as though moving on its own. It tickled her toes, and Cleo giggled as the red light beamed from deep within the core of the tangle. The leaves above her began to tremble, and she heard the whisper, begging her to continue onward, to find *them*, to *seek them out.*

Cleo pulled the final segments of bramble and root away and watched as deep, throbbing light scrambled her senses. The taste of copper entered her mouth, and she found herself struggling to remain standing. She didn't cry out. She felt her eyes grow heavy, the throbbing intensifying and radiating energy and light toward her. She reached into the open cavity of the cleared area and felt the warm, wet interior. The throbbing intensified, and Cleo began to climb into the red cavern she dug out moments ago.

In the crimson light of the world around her, Cleo felt her nose begin to drip. The copper taste suddenly made sense. Sickness came in waves, the pulsing beginning to affect her bowels, her bladder, and more.

Inside, the red cavern seemed endless, and her senses were overwhelmed with the color and throbbing of the world around her. She struggled to keep her eyes open, and when she finally couldn't take any more, she screamed.

She awoke in her bed, her hands and stomach covered in a slippery red foam. She worried it was blood or some other as-yet-unexperienced-bodily fluid, but when she sniffed it, it smelled like maple syrup.

There weren't any maples in the arboretum, but that's what it smelled and tasted like. She called in sick and took a day to think about what had happened in the dream. When she went to bed that night, there was nothing, and the next day, at work, she continued her study of the fungus.

When she trekked into the woods for another sample, she stopped in her tracks, the cluster of trees from her dream suddenly manifest in reality, alive before her, ancient in a way that felt like it belonged there.

The branches stretched to the sky, and she knew immediately that for these trees to exist, they would have to have been planted hundreds of years ago.

There was no throbbing or hum. She approached the cluster, and as she examined the tangle of vines and root, she noted the red just beneath. A deep, bathing crimson radiated outward. She reached down and began to pull the vines and roots apart, the whispers calling to her, welcoming her as their own.

YOU CAN'T WALK IT BACK

"You can't say that," she said, her face red with anger, a term he never imagined was possible, but here it was in reality. After thirty-six years on Earth, here was a woman whose face had actually grown red with anger.

The room, he noticed, had grown dark. As though the sun that head beamed through the windows moments earlier had completely become engulfed by an unfathomable eclipse. No one else in the room noticed, and he had to respond to the red-faced woman in the crowd gathered to attend his reading.

"Well, I sincerely apologize. You're right. My joke was absolutely off-color and inappropriate, and I'm truly glad you pointed it out to me, so again, thank you," he said, genuinely mortified by his choice of words and the way it struck such a nerve with this woman, who had, until her outburst moments ago, remained quiet, enjoying his prose.

"You can't just say something like that, though. I'm just really amazed at how callous you could be. That never came through in your writing," she said.

"I imagine a great many things don't come through in one's writing, but like I said, you're spot-on and absolutely entitled to your outrage. I'll endeavor to be more thoughtful in my interaction and response to readers' questions moving forward. This is actually a valuable learning experience for me," he said, agreeing with the woman. Again.

The gray skies looked angry out the window. He couldn't take his eyes off the parking lot, where parents and children fluttered about, no one seemingly paying attention to the encroaching darkness.

"With so much ugliness in the world, I just can't imagine why you'd add to it." She felt emboldened with this statement. Others in the crowd seemed embarrassed and squirmed in their seats. The staff of the bookstore made no motion to usher the woman back to her seat, and thus she remained at the microphone.

"The world is an ugly place. That's true. I write about it often, as you surely know. But, to that end, humans aren't perfect, right? So, while yes, I'm grossed out and annoyed that I responded to that question in that way, I have to admit ignorance and perhaps laziness in that I didn't truly think my response all the way through, and thus, I made a very human error. We aren't perfect, after all."

The crowd chuckled at that. Some stared at him as though he was speaking another language.

He felt a shift in the atmosphere of the room, as though some of the air had been sucked out, and cleared his throat.

"I just think of your younger fans. Kids, you know?"

He stared at the woman. Slowly, he started to nod. "Sure, yeah, you're absolutely right. This is streaming on Facebook Live right now, I believe, so there are probably some younger fans watching, and to them, especially, I apologize and pledge to do better in the future."

"To them *especially*? What does that mean?"

"Just that, because they're younger, and perhaps not as socially developed or aware of things like sarcasm or the notes of public discourse, some statements could be taken way out of context, and for that, I apologize. It's unfair not to take them into consideration."

"Mmmhmm," she said, her arms folded.

He looked at others in the crowd. Some had assumed the same stance as the woman. They had been lost.

"I worry, often, that we're losing ourselves to a monster," he began. "A monster that wants the world sanitized and scared of the notion of *the other*, something authors write about all the time. To lose our focus and to lose ourselves in an effort to sanitize our opinions, our art, don't we lose the very core of the human experience?"

The room stared at him blankly. A sudden shadow washed inward, engulfing the room. In that moment, he knew all was lost.

The faces of those present suddenly shifted. Amorphous at first, then taking starker forms. They all looked like the woman at the microphone. Their faces angry, red, the looks of scorn focused squarely at him.

He tried to open his mouth to address them, but he noticed the creeping darkness inching its way over the crowd, sliding along the ceiling, spreading over posters of actors imploring children to read in big, white, block letters. The windows along the front and left side of the store, which normally looked out upon the bustling street, were slowly blacking over, making it impossible to see the sun, the town, or any passersby.

He closed his eyes and waited for the darkness to wash over him. Waited for the darkness to wipe him out completely.

THE NEBULOUS THEY

Officer Blatty wasn't entirely sure what to make of Kevin Moore. The man had been arrested earlier that day while at a Times Square movie theatre, matching the profile put together by the headpeepers at Quantico. Blatty had been a good student, and he stayed on top of modern FBI profiling techniques, something some of the older guys in the New York Police Department thought was a waste of time. "Good ol' detective work is the key here," many of his older compatriots said when they caught him studying books written by famous profilers like John Douglas or Robert Ressler.

Blatty was just checking in with the ticket seller at the theatre, a girl named Katherine with whom he often stopped to chat while on his patrol. She was a cute girl, and Blatty was single, so, he was working up the nerve to ask her out. Even though he had been working in the area for almost a year, he felt that any moment now, he'd ask her to dinner. When it came to normal police matters, training with his firearm, understanding the ins and outs of the NYPD, Blatty was a whiz, but when it came to women, he was a rookie.

It was during one of these nervous conversations that the office spotted Moore at the candy counter. Blatty immediately remembered the well-circulated sketch of an individual who died at the hospital, the most recent victim of what the NYPD and FBI were internally calling "the Butcher of Manhattan." The news outlets hadn't yet learned about Moore or his activities, so the hunt was still quiet, with NYPD officers and FBI personnel executing the dragnet with relative secrecy. The killer had been responsible for at least a dozen deaths over the past four months, all with the same modus operandi. Removing one of the victims' kidneys and then carving a series of strange symbols and nonsense into their skin.

It had been a miracle that the latest victim, Ana, survived long enough to give a description and account of what had happened to her. Ana had been working in a small market just off Times Square, and before she passed away at the hospital, she told investigators that she had seen the killer multiple times in the area, and that he possibly even lived nearby. When Blatty learned this, his first response was anxiety, that the killer was in his neck of the woods, but then his nerves turned to excitement at the possibility of catching him, earning some credibility in the department, and maybe using that as a ticket into the FBI.

Blatty excused himself from his conversation with Katherine and made his way over to the candy counter. Moore noted his arrival with a smile and nod and then proceeded to order a Dr. Pepper along with some Red Vines. *That should've been enough right there, ordering Red Vines like a common lunatic*, Blatty would later joke with his co-workers at the precinct, recalling his encounter with Moore.

Once in closer proximity to the man, Blatty noticed a familiar scent. One's olfactory senses can sometimes act as a kind of time machine, recalling a particular moment or place in our pasts. This odor coming from Moore did exactly that to Blatty.

As a rookie with his then-partner, he had pulled over a man for driving recklessly. He was perfectly normal-looking in every way, which should have been a dead giveaway to Blatty and his partner that something was wrong, but that wasn't the clue they needed in order to make an arrest that day.

It was the stench emanating from the man's trunk. His champagne-colored Toyota Cressida was immaculate for an older car, and yet, it seemed saturated with the smell of rot. Like coffee grounds, old fruit peels, human refuse, and festering dairy products all rolled into one.

The faintly sweet smell of fecal matter hung in the air around the Toyota. Blatty, weapon drawn, opened the trunk of the car, and inside was the three-week old rotted corpse of the driver's grandmother. Her skin had bloated and swelled with fluid, and her teeth were missing. Her eyes were yellow, and her mouth, from what Blatty could tell, was twisted into a rictus. *That smell*. It was the worst thing Blatty had ever experienced as a police officer. And it was, by far, the worst thing he ever smelled.

Yet, here it was again. Coming from a man and not the trunk of an old Toyota.

When Blatty asked Moore which movie he was seeing, Moore just smiled. There was a tiny bit of red on his neck, and a small scratch on his cheek, and Blatty immediately became more suspicious.

Moore, who didn't fit the traditional profile of a serial killer, was athletic-looking and African-American. Most serial killers weren't African-American, but here he was, in the flesh. Blatty checked on Katherine, who was watching the exchange between Moore and Blatty closely, her hand on her cell phone.

"Sir, could you come with me?" Blatty asked. They stepped out of line, and Moore took a sip from his Dr. Pepper. He stared at Blatty, his eyes glassy and wide, as though he were in another place, mentally.

"Do you hear it? That music?"

Blatty listened, his hand slowly moving and eventually resting on his sidearm. "I don't hear anything, sir. What's your name?"

"You already know my name, Officer Blatty."

Unnerved hearing his name, Blatty was about to ask how he knew it but then remembered that it was on his badge. "Sir, do you have any identification on you?"

Moore shrugged. "It was supposed to be a beautiful movie, too. One of those life-affirming charmers, you know?"

"Sure, pal. Do me a favor. Take a seat right there." Blatty turned to Katherine and nodded, and she called the police. Blatty used the radio on his shoulder to call in the situation. "Is that blood?"

"Is what blood?"

"On your collar. On your shirt. That looks like blood."

"Doesn't everything look like blood, Officer Blatty?"

Blatty just stared at Moore. "Sir, do you have any identification on you?"

"What *is* identification, after all? What if I was switched at birth, and my identification said one thing, when in fact, I was another. Would identification matter then?"

"That's an excellent question, sir," Blatty said, nodding. "Let's just wait and see, okay?"

Moore smiled, nodded, and continued to drink his soda. The bag of Red Vines sat beside him on the bench. Katherine walked over and told Blatty that she called the police, and Moore stared at her. "Katherine, you're very tricky, working with Officer Blatty like that. You will do well, once *they* arrive."

Soon after, Moore was being loaded into a police van that would take him to the precinct. Blatty was debriefed by his commanding officers, along with the FBI agents who had been sent in to provide guidance and catch the killer. Blatty impressed the agents, discussing how in the end it was the victim's account and description that informed his instinct. The agents asked if Moore said anything strange to him, and Blatty recounted the conversation in the lobby of the theatre. The agents spoke to Katherine, who was a little shaken up by the entire ordeal. Nobody seemed bothered by the smell of rot coming off Moore.

What *did* bother everyone was that Moore refused to speak to anyone. He was asked a battery of questions and shown pictures and indicated exactly zero response to anything. When the FBI agents decided to get a little physical with him, even then, he didn't utter a peep. Eventually, Moore made one statement: "I will only speak to Officer Blatty."

The agents were annoyed by this, and only after two more hours of questioning, only to be met with the same response, the same seven word statement from Moore over and over, *I will only speak to Officer Blatty*, did the agents finally relent. Blatty, who understood the gravity of the situation perfectly, was given a crash-course on how to address and manipulate Moore into giving up as much information as possible by the agents. Whiteboards and smartboards were filled with notes and strategies that usually took the FBI years to teach to their best agents, but here it was being boiled down into a few minutes.

A familiar pang of anxiety came over Blatty. His sergeant didn't want him going into the room with Moore, since Blatty certainly wasn't his most experienced officer, but there wasn't much choice. The young officer had his vest and uniform on, and he was permitted by both Moore and the agents to enter with his sidearm.

When Blatty entered the interrogation room, the stench hung in the air, like dishes that had been sitting in the sink entirely too long. Blatty remembered his first murder, down in Harlem, the dishes piled high, a wife with a steak knife buried in her throat. Blood, ancient, crusty dishes and stagnant water. He'd never forget it. Blatty stifled a gag and sat down opposite Moore.

"Why haven't you asked her out yet?" Moore asked as Blatty sat down.

"What? Who?"

"The girl at the movie house. Katherine. Don't play stupid."

"Just haven't worked up the nerve, I guess," Blatty admitted. "Do you know why you're here?"

The FBI had told Blatty not to let the conversation get personal, and here they were, getting personal with the first question. In Blatty's mind, the concept of approaching Moore on his own ground, in a more honest and open fashion, was the key to success. Speaking to Moore and not playing the FBI's games of manipulation would, hopefully, result in Moore giving Blatty everything they were looking for. And Blatty had nothing to hide. His entire life had been relatively boring and without incident. Blatty was a model police officer, by the book, honest, and *good*.

"You shouldn't wait, you know? A girl like that, she's ripe and men know it," Moore said, smiling. Blatty noticed that Moore was the type of man who could easily be passed on the streets of New York City and not be noticed. He was perfectly average in every way.

"Why do you think you're here, Mr. Moore?"

"Because I killed a bunch of people, and that little Puerto Rican girl lived long enough to give you some information about what I look like, and your police department was somehow smart enough to keep it a secret? Ana, right? That was her name?"

Blatty stared at Moore. In all the videos he saw and information he read about suspects accused of murder, none had ever outlined their situation so succinctly. "Her name was Ana. That's correct."

Moore nodded. He sighed and leaned back in his chair. His hands were shackled together with handcuffs, looped through a metal bar on top of the table between them. "When I removed her kidney, she pissed herself. Did you know that? I bet you did. The human body is deliciously strange, all sorts of crazy shit happens to it when you start applying certain pressures. Removing a kidney, for example, results in the involuntary loss of urine. How delightful!"

"Why do it? What do you get out of it?"

"Out of what? Exploring the human body with knives, scissors, and Exacto blades? What a dumb question. Why not ask me what I *don't* get out of it?" Moore said, laughing.

"Fair enough. Why the kidneys, though? Why not take something a little more symbolic, like the heart or the eyes or something?"

"Now *that*'s a good question, Officer Blatty," Moore said, smiling. "The kidneys are what *they* eat."

Blatty stared at Moore. *They?* He leaned back in his chair, and looked toward the two-way mirror into the observation room of the station, where he knew the FBI agents were hanging on every word. "Who are *they*?"

"It would be so much easier to just show you who they are, but," Moore jingled his handcuffs. "They're everywhere. At all times. They see things. They know things. They're us, but they're also *them*."

"You have to understand that what you just said doesn't make a lot of sense, Mr. Moore."

"To you, maybe. To the agents behind the glass, maybe. But to some, it makes perfect sense."

Blatty stood up and walked to the wall. He crossed his arms and leaned against it, thinking. "Tell me about them. Why do they make sense to you?"

"Well, because I've seen them, Officer Blatty. They came to me, asked me to get them what they needed," Moore explained, his matter-of-fact tone of voice unsettling to Blatty.

"Why couldn't they get what they needed on their own? Why ask you?"

"Because I was available to them. I was in the right headspace, man, that's all," Moore shrugged. "Could've been anyone, really. You, even, if you were in that zone, you know?"

"What 'zone' is that?"

Moore shrugged. "I was at work. Bored as usual. Running figures. Making the company money. My secretary informed me that my lunch date with Paul Denton was being called off because Paul couldn't get away from the office. I guess I was just annoyed. And that's when they *slipped in.*"

Blatty stared at him. "So because your lunch date was cancelled, you started killing people and cutting out their kidneys?"

Moore rolled his eyes. "If you're just gonna give me the runaround, then just lock me up and let's just wait for them to get here. You're supposed to be cool about this, Officer Blatty, not all boring and running the FBI's shitty playbook, page by page."

"I'm sorry. You're right."

Blatty sat back down. The smell was overpowering to the point where his eyes began to sting a bit, like chopping onions.

"Please continue," Blatty said, rubbing his eyes.

"You okay? Something in your eye?"

"You stink, Mr. Moore. You smell like --"

"Like *they* do."

Blatty stared at Moore. "I wish you could explain who *they* are."

"They will be here soon enough. They have what they need now. Ana was the last one, of course. I was going to the movies to celebrate their arrival."

There was a low rumble, like the sound of thunder. Blatty looked at the two-way mirror, then at Moore. "Did you feel that?"

"When they arrive, it will feel like pins and needles all over your body. Do you feel it?"

Moore was right. Pins and needles, starting at Blatty's toes and working its way up, as though his entire body had fallen asleep. Another sound of thunder. The lights in the interrogation room flickered.

"What's happening?"

Moore smiled. "They are *here*."

With that, Blatty stood up and walked to the door. When he opened it and stepped into the station, he saw that everyone, including the FBI agents, had gathered at the front doors and windows looking out onto the street and the city. Blatty walked over and joined them.

In the distance, hovering over the skyscrapers, was a massive purple cloud, pulsating with red lightning. The tremors grew more aggressive, and furniture began to topple over in the station. Everyone seemed paralyzed watching the cloud grow and slowly engulf the tops of buildings. People on the streets watched, too, transfixed by the incredible sight.

Blatty watched as tendrils slid out of the cloud and began crawling their way down the skyscrapers. He stepped out onto the street, through the crowd of officers at the door of the station, and stared. The glass of the buildings shattered under the pressure of the tendrils. Concrete, metal, and glass rained from the sky.

As Blatty watched the buildings around him become engulfed by the clouds and the thick tendrils, he thought he saw a multitude of eyes in the darkness of the nimbus. Blinking furiously, pink, darting around in every direction, but only for a moment. Unable to comprehend what it might have been, Blatty sat down on the sidewalk and listened to the screams of the people around him as the dark purple tentacles swarmed down from the sky.

APPLE VALLEY

North of Resting Hollow, New York, is a small region of land known as Apple Valley. The area, once home to clusters of Native American tribes, had long-since been resettled by Dutch colonists and small smatterings of Irish and Polish families, all looking to farm the region.

Apple Valley has two state schools, a community college and a high-ranking state university, and is littered with old farms, cider mills, small towns, and more. A gas station, one of the few in the area, sits at the foot of a mountain, at either the beginning or end (depending on your point of view) of a long stretch of highway that either curves up, vanishing into the oak trees and blueberry bushes that once littered the skirt of the mountain, or down, into the valley itself. The gas station, simply called Apple Valley Fuel & Rest, sees many visitors and goes through oceans of coffee every day.

It is at Apple Valley Fuel & Rest that Gart Sloan has stopped. His bladder, loaded with coffee purchased at one of the dispensaries in Resting Hollow on his way up the mountain to meet with a potential client, had been pulsing for the better part of the last hour, but Gart hated stopping. His dad had always instilled the virtue of having a strong bladder, able to travel insanely long distances before ever having to stop. Gart was like that usually, but not today. His bladder trembled at the notion of traveling up the mountain without relief.

Gart entered the convenience store portion of the gas station and looked around for a clerk. He didn't need gas, and he wondered if he had to buy something in order to use the bathroom. A clerk, her name tag reading "Chloe," eventually emerged from a back room. She looked tired, in her twenties, eyes heavy and dark with makeup. A tough-looking gal, but friendly enough when she greeted Gart. She looked like she had a few hard years of living under her belt.

"Can I use the restroom?" he asked, looking around.

"Customers only, but, here," she said, handing him the key. "It's out back."

Gart bolted toward the entrance of the convenience store and made his way around to the back of the store. In broad daylight, he could see stacks of boxes, cartons, and more. Discarded packaging, a broken office chair, and a mop bucket swarming with mosquitos were near the entrance to the bathroom. He slipped around these things and ducked into the bathroom.

Once inside, Gart flipped the switch, but the light wouldn't turn on. He grabbed the broken office chair and propped the door open, the buzzing of flies the only sound. He looked around the bathroom, which was remarkably bare bones other than a blackened room next to the toilet, separated by a thin bed sheet, hanging barely a foot off the ground. The breeze from outside caused it to ripple lightly. Gart walked over to the toilet, unzipped his pants, and began relieving himself.

While going, his eyes drifted toward the curtain. The darkness on the other side of the thin fabric was strange because it extended fairly deep, and Gart imagined that at some point it would jut up against the freezer or the small area behind the counter where cigarettes and chewing tobacco were stored. He couldn't quite figure out what this area was used for. Storage, he imagined, but in total darkness he couldn't make anything out. He looked at the opening along the bottom and saw nothing. Peeing was taking forever, but it felt amazing in the way that bladder relief usually did after a long drive. He exhaled softly, his voice echoing from the dark space behind the curtain.

His mind wandered. He thought about the meeting he had later that day. Insurance paperwork. Nothing too crazy. Just some signatures and that was that. He had to serve as a witness to the papers being signed, hence, why he had to make his way up the mountain to meet with the client. This wasn't uncommon, just inconvenient. Gart's job took him all over upstate New York, the metropolitan area, and Long Island. He was very good at his job, and many of the higher profile clients found their way into his service, something he took pride in. The one thing he hated was wearing a suit. Back in the office he was strictly a t-shirt and jeans kinda' guy, and since he was so good at his job and had a way with clients that made them want to work with him, the bosses didn't mind his more relaxed approach to "office casual." Gart always said that the guys who invented business attire were all dead anyway, so why continue the trend?

Another sigh. This time, Gart paused. It didn't come from him. Confused, his mind racing, he turned to the curtain swaying lightly in the breeze next to him. "Hello?"

A chill went up his spine, and he prayed he'd be done pissing soon. Deciding to pinch it off, he tucked his member back into his pants, zipped up, and made for the exit. He kicked the office chair out of its place as a wedge, and the door slammed shut behind him.

***

Back in the car, Gart continued his drive up the mountain. The man with whom he was meeting was a high-profile therapist from Manhattan who retired to the mountains, fed up with life in the city, and fed up with the day-in-day-out of psychotherapy and treatment. Patients either got better or didn't. It was almost a 50/50 shot, and when they didn't get better and found themselves released from the hospital, the results were often bloody and devastating not only to themselves but often to those around them. Dr. Harrison was a kind man when he started practicing, and believed in what he was doing in the beginning, but like in so many professions, he burned out towards the end.

Gart knew this from multiple discussions with the doctor over the phone. The doctor wished to add to his life insurance policy in an effort to protect his assets and provide a better future for his relatives, few as they may be, should something happen to him. The paperwork was drawn up, and Gart got it pre-approved by his bosses and by Dr. Harrison, whose stately manor in the mountains was something of legend to those in Resting Hollow. It was built to spec and was considered the largest private residence construction job in Apple Valley history, with a supposed twenty rooms and a massive garden, which many of the locals referred to as "the maze" due to its high ivy-covered walls dotted with roses and other flowers. It wrapped in a circle all around a black and white marble and stone path and tall brick walls, leading to a black gate at the entrance. Harrison's home was a sight to behold.

Gart had only seen the home in pictures, and when he saw the maze he smiled, thinking of *The Shining*, his girlfriend's favorite movie. Pictures were impressive, but being able to see the place in person would be something special. Gart wouldn't have time to spend getting lost in the flower and ivy maze of Harrison's backyard, but he thought about it. If he had a few extra hours, he'd love to explore the grounds and the rooms of the mansion while talking to Harrison and learning about the man's career. Harrison had treated some famous figures throughout history, and now, in his eighties, he was free of tongue, telling Gart stories over the phone about his treatment of baseball players, actors, politicians, and more. Harrison was forced to sign a variety of non-disclosure agreements, but in his elder years he didn't seem to give a shit about them. He had outlived most of the people he treated, so he didn't think it mattered much to talk about Jackie Gleason or Richard Nixon's nocturnal proclivities.

Harrison's career had been dotted with a variety of controversies, from his experimental psychopharmacological treatments to his extreme therapeutic endeavors that included past-life regression, intense physical treatment, shock therapy, and more. The doctor was often accused of having a greater connection to the Nazi doctors of the past, operating with limited morality in an effort to seek the greater good for mankind. Harrison was protected by politicians, journalists, and more, people with high standing in the community who felt his methods got results, and thus he never lost his license and was able to maintain a position of authority at the most prestigious hospitals in New York.

In the seventies, when Geraldo Rivera's expose' of the mental health system aired on television, Harrison had only a passing cause for alarm, knowing that he had the backing of enough heavy-hitters in the United States to keep his hands clean. The doctor saw some of his own patients in Rivera's news piece, but once the hospitals began to get shut down, Harrison assumed a more authoritative and ceremonial position, practicing less and operating in a more observational capacity for his various proteges and doctors-in-training than ever before.

Gart's interactions with Dr. Harrison had been largely pleasant, but his research into the man's career only turned up so much. Hearing Harrison talk about previous patients who had a level of fame was always interesting, so Gart was hoping to hear some more in person once he got to the estate. Harrison's wife had gotten dementia, and the doctor worried that Alzheimer's or another kind of disease that set largely in the mind was in his future, too. His wife, Caroline, spent most of her time shuffling around the house looking at furniture, paintings, and other items as though they were brand new, and Harrison wasn't sure what to do. All of his breakthroughs in mental health and therapy couldn't help his wife. Having Gart come to his home and set up his estate would be helpful.

***

When Gart arrived at the manor, which was nestled deep within the wooded confines of the mountains that flanked it, he was immediately taken aback by the size even though he had seen it numerous times in pictures. The brick wall, covered in ivy and mortar in patches throughout, stretched ten feet into the sky and featured adornments of black spheres of metal, almost like crystal balls in their reflective qualities. Gart stood and stared into one, seeing his own suited reflection. The massive gate was locked in place, and he pressed the intercom on the brick facade in a small opening of ivy. The driveway, composed entirely of gravel, stretched in a large loop with a fountain in the middle, the water off, and statues of strange fish that Gart had never seen before molded into the cement with jeweled adornments.

The intercom sparked to life. "Mr. Sloan?"

"Yes, Mr. Harrison, this is Gart Sloan with Irwin Life & Estates," Gart said into the intercom. He continued looking through the gate, obsessed with the fish on the fountain. Some were multi-headed. Some had human faces and human appendages. A feeling of unease ran through Gart's body.

"Thank you for coming, Mr. Sloan. Please come in," Harrison said. His voice was powerful, even as an older man, and he spoke carefully, his words measured. The air of formality wasn't lost on Gart who, after dealing with multiple high-roller clients, felt that Dr. Harrison was a different breed entirely.

The gates squeaked open and Gart drove through slowly. As he swung his car to the right, he circled the fountain, noting the designs of the fish again. The human faces of the fish looked like they were filled with anguish, and the faces made Gart uncomfortable. Once at the foot of the steps leading to the front door, Gart exited his car and grabbed his briefcase from the back seat. When he looked up, Dr. Harrison was standing at the top of the steps. He was wearing a gray Miskatonic University hoodie, his alma mater and where he spent time teaching in the eighties. His jeans were splotched with what looked like brown paint, faded, having gone through the wash multiple times. He was barefoot. He was taller than Gart imagined, the pictures he'd seen never really doing justice, and his hair was a sharp silver, almost glittery in the afternoon light of the mountains.

"Hello, Mr. Sloan. Welcome," Dr. Harrison said, extending his hand. Gart shook it and smiled warmly.

"It's a pleasure, doctor. Thank you for taking the time. I promise it'll be brief and as painless as possible," Gart said.

Harrison smiled as the two walked into the home. To call it a home felt reductive, since the foyer alone was bigger than most homes. The entryway was cavernous, the walls lined with books, which Gart thought was a way to intimidate lesser educated individuals (such as himself), and the titles varied wildly from the classics of American literature to strange, confusing titles like *The Treatise of the Soul, Intermittent Dreams*, and numerous titles about Tibet. Gart examined them briefly and noticed a few were written by the doctor himself.

"Dr. Harrison, I believe *wow* is an understatement," Gart said, following Harrison through the entryway and into the rest of the house. A massive marble staircase led upstairs, separating in two directions, one leading down a long hallway, the other a catwalk lining the foyer, three rooms leading from it.

"Thank you, Mr. Sloan. My life's work was good for something after all," Harrison said. He was always pretty self-effacing and funny in his previous conversations, so Gart was relieved when the tension was cut early.

"I tried reading one of your studies on Freud's inaccuracies with psychoanalysis, but I'll be honest, it was beyond me," Gart said. "I think that means I'm what you may clinically refer to as an 'idiot.'"

Harrison laughed. "That study was an interesting one to do. My test subjects were all pretty open, and the ones that weren't, well, they came along eventually."

"I must say, I haven't ever spoken to a therapist or a shrink before."

"Well, you're Irish, correct? Or of Irish ancestry?"

Gart nodded.

"Well, I think it was Freud who said that your people are immune to psychoanalysis," Herrison said as they entered a large study, more books on the walls, scattered busts and statues of figures Gart didn't recognize, and some fantastical-looking creatures, many tentacled, many with impossible physicality. "I've never had a problem with you micks, though."

Gart laughed, nervously. "This study makes my home office look like a child's playroom, doctor. I'm more and more impressed every second I spend here."

As Harrison walked Gart to a leather seat at the large oak desk at the far end of the room, backed against a large stained glass window, Mrs. Harrison walked past the door, wearing a long red robe, a sleeping mask propped on top of her head, held in place with a messy tangle of white hair. Her skin was thin, blue veins clearly visible, and she looked weak. She stopped in the doorway a moment and looked inside. Dr. Harrison greeted her, kissed her on the cheek, and walked her away from the room. He almost seemed embarrassed by her presence, and upon returning his entire countenance had changed.

"I'm sorry about that. My wife can be disquieting to some," Harrison said, sitting at what Gart imagined was his normal seat in the room, opposite him at the desk.

"Not at all, doctor I'm sorry that she's going through such a difficult time," Gart said, taking the paperwork from his bag.

"Diseases of the mind are the worst kind, Mr. Sloan. Never forget that. A mind filled with terrors never truly gets the rest it needs and thus is never able to truly repair itself during times of rest," Dr. Harrison said. Gart listened carefully, as though receiving wisdom from a great sage. "The mind is the key, you know? The key to everything. One who masters the mind can master all things. That's what I've dedicated my life to. Mastering the mind and the maladies that malign it."

"That was a lot of 'm' words, Dr. Harrison. Perhaps a book of limericks is in your future?" Gart joked. Dr. Harrison smiled.

"Mr. Sloan, truly, I thank you for coming. This entire process has been so painless and helpful. Thanks to you and your team, it's truly been remarkable. I usually dread having to deal with paper-pushers, but every chat we've had has been enlightening."

"I'm glad to hear it, doctor. We aim to please," Gart said, looking over the paperwork.

From the corner of the room, Gart heard a familiar sigh. He turned quickly and checked, nothing but a statue of Poseidon, his trident pointed squarely at Gart's face.

"Everything alright, Mr. Sloan?"

Gart nodded. "Must be tired, doctor. Long drive. Weird thing happened when I stopped at the gas station -" He trailed off, not wanting to bore Dr. Harrison with the incident in the bathroom. He figured the doctor might use the case to analyze him, and he was worried that once that Pandora's Box was opened, there would be no going back. It wasn't that Gart was afraid of therapy or afraid of seeing a therapist, but he grew up under the impression that things were often better left unsaid. *Maybe Freud was right about the Irish,* Gart thought.

"How about a drink, Mr. Sloan, to celebrate the securing of my legacy? Normally, I'd open a bottle of some French nonsense with my wife, but alcohol combined with her vanishing memory isn't a healthy cocktail," Dr. Harrison said, rising from his seat. "You a whiskey man?"

Gart was more of a beer guy. The basics. Whiskey was essentially lost on him, but he wasn't one to refuse a free drink, especially from a high-profile client whose own tastes were probably more finely developed than his own.

"Sounds wonderful, doctor. Thank you," Gart said, rising and walking with Harrison to a small cart in the corner of the room. There were multiple bottles of liquor, snifters of brandy, and more. Dr. Harrison poured a glass from a large crystal container, sniffed it, then handed it to Gart. He then poured himself one from the same bottle, and the two toasted.

"To new beginnings, Mr. Sloan," Dr. Harrison said.

"To securing your legacy, doctor."

***

By the time they finished the bottle of whiskey, Dr. Harrison was sitting on a nearby couch, and Gart was on a wooden stool facing him. They had been discussing Harrison's life, his work, his famous patients, and more. After a couple of hours chatting with the doctor, Gart began to feel very tired, even with the thirty-plus ounces of coffee he chugged during his drive to the estate. He checked his watch and, seeing that it was only four thirty in the evening, decided he needed to sober up quickly if he was going to make it home in one piece.

"Another drink, Mr. Sloan?"

Gart shook his head. He was feeling the whiskey and struggled to keep his head up. "I'm sorry, doctor. I don't normally drink liquor."

"That's alright, my boy. Just relax. Here, let me help you to the couch. Set down for a spell." Dr. Harrison moved swiftly, helping Gart to his feet and ushering him to the couch. For a moment, Gart thought Harrison's feet looked like gnarled little fists, scrunched up as they moved across the carpet. On the other hand, the Poseidon statue suddenly resembled Jesus on the cross, eyes pleading and wide, so Gart didn't know what to think. Harrison gently placed Gart's head down on a pillow and laid a crocheted blanket over him.

"Thank you, doctor," Gart said, dozing off almost immediately.

When Gart's eyes opened, he was still in the study, but the doctor was nowhere to be found. The paperwork was on the table next to him, signed and taken care of. Gart rose slowly, checked his phone, and saw that somehow four hours had elapsed. He had five texts from his girlfriend, so he texted her back with a simple *Sorry babe, got stuck bullshitting with the doc, on my way home now.*

He stood up, a little groggy, with a light pounding behind his eyes. The lasting effects of the whiskey, he imagined. He checked his pockets for his keys, found them, and grabbed his briefcase. He tried opening the door to the study, but it was locked. "Dr. Harrison?"

Gart turned toward Harrison's desk and thought maybe the doctor locked him in the room on accident, or maybe in an effort to keep his senile wife away from him. Maybe it would startle her to find him sleeping on the couch? Gart couldn't find a key to the door and there was no other exit, so he sat down at the doctor's seat at the desk and looked out the window, through the stained glass.

The glass obscured his view, creating a ripple effect on the back yard. Gart thought he saw a figure, tall, thin, pale, and blurry, standing at the opening to the flower garden. He called to the figure, but with the distance between the house and the garden, as well as the thickness of the stained glass, whoever it was surely couldn't hear him.

Gart walked to the bookcase and started examining the titles. They were largely similar to the ones from the foyer, and he hadn't read any of them. One of the titles caught his attention, *A Mind, Flayed*, written by someone named Penn, and he touched the spine of the book. A sudden metallic click caught Gart's attention, and he turned his head toward it: the door. He walked over and turned the knob again. Surprisingly it opened. He stepped out of the office and into the large hallway, looking in both directions for any sign of his host.

He checked the knob. The key was lodged in the lock, so he removed it, intending to return it to Dr. Harrison later. He started toward the entrance of the home but found himself blocked from it by chain link. The entryway of the house remained the same as it was before, but now there was a thick chained fence between himself, the door, the steps, and his car. He looked to the side and saw a padlock holding the fence in place. Walking over to it, he thought for a moment that the key in his pocket would work, but upon examination he knew the key was too large to fit.

A sound of shuffling feet down the corridor to his right caught his attention. "Dr. Harrison?"

He remembered that Harrison's wife shuffled around, dazed and lost in her own thoughts, memories, or dreams, claimed by the Alzheimer's. Dr. Harrison was barefoot, though, so, the shuffling might have been his. Either way, Gart was anxious to head home. At this rate, the drive from Apple Valley would take around two hours, and he wasn't looking forward to driving down the mountain in the darkness.

"Doctor, I believe you might have forgotten about me," Gart called down the corridor, into the darkness. With the sun down, he took note of how black the interior of the home was, and when he got near a window, he noticed it had started to rain. Lightning struck, and he remarked at how unbelievably terrible his luck had turned. *Definitely a two-hour drive, now.*

  Gart searched the walls for a light switch but couldn't find one, so he used his phone as a flashlight to illuminate the way. As he made his way down the corridor in the direction of where he thought the footsteps came from, a flash of lightning caught his attention out the window. Thunder followed about two seconds after. He remembered how his dad used to tell him that during a storm, the number of seconds between the lightning and thunder was how many miles away the lightning was. Based on this estimate, the lightning was about two miles away. Pretty close, overall. Gart was never a fan of storms. When he was a child he would hide under his bed, usually with his GI Joes, X-Men, and MASK figures surrounding him, his "army" as his dad used to refer to it.

  As an adult, Gart still wasn't a fan of storms, mostly because they often resulted in added driving time, or, in the case of how most drivers were in Resting Hollow and on Long Island, accidents on the road. *Everyone forgets how to drive in the god-damn rain*, he often thought as he passed accidents on the road or when he was stuck behind minivans and other slow-moving cars.

  More footsteps. Gart paused a moment, listening carefully, only now they somehow sounded as though they were *behind* him. It was impossible, of course, and he realized that it was his mind playing tricks, but he turned and looked anyway. When he saw Dr. Harrison's wife standing in the foyer, about sixty or so feet from himself, he froze.

She was completely nude, her aged body drooping and bloated. She was also soaking wet, and Gart wondered if she was who he saw outside. Her mouth was agape, and her eyes were cast to the ceiling. In her hand was a candle, dripping onto the floor, pink driblets of wax clustering at her wrinkled, fist-like feet.

"Mrs. Harrison," Gart began, searching for what to say. "I'm Gart Sloan. I'm with the insurance company. Your husband and I had a meeting, and I guess I was feeling sick. I'm sorry to disturb you."

He started walking toward her, but she remained completely frozen, her eyes cast at the ceiling. Gart wondered what she was looking at, but because he was in the corridor and she was in the foyer, he couldn't figure it out. He remembered that there was a hallway above the one he was in, upstairs, running along the eastern side of the house, so it was possible that she was watching something in the darkness above her. He stepped closer to her, slowly, and watched for any sign of movement. She just stood, dripping with water, the candle dripping wax.

"Ma'am?"

He was within twenty feet of her now. He put his phone back into his pocket and removed his jacket to put around her and thought maybe he'd take her back to the office and help her lie down, maybe cover her with the same crocheted blanket he woke up in. When he got within five feet of her, she took a step backward and screamed, her eyes dropping and landing on him.

They appeared light, almost milky, with deep purple pupils, something he hadn't noticed before. She swung the candle at him, connecting with his arm, sending wax everywhere and causing the candle to flicker out upon impact. He recoiled, and she started up the stairs, moaning and giggling to herself as she went.

Gart watched her move. As she disappeared down the upstairs corridor, he started up after her. He still didn't know where Dr. Harrison was, but he certainly couldn't leave the man's wife running around, naked and soaking wet in their cold, enormous mansion. Basic decency wasn't lost on Gart, and he certainly didn't want to look like a bad guest to one of the firm's biggest clients.

***

Moving up the stairs, Gart heard whispers behind him, toward the front entryway. With a sharp turn, he realized there was nothing there, and the shadows dancing around him, courtesy of his flashlight, only added mounting stress to the situation. Gart was more annoyed than worried at this point, and he only wanted to get the hell out of the estate. As much as he would have liked to explore it more, he knew that his girlfriend's ire would far outweigh his excitement for a rich old man's mansion.

When he made it up the stairs, he noticed there weren't any rooms lining the hallway; instead, the hallway led to nothing. As he walked, he made mental notes of the paintings, statues, and busts he passed along the way. More animals, more strange figures, more mythology. He passed what he imagined was a fertility idol, a feminine figure with a swollen, distended belly. No face. Long, dreadlocked hair running down her back to the rump of her ass. Breasts, enormous, nipples erect. Gart wanted to take a picture of the idol to send to his girlfriend and friends, but he didn't and opted instead to conserve his phone's battery and keep the flashlight app sparked and lighting his way. Once near the end of the hallway, he found a recessed portion of the wall made of dark stone. Touching it lightly, he was amazed at how cold it was and recoiled in surprise.

When Gart turned around, a crack of lightning sent him into a spiral. The corridor, which had moments ago been lined with deep orange walls, paintings, statues, and more, had vanished. In many of the artworks' places, doors. Doors that weren't there before. The fact that Mrs. Harrison had vanished disappeared from his mind, replaced by the impossible geometry of the space around him.

"The fuck?" he whispered to himself, secretly praying that *someone* would answer. Maybe he really did miss the doors. Maybe the paintings weren't really paintings. Maybe he was losing his god-damn mind. Gart tried to open the door nearest to him, but it was locked. He took the key from the office out of his pocket and tried it. No good. He moved on to the next door. Same thing. The next. Same. Before the end of the hallway, he tried the last door, and, surprisingly, it was unlocked. It opened over a large garden with a small stream running through it. There was no rain, and the sun was shining, so much so that he felt the heat on his skin for a moment, stumbling out into the garden, but he held onto the doorknob and pulled himself back into the hallway. He looked out at the garden and realized it stretched far beyond the space of the home.

The garden that he saw from the stained-glass window, the one he had seen in so many pictures of the estate, would have been about thirty feet to his right, but where that should have been there were thick trees, blueberry bushes, and flowers. The scene was positively bucolic. A rustling in a thicket of blueberry bushes caught Gart's attention, and he half-expected to see Mrs. Harrison emerge, draped in butterflies or doves or some other perfect creature of nature, but instead, a large stag ambled through, its mouth full of leaves. Or, at least, he thought it was a stag. Spotted with white against its light brown covering, the creature had one massive horn protruding from its head where a pair of antlers might normally be. The horn, which curved slightly, had vein-like markings of blue along it, and extended possibly three feet into the air.

A chirping of birds echoed in the air, and as they broke into Gart's field of vision, he was taken aback by their coloring. Or rather, their lack of coloring. They seemed composed entirely of light, with enough form that he could make out their wings and long, thin, tail-like feathers not dissimilar to birds-of-paradise. The light shimmering in the sun created a spectacular rainbow that Gart had never seen in an animal before. They fluttered in the air for a long time, eventually disappearing into the tree line.

***

A crack of lightning caused Gart to jump, and the door slammed shut. When he jiggled the knob, it was locked. He regretted not letting himself fall into the open space. He wanted more. He sighed, looked around, and continued back to the staircase in the main hall. At the top of the stairs, Gart's eyes went wide when he saw that the upper stairwell on the opposite side of the mansion had vanished completely. Rain streamed in, and lightning could be seen in the distance. Dark, heavy-looking clouds. The storm looked ugly, and the maze/garden was drenched. Water pooled in spaces, and the flowers drooped under the weight of the rain.

"Jesus Christ," Gart muttered under his breath. He examined the mansion and saw that pipes were exposed, as though the building had been severed cleanly, like a massive brick, metal, and concrete cake expertly sliced by a gourmet baker. Water poured from the pipes, and sparks exploded from cut electrical wires. The mansion was exposed to the elements, and the wind pushed leaves, flowers torn from the massive maze bushes, and more into the foyer.

The front gate remained in place, blocking the front door. Gart walked down the steps and thought maybe now he'd be able to get to his car. Walking down the stairs, he felt the steps creak and begin to sag, as though the entire structural integrity of the home was unraveling due to the sudden sectional removal of the house's west wing. He walked slowly, making his way to the marble ground of the first floor, and as he grabbed the railing heading down, his grip loosened and he fell, confused, downward, the marble floor below him becoming fluid, a swirl of black and white. He splashed into the ground, finding the once-stiff marble floor suddenly light as water. He began sinking, unable to breathe, and in his panic, his mind raced, neurons firing maniacally, until finally, everything went black.

***

Gart's eyes opened and he was face down on cold, wet stone. The rain was pouring down, and he was soaked. His phone lay next to him, drenched and broken. He stood up and looked around. The high walls, the ivy, the flowers. The dark, gray sky. He was in the center of the maze.

A scream pierced the low, distant rumble of thunder. High-pitched, shrill. It stood out against the sound of rain pummeling the stone and walls. Gart checked his pockets and was thankful that his keys were still there. He was worried that in the fall off the stairs they had become lost in the lake of marble he was swimming in moments earlier. His sudden swimming lesson was still playing in his mind, and he couldn't shake it. He felt as though he was drowning, his lungs struggling for air, but here he was, awake and alive.

Gart immediately started climbing the ivy-covered walls, but they were far too slick, and he couldn't grip anything. Cursing under his breath, he brushed the bits of flowers and ivy off of himself and looked at the three possible avenues of exit before him. Wind, rain, and debris were whipping through each path, and he decided that the middle was the way to go.

He continued through the maze, passing more statues and busts of figures he couldn't recognize, more of the human-faced fish creatures from the fountain out front. He stopped and examined a triptych that seemed to show a human man's transformation into a fish-like creature. A phrase in a language he didn't recognize was etched into the stone: "Ph'nglui mglw'nafh Ngyr-Korath R'lyeh, wgah'nagl fhtagn. Grah'n stell'bsna, cch' ebunma."

"Fa-nig-lew ... huh?" Gart muttered, trying to sound out the jumble of letters. "Whatever."

Another scream. This time, closer. Gart looked around, startled, and walked faster toward what he hoped would be the exit. Remembering how big the maze was, he knew he wasn't exactly close, but was hoping he was at least making headway. The deep, lush green of the maze was only broken up by a random statue of something insane, or a birdbath, or a stone lantern that couldn't be lit because of the constant, oppressive rain.

After walking for what seemed like half an hour, Gart paused for a moment and leaned against the wall, thinking that he should have found the exit by now. There should have been another branch of the maze that led in another direction, not just a long walk through green corridors under a dark, ugly sky. He hadn't heard the scream in a while, nor had he seen any more of the strange, nonsensical writing.

"Missssssterrrrr Slllooooooooooannnnn …" a voice hissed to his left, the direction he had previously been heading. Gart lifted his head and saw a figure, hunched over, head low, soaking wet, and carrying a piece of rotted plywood in a tight fist.

The figure resembled Dr. Harrison, but instead of his normal, elderly features, his skin looked gray, his cheeks sunken in, his eyes set deep in his face. The flesh on his head was sagging, as though he was wearing a Halloween costume that was two sizes too large for him.

"Doctor?" Gart rose and took a tentative step toward him. The doctor, or whatever it was, twitched. Gart immediately froze and raised his hands in an act of submission.

"Impervious … to … psychoanalysis?"

The thing that might have been Dr. Harrison swung the piece of wood wildly, and Gart ducked backward. He scrambled to his feet and sprinted back towards the center of the maze. He found himself back at the maze's center in what felt like only a couple of minutes. It didn't make any sense. Nothing was making sense. *What is this place?*

In the center of the maze, before, there was absolutely nothing. Upon returning, Gart was surrounded by statues, all of the same thing: a large, human-like figure, female, winged, her white stone body bound with what looked like black leather straps, blinded with some kind of metal-spiked, Medieval-looking wrapping. The figure's body twisted, its face racked with agony, frozen. There were around thirty of the statues in the center of the maze, and Gart's mind raced to understand how this could happen. The statues looked heavy. It would have been impossible for someone to move them into place while he was gone, even in the half hour of distance between him and where he was in the maze. The statues' arms were outstretched toward the sky, as though they were seeking a salvation Gart wished they'd receive.

The statues were slick with rain. The thunder and lightning had picked up, moving closer to the house and the mountain. Gart examined one of the statues and, finding it strong enough, placed a foot on its base and began to climb it in an attempt to get a view of the area around the maze. When he was up high enough, he craned his neck, spotting the estate, the mountain, and more. Something was wrong, though, and Gart's mind couldn't put it together at first.

Oh my god. When it finally hit him, Gart stumbled off the statue and fell to the ground. From the view of the estate and the mountains surrounding him, the maze stretched for miles in every direction. Gart's heart was racing. He didn't know what to do. Panic was setting in. He heard the sound of stone scraping across the ground.

Did that statue just move?

Rising slowly, soaked to the core, Gart's eyes moved from statue to statue, trying to locate the source of the sound. The statues at least *seemed* to be locked in place, but Gart wasn't sure. Another shift of concrete behind Gart alerted him, and he spun, confused, feeling anger beginning to swell inside.

"What do you want from me? What do you *want*?" he screamed to no one. To the statues. To the rain and the sky.

A clap of thunder answered him. He recoiled, terrified, feeling as though the lightning smashed the ground at his feet. A spark of electricity in the air confirmed this, and he felt every electron in his body crackle to life. Filled with energy, he bolted full speed down another corridor of the maze, his shoes slipping along the marble and brick. He heard the statues moving behind him, flooding into the various corridors of the maze.

Another feminine scream rang through the air, and he continued gasping for breath. He heard Dr. Harrison on the other side of the wall, calling his name, "Mr. Sloan," repeatedly, his voice frantic and confused, almost distant-sounding. Gart began to cry, feeling his heart pounding, almost exploding from his chest, turning down corridor after corridor in a desperate attempt to put as much time and space between himself, the statues, and Dr. Harrison.

***

Eventually, the exit was in sight. Gart kept up his pace, running at full speed toward what he hoped was freedom. He exited the maze, nearly keeling over from the stress of running. When he lifted his head, a clap of thunder and flash of lightning rang out like a snare drum, and the madness set in. He couldn't understand what he was seeing. Dr. Harrison, wearing a white lab coat, and his wife, looking perfectly rested and well. She was wearing a long coat, white, with a name tag. Gart stood and watched them as they worked over a body on a stretcher. Next to them was a piece of machinery with two large dials and two cables that were connected to the body's head.

"Dr. Harrison?" Gart whispered, his voice harsh and strained. He had been screaming while he ran, and his voice had completely escaped him.

Dr. Harrison and his wife completely ignored him, instead disconnecting the cables from the body on the table and wrapping them up on the machine. Harrison's wife wheeled it away, and Gart knew instantly that it was an electroshock therapy device. How he knew, now *that* was a mystery. Gart approached Dr. Harrison and stood next to him, looking down at the body.

"Time of death, 11:17," Dr. Harrison said, making a notation on a small chart at the foot of the stretcher. It had stopped raining, and the sun was beating down from above. Gart's clothes were miraculously dry.

Gart's body, both the one on the stretcher and his own standing next to it, looked exhausted from the ordeal. Gart felt a sudden tightness on his temples and, noticing the red marks where the electroshock device was attached to the body on the stretcher, realized that the pain he felt would be temporary. The body laid before him sighed, and Dr. Harrison caressed Gart's head on the stretcher. The Gart on the stretcher looked peaceful. He was thinner, almost gaunt, his cheeks sunken in. As his face relaxed, the Gart standing over him relaxed too.

Light swelled around both Gart Sloans. And in a flash, they both were gone.

PLAYING GOD

"Clark, you need to take a break from that thing. We're going to my mom's and we'll be late if you don't hop in the shower now," Deb said, packing a tray of cookies into a large, reusable grocery bag.

The "thing" in question was an Xbox One. More specifically, the game *Digi-Life*, a life and character simulation game that Clark became obsessed with after buying it for $7.99 during a Black Friday sale on the Microsoft store. Clark, who was typically more of a *Call of Duty* guy, found himself addicted to the everyday in and out of controlling these digital characters' lives. It was easy to fulfill their needs, as what they "wanted" was indicated by a colored sphere above their heads.

Red - they were angry and needed to do something fun to cool themselves down.

Blue - they were sad and wanted to be cheered up.

Pink - they were in love.

Orange - they were laughing.

Brown - they needed a shower.

Yellow - they were hungry.

Green - they were perfectly fine and had no desires to be filled.

His characters, modeled after himself and his wife, Deb, were near-perfect facsimiles, down to the red streaks in Deb's hair and Clark's predilection for wearing shorts in the winter time. They dressed and acted largely the same way that the real Clark and Deb did, with few differences, mostly how hungry Deb's avatar always seemed to be and how Clark's character always seemed to need a shower.

Clark navigated to the game's menu, saved his progress, then switched the game off.

* * *

At Deb's mom's house, he found himself daydreaming about his plans for the avatars. His character was on a career path to be an astronaut, which would allow his character to explore space, visit other planets, and possibly even set up a colony.

Avatar Deb, however, was locked into a career as a chef, working night hours and having an opposite schedule to Clark's avatar. In real life, Deb and Clark were both teachers, but Christmas break was in full-swing, and Clark had nothing but time to play his game, which annoyed Deb more than anything, since she saw their time off as time to do things together. Instead, she found herself planning and grading papers while Clark ignored her for the digital versions of themselves.

Clark was shifting a piece of cake around on his plate while Deb and her brother and parents talked about the upcoming holidays. He was lost in his own world, imagining trips to other parts of the game that he and Deb could take, exploring a digital version of Dracula's Castle thanks to the Halloween downloadable content he purchased (without Deb knowing), or possibly visiting the Grand Canyon, courtesy of the *Digi-Life Vacations Pack* that came free with his initial purchase on Black Friday. He never cared about the Grand Canyon in real life, but something about taking his avatars there excited him, and he looked forward to seeing how the game rendered and created the world he had seen only in pictures.

"Babe? Want more coffee?" Deb asked, finally getting him to pay attention to the conversation at the table.

"Hmm? Sure. Thanks," he said. Clark talked about school with Deb's parents while more coffee was poured into his cup. Deb's brother, Mitch, a college student preparing for his career as a barista by studying philosophy, was a gamer too and asked Clark if he'd been playing anything new lately.

"He's *obsessed* with this dumb game where you control people and their lives," Deb shouted from the kitchen. "*Digital People* or something."

"*Digi-Life*? I heard that was good. They're always updating and adding content," Mitch said.

"It's great. There's a lot to do, and really, it doesn't end. Unless your avatars die, I guess," Clark said. "I haven't had any die on me, but they do age, which is kinda' funny to see."

"You play that game, Mitch?" Deb's mom asked, feigning interest.

"No, but I think I know what to get Clark for Christmas, now. I think the summer pack is available for pre-order."

***

At the end of the night, Clark and Deb returned to their tiny house in the southeastern part of Resting Hollow. It was an older area of town where many of the houses had been remodeled and old-time charm was beginning to give way to apartment complexes and superstores. The two sat and watched *It's a Wonderful Life* on TV, and then Deb went to bed. The second she was in the bedroom, Clark flipped on his Xbox and started playing *Digi-Life* again.

He walked Deb's avatar into a clothing shop in the town of Seaside Paradise where he chose to have his characters live. The town was exactly what it sounded like, a seaside paradise, filled with beaches, bikinis, surfboards, and more. Their expansive estate (purchased as downloadable content for $2.99) sat on the shores of the westernmost part of town, bordering the ocean.

In the clothing shop, he began playing dress-up with Deb's avatar, trying on different outfits and accessories to "freshen" up her look. Between outfits, Deb stood on the screen, her nude bits pixelated, her cartoony face adorned with a smile. Clark found himself staring at the avatar's body. He looked up a cheat online to keep his avatars the same age they were and entered it. The words "Cheat Enabled" popped up on screen.

Clark looked at avatar Deb's pixelated bits, then at the rest of her body that wasn't pixelated. He saved his game, then went to sleep.

That night, he dreamed of the game, walking around Seaside Paradise as a real person, the sun shining above him in a pixelated sky. He could feel the heat and smell the ocean, and when he entered the same shop where he dressed his wife, he saw her, standing in the changing room, nude, parts of her body still pixelated.

***

Clark awoke the next morning and noted the surprising arousal he felt having "seen" avatar Deb's body up close in his dream the night before. He looked over for the real-life Deb but found she wasn't there, so, sighing, he got out of bed, took a shower, and headed into the kitchen, where he heard her clanging away on pots and pans. No doubt she was putting together some kind of treat for Christmas Eve at their friends' house, which was the following night.

"Hey babe," she said, kissing him. He squeezed her ass, and she playfully slapped his hand away. "Excuse you!"

"Sorry. Had a dream. Woke up all kinds of bonered up," he said, sitting down at the kitchen table and eating a banana.

"Is 'bonered up' the technical term?"

"That's correct," he said, peeling the banana.

"I think it's going to snow today," Deb said, looking outside. The news reports for Resting Hollow indicated a snowy Christmas was in the forecast, which was nice because after the holiday nonsense wrapped up with their families, Clark knew he'd be returning to Seaside Paradise for some fun in the digital sun. Clark couldn't shake the dream he had. He remembered the feeling of the sun and wanted more.

***

Deb spent the day planning lessons for class and working in the kitchen while Clark sat on the couch, pouring over every aspect of his avatar's digital life. He started an affair with a new neighbor, inviting her over while his digital wife was out, and sleeping with her in their bed. On more than one occasion, Clark found himself staring deep into the television, his fingers and hands moving on their own, guiding the on-screen characters around.

"Are you still playing that game? Maybe try something else, jeez," Deb said, walking in front of the television. "You've been playing for five hours."

He stared at her and shook his head. "Really? Five hours?"

Deb looked at the house on the television. It looked different. Bigger than previously, and more scattered than before. Bathrooms and bedrooms placed at different spots all over the house. Closets filled with bizarre paintings, most of animals, red and dark with white stripes. Impossible creatures. Clark's avatar stood in the center of the living room, staring directly upward, almost as if he was staring at Deb. The spherical indicator above his avatar's head was brown.

"Did some redecorating, huh?"

"I guess so," Clark said, rubbing his eyes.

"Looks like a Francis Bacon painting, babe. You're going nuts. Maybe go back to killing terrorists in *Call of Duty* for a while," she said, heading back into the kitchen.

Clark stared at the screen. He panned around the house using the controller, trying to find Deb's avatar. He checked every new room but couldn't find anything. Eventually, he came to a small closet off the main hallway downstairs in the mansion. He clicked it and the walls turned opaque, letting him see inside.

There stood Deb, her sphere blue, crying animated tears. The door to the closet was locked, and her avatar couldn't get out.

***

That night, Clark and Deb ate dinner and went to a movie. When they were driving home, it started to snow. Huge, thick snowflakes, sticking to the windshield, but not the road. It was a pretty snow, not the kind of cold, insulating snow that kept people indoors, and off the roads.

Clark was unnerved at the changes to the house, and even more so by the fact that he somehow lost five hours to the game without realizing it. When they got home, he and Deb went to bed and made love.

Afterwards, as Clark lay there unable to sleep, he turned his head to watch the snow fall out the window. He couldn't stop thinking about the game, the house, and the avatars themselves. He had never seen his own avatar stare into the sky, almost as if the screen wasn't there and the game itself wasn't just a jumble of code and information generated from a pool of ones and zeroes.

There had been games that broke the fourth wall before, lead characters engaging with the player. Media was full of instances where characters often addressed the audience or reader or whatever the case may be. Shakespeare didn't shy away from it, and neither did the classical Greek writers, utilizing the chorus to provide information to the audience that otherwise might be ignored or forgotten.

Could the company behind *Digi-Life* be doing the same thing? Could they be utilizing their game to make some kind of commentary on life simulation? Clark had researched the company, and they were responsible for a slew of other titles, most of them military shooters or adventure games set in various countries, none of which had much value beyond surface entertainment. *Digi-Life* was a departure for them, created by a smaller team at a tiny development studio in Rhode Island and which had dedicated nearly two decades of game development and research into an expansive life simulator. Millions of gamers were hooked, and people talked a lot about their various digital lives on Reddit and other forums, but none were having the issues Clark was having. Losing time to a game was possible, sure, but not common.

***

Christmas Eve came and went, with Clark and Deb spending time with family, having dinner, and engaging in conversation about their lives. Deb's parents put pressure on her to have a child, which Clark wasn't against, but with their financial situation, he knew it would be a severe strain. Deb was in her tenure year at school, and Clark had only gotten tenure the year before, so, the stress of a child on Deb would be too much. She found cooking and baking to be a way to de-stress, and Clark turned to gaming for the same reasons.

That night, Clark sat, controller in hand, and stared at the television, which was powered off. Deb had gone to bed, affected by too much eggnog, but Clark was wide awake. He thought about playing another game, but he felt this impossible urge, a draw to see what was happening with his digital home and life that was too strong to ignore.

When he powered on the Xbox, the screen highlighted his dashboard, showing the cover art for *Digi-Life*, along with other games he had been playing previously. He thought about playing *Battlefield V* or returning to *Far Cry 3*, but only for a moment. Those games and their murder festivals would always be there. *Digi-Life* needed to be played. He clicked the art and the game loaded, faster than usual, taking him directly to his digital home.

The extra rooms were gone, replaced instead with sealed-off, cement-looking blocks. He clicked the blocks, and instead of turning opaque they remained solid. He looked around the house and found Deb sleeping in the large, expensive king-sized bed he purchased for the couple, far swankier than their meager real-life queen bed purchased at IKEA, which had broken twice since purchase. Standing next to the Deb avatar was Clark's avatar, covered in filth, the sphere above his head brown. He seemed to be staring at the sleeping Deb character, and was nude, digital obscuration covering the area where his avatar's genitals might be.

Clark clicked on his avatar and directed him to the shower, and the avatar followed the orders of his master, standing beneath the digital spray of water, then emerging. The sphere above the character's head remained brown, and Clark was confused.

Usually a shower turned the sphere green, and when he checked the needs of the avatar, all were seemingly fulfilled. He wondered if maybe his game file had gotten corrupted by the new downloadable content, or by an update to the Xbox's operating system, so he saved the game, powered off the Xbox, and did some research. No one online was seeming to have the same problems as him, but he uninstalled and reinstalled the game anyway just to be sure.

When he booted the game back up, he saw that the house was exactly the same as it was before, only now, the Deb avatar was awake, and sobbing, nude, in the bathroom, the sphere above her head blue. Clark clicked on her with the controller but couldn't get her to follow any of his commands. He searched the house for his own avatar and found him in the back yard, head turned toward the screen, seeming to stare directly at him. It was night in the game, and the back yard wasn't well lit. Clark's avatar was still nude and was filthy again.

***

The following morning, Christmas, Clark awoke on the couch, controller in hand, television on, but Xbox off. He figured the system must have timed out due to inactivity, but he couldn't remember the last thing he did in the game. He was struck with a pang of annoyance that something might have happened that he'd have to re-do, but when Deb came down the stairs, the two had breakfast, exchanged gifts, and relaxed on the couch before having to head out for visits to their families and friends.

Throughout the day, even with the hectic atmosphere of the holiday, Clark found himself thinking about the game and about the weird things that had been happening with his characters. He'd check on them periodically, but it was always the same: Deb crying or sleeping, always nude, even when he'd try to put clothes on her, and his avatar covered in filth and staring at himself through the television screen. Clark zoomed the game's camera in on his digital self as close as possible, got up, sat on the floor in front of their enormous flat screen, and watched his digital self for any kind of movement. He noticed that his digital self's eyes were locked on his own and that they followed him as he moved.

"What's going on?" he whispered at the television. He noticed that when he moved his mouth, his avatar's mouth moved too, but the jumble of nonsensical sounds and words the avatars usually made was replaced with eerie silence. Clark opened his mouth again, and his avatar did the same. Clark then raised and placed his hand on the television screen, and after a moment, his avatar raised his hand, too, and placed it in-line with the hand on the screen.

"What're you doing, weirdo?" Deb asked, walking into the room.

"Huh? Nothing," Clark said, falling backward, away from the television.

"You'll hurt your eyes like that, babe. Listen, I'm gonna meet the girls for dinner, okay? I'll grab you something while I'm out?"

"Sure thing. Thanks, babe," he said, rubbing his eyes.

***

That night, at home alone, Clark played the game, staring at the house and watching his avatar operate on his own. The avatar was doing things he had never done before and was acting drastically different than he ever had previously. He watched as his avatar-self initiated sex with the avatar of Deb over and over, until eventually, Deb sat in one of the bathroom tubs, crying, the sphere above her head remaining a constant blue.

The avatar of Clark, meanwhile, had begun a garden in the back yard, growing all manner of flowers and plants, and Clark noticed his gardening skills had gone up dramatically between times when he was playing and times when he wasn't. He knew that the game would sometimes play itself, with characters working on skills and activities while the actual player was away, but this was different. Clark's avatar had seemingly abandoned his astronaut career path and instead focused solely on gardening. Always in the nude. *This would explain why he's always filthy*, Clark thought.

Clark's avatar began having relationships with other characters in the game, often engaging in the game's version of sex in front of Deb, who stood in the corner of the bedroom crying while her digital husband ravaged the neighbors, the mailman, the pizza delivery avatar, and more. Clark sat, controller in his lap, while the game played itself. He imagined himself in his avatar's shoes, and before he knew it, he was aroused at the thought of living such a bizarrely primal and unfettered lifestyle.

Clark squeezed himself through his pants, and after a while he began pleasuring himself while watching his avatar engage in activity with all the other avatars in the game.

Later he watched his avatar drag Deb by the wrist and throw her into a large hall closet outside the bedroom, locking the door so she couldn't leave. Deb's avatar cried and stomped her foot, her sphere changing from blue to red, then back to blue as she curled into a fetal position and cried.

Clark's avatar went into the yard and began working in his garden, and when Clark used the controller to zoom in, he noticed that a section of all the flowers looked like Venus flytraps. He took out his phone, and looked up the various plants one could grow in the game, and found that Venus flytraps were available once an avatar's gardening skills were maxed out. He checked his digital self's stats and saw that the skills were, indeed, increased to the max.

The various characters with whom his avatar had been having sex were scattered around the expansive mansion, most in their underwear, some nude, looking like a scene from *Caligula*. It was a strange visual, all of these characters walking around the home, eating food, drinking booze, and ignoring the cries of the closeted Deb.

Clark suddenly felt disgusted with himself, realizing that he was somehow enjoying watching the game play itself in such a strange way. The characters, who were normally cheerful, friendly, and sweet to one-another, had somehow taken a dark turn, and when Clark checked their stats, he noticed they were all in love with the Clark avatar, which made it easy to bed them.

Clark didn't understand why this was happening, as he had spent most of his time exploring the game's world, working as an astronaut, and buying furniture for the digital mansion he and his wife's characters lived in. His arousal over the game's dark turn shook Clark to his core.

He saved the game and turned it off.

***

In the shower, he leaned against the wall and let the water cascade over him. He wasn't big on resting in the shower, but he had nothing else to do and was feeling sorry for what he watched happen in the game moments earlier. He felt *dirty* about it all. The water coming off his body was clear at first, but eventually, he noticed a small trail of dirt coming off his legs. He examined himself and didn't notice any kind of filth or grime, so he examined the tiled walls and noticed that they, too, were clean. It was Deb's job to clean the bathroom this week, and she always did a great job, so Clark couldn't figure out where the dirt was coming from.

He got dressed, went downstairs, made himself a drink, and by the time he was back to the couch, Deb had returned with dinner, a chicken quesadilla and fries. The two sat, talked about her girls' night, and relaxed. When Deb asked him how his night was, he told her "fine," and that was the end of their conversation.

He decided that telling her he masturbated to his avatars was a bad idea and would probably make him look ridiculous, so he kept it to himself. But the idea remained with him, nagging at him, long after he stopped playing. The idea of being turned on by an amalgam of pixels, colored and crafted to resemble people, was weird to him, certainly nothing he'd ever felt before. The closest was probably the time he popped an erection while watching *Batman - The Animated Series* and Poison Ivy appeared on the screen, but other than that, never before.

He went to bed before Deb, and when he finally drifted off, his dreams were filled with images of the *Digi-Life* house, pixelated and very much resembling the game, but this time, it was on fire. In the bathroom, nude, digital Deb stood in the shower, creating a noose. There were no nooses in the game, or at least none that Clark knew of, but here she was, knotting together a noose made of digital rope.

In the bedroom, his avatar sat, covered in filth, his eyes bright against the darkness of the dirt. The avatars had no spheres above their heads, but they appeared pixelated.

Clark watched as Deb finished the noose, wrapped it around her neck, and stood on the edge of the bathtub that Clark watched her cry in earlier while playing the game. "Please don't," Clark said, but Deb, even with her pixelated, cartoony face, looked exhausted and broken. She stepped off the ledge of the bathtub, and swung backward, the sound of her flesh slapping against the tiled wall.

Clark stood, watching her a moment, but didn't move. He didn't make any effort to save her and instead was joined by his avatar, the two of them sharing a brief look as Deb's naked, digitized body swung and writhed around above the tub, her feet frantically slipping and smashing against the porcelain, echoing loudly in the bathroom.

"Help her," Clark said to his avatar.

The avatar looked at Clark and smiled. He opened his mouth to speak, but instead, the weird, jumbled language of the avatars emerged. He started screaming, and suddenly Clark felt a wave of panic wash over him. The avatar of Clark grabbed his arm and pulled him close, so close that Clark could smell the filth and dirt of his avatar counterpart.

***

When Clark opened his eyes, he looked out the window and saw that it had snowed heavily overnight. He rose slowly, rubbed his eyes, and looked down at the bed - dirt where his arm had been resting. The arm his avatar had grabbed in his dream. Confused, he stood up and went to the bathroom, where Deb was showering.

"Morning, babe," she said, pressing her butt against the glass of the shower.

He laughed as he brushed his teeth. "I had the weirdest dream, about the damn game."

He heard her make an exasperated sigh and imagined a roll of her eyes to go with it. She turned the shower off and stepped out, grabbing her towel as she moved. "What else is new?"

"I know, I know, but look," he said, showing her the dirt on his arm, in the shape of a hand. "This happened in my dream."

"Why are you so dirty?"

"Deb, it's from *the dream*. The dream about the game. I woke up with it like this. It's not like I went out this morning and did some gardening or whatever. It's fucking snowing out," he said, his voice frantic.

"Relax, babe. You probably just brushed up against something last night before bed, and it stayed on you. Hop in the shower. Breakfast will be ready in a bit. Then I have some lessons to plan," she said, giving him a kiss on the cheek as she slipped out of the bathroom.

Clark stood and looked in the mirror. His eyes looked sunken in, and the dream was weighing heavy on his mind. He and his avatar, side by side, watched his wife's avatar commit suicide, and neither of them did anything about it. He was worried about what this might mean, and worried he was starting to go crazy.

***

That afternoon, while Deb worked on her lesson plan, Clark uninstalled the game from his Xbox's hard drive and clicked "Remove from Library." Once *Digi-Life* was erased, he turned the Xbox off, went and kissed Deb, then decided to shovel the walkway to their front door.

Outside, Clark scraped the shovel along the cement walkway, lobbing the snow onto the lawn that lined the front walk of the house. His back was aching after about ten minutes, but he knew it wouldn't be much longer. He remembered his dad always told him it was smart to get ahead of the snow and shovel a bit, even as it came down, to lessen the load later. It was while taking a break to re-tuck his scarf into his jacket that he noticed a dark figure standing in the light snowfall, in the space between the house and the fence that lined their property.

The stark white of the world around him helped shape the figure into that of a man, even though the flakes continued to fall from the sky, sometimes obscuring his vision. Clark squinted and saw that the figure was his own, rather, was his avatar's, covered in filth and watching him.

"Hey!" Clark shouted, dropping his shovel and walking toward the avatar, who stood firm, his breath creating small puffs in the air.

When Carl reached the area where the avatar stood, he looked around. The figure was gone. He looked down and saw two filthy footprints in the snow quickly filling up with fresh powder. Clark knelt down and examined the prints. They were his own. The outline of his own toes. The shape of his own foot. The dirt, mixed with flecks of red and pieces of green grass, was light but very present. There were no other tracks in any direction.

***

Clark entered the house and looked around. The lights were off, and the heat wasn't on. He worried that maybe the electricity had gone out in the snowfall, so he made his way to the circuit box, popped it open, and examined the fuses. Multiple fuses were missing, and he noticed a crunching sound under his boots. When he lifted his feet, he noticed the fuses were smashed to pieces.

"Shit," Clark said, under his breath. "Deb?"

Clark walked around the house and couldn't hear his wife anywhere. He entered the bedroom, but she was nowhere to be found. Eventually, after looking around the entire house, which didn't take long, he entered the bathroom, and when he did, he froze. Hanging in the bathtub was his wife, nude, her body slashed apart, and blood everywhere. The white tile of the walls was coated with her blood, and Clark noticed something scrawled on the wall behind her.

Written in her blood was "Play The Game."

Clark ran his hand along Deb's face, tracing her cheeks. Panic, sadness, and anger filled him, and his brain exploded with a variety of emotions. He started weeping, cradling her body, pulling on her, but when he realized how well-fastened she was to the frame of the sliding tub door, his hands slipped from her wet body, and he fell backward, covered in Deb's blood.

***

In the living room, Clark sat on the couch, staring at the television.

He flipped the Xbox on, and as the system came to life, he noticed a heavy scent of rust in the room. He took the controller in his hands and noticed that every single game he had installed on the Xbox was replaced with *Digi-Life*. No more *Call of Duty*, *Battlefield*, or *Stardew Valley*. In their place, *Digi-Life*, *Digi-Life*, and *Digi-Life*. There was nothing else. The fact that his Xbox and T.V. were the only things getting power in his house sent a shiver up his spine.

"Jesus ..." Clark whispered, still covered in his wife's blood. He clicked on *Digi-Life*, the only choice he had, and the game came to life. On the screen was a perfect reproduction of his own home. Not the once-sprawling mansion, but the one he was sitting in currently, down to every single detail. On the couch in the living room on-screen was his avatar.

The mood sphere was nowhere to be found. Clark moved the sticks of the controller around, shifting the screen to the bathroom. In the bathroom, Deb's body hung in the tub, digital blood everywhere.

Clark navigated back to the living room and noticed something on the coffee table in front of his avatar. He clicked it and a small information balloon appeared reading "Kitchen Knife." Clark zoomed in on the knife. It was covered in blood.

Clark leaned back on the couch. On the table in front of him, the same knife, in the same position. He reached for it, picked it up, and held it in his hands. It looked like a mesh of pixels, but it was there, in reality. The blood even looked pixelated, almost cartoony in the dim light of the living room. Snow continued to fall outside. In the game, Clark's avatar held the knife to his throat.

He felt his arm move, on its own, raising the knife to his own throat. He watched the screen as his avatar smiled and slid the knife across his neck, his throat erupting into a waterfall of digital blood. Clark, in reality, did the same, blood pouring from his throat as he slid the knife across.

GNATS IN THE TEACHER'S LOUNGE

When Mr. Hayes sat down at the computer tucked in the corner of the teacher's lounge, it was the first time he noticed the flittering of tiny bugs in the air. At first, he thought they might have been dust particles, but when they flew in his face while he was typing up a PowerPoint presentation on *The Monkey's Paw* to use for his 8th graders, he knew they were gnats. Other teachers complained about the deluge of tiny winged nuisances that had invaded the teacher's lounge at Belvedere Public School, but not much had been done about it.

He thought about the police officers who came by the school earlier that week, inquiring about a missing child. The child wasn't one of Mr. Hayes' students, so he wasn't questioned, but he remembered seeing the child in the hallways, usually running, and even remembered asking the boy to slow down once or twice.

"How is this *our* job to take care of this shit? Don't we have an entire janitorial staff that should be cleaning this fucking place every night?" Mr. Gregson asked. He was older, in his fifties, twenty years of teaching under his belt, and anxious to retire. He had been in the school district his entire career, and he knew the families and culture of the area. His own kids went to the school when they were growing up.

"Maybe some Raid will do it? We could always spray after school," Ms. Sachs said. She was young, pretty, in her second year teaching at Belvedere, and still excited every day to step into the classroom to teach the kids about the miracles of mathematics. Thick glasses hid deep purple eyes, which Mr. Hayes had never seen before.

"*Raid*? Jesus Christ bananas, Kit. That shit is *toxic*. It's against OSHA regulations to spray that. Read your contract," said Mrs. Barbara McCauley, also known as "the battle axe" to those who ducked her in the hallways. She ruled the Foreign Language Department with an iron fist, and she had the steely will to go with it. A thirty-seven-year veteran, and about fifteen years past her expiration date as a teacher, Mrs. McCauley was often referred to as "a fountain of information and experience, from which one should not draw water."

Mrs. McCauley sat in her usual spot in the teacher's lounge, beneath the large row of windows overlooking the front of the school, eating reheated meat skewers. Mr. Hayes did everything he could to avoid interactions with her. Mr. Gregson, too, even as the school's union representative, avoided her like the plague she was. Every year, he helped administration come up with a suitable retirement package, often including additional benefits that wouldn't ordinarily be offered, in an effort to get her the hell out of the school and into the sweet abyss of retirement.

Mrs. McCauley had no intention of retiring any time soon. She remained at the school, making life hell for her students and her co-workers. The ranking veteran, she assumed control of the Foreign Language Department twenty years prior, and had yet to give it up. The other language teachers scurried around the school, kowtowing to her every whim and desire. They were an army of sycophants, but with no possible reward in sight.

"Mrs. McCauley, perhaps they're attracted to whomever is heating up fish in the microwave? That smells *delicious*, by the way," said Mrs. Linscomb, a twenty-five-year veteran and chairperson of the English Department. She was, essentially, Mr. Hayes' boss, but was the polar opposite of the tyrant, Mrs. McCauley.

Ms. Sachs smiled to herself. Mr. Hayes always noticed her smile. He described her often to friends, saying that she had one of those smiles that seems like she has too many teeth. "Like a Julia Roberts-type situation," Mr. Hayes would often say, drunkenly, at the local Applebee's, where he'd meet with friends for drinks on Fridays. The fact that he was Ms. Sachs' senior by nearly a decade wasn't lost on him, and thus he never said anything to her about his almost painfully obvious crush.

"I'd be happy to warm my other skewer up for you, Mrs. Linscomb," Mrs. McCauley said, her voice dripping with sweetness. She popped the skewer into her mouth and bit down on the wet-looking meat. She began chewing it, loudly, staring at Mrs. Linscomb, who simply smiled, gathered her paperwork, and walked out of the teachers' lounge.

Mr. Hayes finished his PowerPoint and had next period off, as well. The other teachers filed out, except Ms. Sachs. She had next period off, too, and she often remained in the lounge, reading a magazine or grading papers. Mr. Hayes, though finished, remained, too, and sat down on the large leather couch under the windowsill that faced the front of the school, where Mrs. McCauley had been previously.

The gnats hung in the air, and Ms. Sachs swatted them with her magazine. "This is gross, right? This *has* to be a safety hazard."

"Or at least a health hazard," Mr. Hayes said, looking up from his phone. He was pretending to scroll through Reddit but was really locking himself in a knot trying to figure out what to say to Ms. Sachs to get her to fall in love with him.

"Something's going around. I've had a few students drop like flies lately. Sick for a few days here, a few days there. A couple haven't been in school in more than a week," she said, genuine concern in her voice. Mr. Hayes hadn't noticed any missing kids from his own classes, but he taught a different level than Ms. Sachs. She mostly taught 6th grade. He taught mostly 8th. Plus, English and math were at complete opposite ends of the educational spectrum, so they didn't even overlap in staff meetings, typically. The only time they really had together were the two periods they both had off. Eighty-four minutes of relaxation in the middle of the day, where they both sat, typically in silence, today being the first time they'd really spoken since the time Ms. Sachs started working at the school.

"I hadn't really noticed, honestly. My kids are completely out of their minds this year," Mr. Hayes said, quietly. "Some can barely string together a sentence when I need them to."

"I was so bad at ELA when I was in school," she said. "I don't miss writing essays."

"I don't miss PEMDAS or whatever you guys call it now," he said. "Or FOIL. Is FOIL still a thing?"

She laughed. That extra-toothed smile. "FOIL no, but PEMDAS, yes. Math isn't too different from ELA. It's all about language and communicating ideas."

"I never thought of it like that," he said. He wondered if maybe she was messing with him. From the little he knew about her, that wasn't her style, but then again, maybe it was. He barely knew her, outside of appreciating how pretty she was, and even then, he felt like a creep due to the difference in age.

"Language is language, right? Communication is fluid, and we create bridges and connections through discourse, right? That's all math is, a way to communicate ideas. You ever see that movie *Arrival*? It's what made me want to teach math," she said, rather, gushed.

"That's the one with the girl who played Lois Lane?"

"Who's Lois Lane?"

"She's a reporter from *Superman*. She's Superman's girlfriend, or maybe his wife, I don't know. But she's the same actress. Amy Adams, I think," he said nervously.

"I don't really know Superman, Mr. Hayes," she said, averting his gaze. She suddenly seemed nervous, which was her usual speed outside the classroom.

"You can call me Karl. Mr. Hayes was my dad," he said.

"And you can call me Kit, or, I mean, obviously, you always *could*, but, well, you know," she stumbled.

"So, a movie made you want to teach math?" he said, after a long, awkward silence. She went on, discussing theorems and concepts he knew nothing about, and furthered the connective tissue between language and math, and the writings of Ted Chiang, as well as Galileo.

The gnats were pervasive, buzzing in their faces frequently.

He was legitimately interested in what she was saying and desperately wanted to make more of a connection with her, so he dangled on every theory and word she uttered. Her nervousness disappeared when she talked about math, her normal, semi-awkward teacher's lounge persona stripping away during conversation.

Mr. Hayes even started telling her about Superman, explaining who Lois Lane was, and she seemed genuinely interested, asking questions and being a good listener. Years of teaching had taught him to spot a good listener a mile away. When the bell rang, they were lost in conversation and had to quickly pack their work and scoot out of the room. They shared an awkward goodbye, swatting gnats and waving to each other, and disappeared down the hallway toward the math and ELA wings of the school.

***

After school, Mr. Hayes spotted Ms. Sachs in the parking lot, and she waved before ducking into her Honda. Mr. Hayes remembered that he left his ski cap in the teacher's lounge closet, so he slipped back into the school, saying hello to some of his students who stuck around for after-school activities. When he unlocked the door to the teacher's lounge and dipped inside, he was struck by the fishy, almost metallic smell that hung in the air.

The gnats were everywhere. In the span of only a few hours, they had gone from a nuisance to a disgusting cloud of black hovering near the fluorescent lights of the lounge, near the refrigerator, and in the sink. The lounge reminded Mr. Hayes of the scene from *The Amityville Horror* when the flies swarmed Rod Steiger. When Mr. Hayes left the lounge after grabbing his ski cap, he wondered if Ms. Sachs had seen *The Amityville Horror*. He decided she probably hadn't and started making a mental list of movies he'd love to watch with her but knew that he probably never would.

***

The next day, when Mr. Hayes arrived at school, he said hello to some co-workers and made his way to the lounge to hang his coat and cap. The wind was howling outside, and when he entered the lounge, two janitorial staff were cleaning behind the refrigerator, in the sink, and all over the lounge. "Bugs," one of the janitors said, and Mr. Hayes nodded, putting his lunch bag in the fridge.

In his classroom, Mr. Hayes unpacked his work, set up his lessons for the day, and rested his head back, closing his eyes.

"Good morning, Karl," a nervous, sweet voice caused him to jump, nearly falling back in his chair. When he collected himself, he realized that it was Ms. Sachs.

"Good morning, Kit," he said, trying to straighten himself up.

"You know what?" she asked, eyes bright behind her thick glasses.

"What's that?" he said, swatting a gnat away. Somehow they had found themselves in the hallways upstairs in the ELA wing of the school.

"We both have 'K' names! How funny is that?" she said, with a smile.

He stared at her. "You're absolutely right."

She just smiled. The moment between them became slightly awkward and when she realized it, she scurried away down the hallway. The math wing wasn't near the ELA wing, so he realized she had to walk from almost the other end of the school to tell him her silly observation. *Not silly. Cute,* he thought.

***

The day went by and was uneventful. Two students failed a quiz he gave on *The Monkey's Paw*, and he wasn't shocked, because those two students were often failures when it came to his quizzes. Mr. Hayes didn't believe in multiple choice and instead relied on essays to gauge student understanding, and these two boys, in two separate classes, simply couldn't rise to the occasion and were on the failing end of the academic. Of course, because public schools on Long Island would not allow a student to fail, Mr. Hayes was forced to pass them with a grade of sixty-five, the bare minimum the administration of the school would allow. Mr. Hayes didn't mind. He was paid well, and in the end, these boys probably had a future in manual labor, so he stopped caring.

At lunch, in the lounge, Mr. Hayes was sitting with Ms. Sachs, talking about math, ELA, and more. They discussed *Arrival*, which Mr. Hayes re-watched the night before, as well as the coincidence of their names. The lounge, which had been clear of gnats that morning during the janitorial scrubdown, had become re-infested with the winged pains. Mrs. McCauley seemed to ignore them while eating a plate of gray meat, and Mr. Gregson, red-faced and angry, ranted about what to do about the "damn bugs."

Mr. Hayes and Ms. Sachs were lost in their own world, something Mrs. Linscomb noticed almost immediately. She was walking out of the teacher's lounge, passing behind Ms. Sachs, and glanced at Mr. Hayes, smiling and gesturing to the pretty math teacher as she went. Mr. Hayes couldn't help but smile. Catching this, Ms. Sachs smiled and, as usual, lit up the room.

"I'm going to make a trap. We use apple cider vinegar, and some other common household cleaning things, and boom, we trap the fuckers and they die," shouted Mr. Gregson.

"I'm allergic to apple cider vinegar, so, absolutely not," Mrs. McCauley said with a finger wag. Mr. Gregson stood, deflated. "You put that out, and you'll have a union complaint on your hands."

"Fine. No apple cider vinegar for Mrs. McCauley," Mr. Gregson said through gritted teeth. When he left, Mrs. McCauley smiled, pleased as punch with her dismissal. The gnats rested on the arms of her chair, and some on her actual arms, and she didn't swat them at all. Mr. Hayes had read that they had four razorblade-like mouth pieces that they used to slash flesh, drinking the minute amounts of blood that came to the surface. He imagined Mrs. McCauley's arms, microscopic slashes scattered, ribbon-like, all over her. The thought turned his stomach and he must have made a face, because Ms. Sachs put her hand on his, and brought him back down to Earth.

"You okay?" she asked, her voice drawing him back to reality.

"Yeah. I just feel a little queasy with all these gnats and flies and stuff. It's gross," Mr. Hayes said, swatting the air. She hadn't moved her hand yet. He didn't want her to.

"We should go out for lunch tomorrow, scoot out of here for a couple periods, maybe go to that pizza place around the corner?" Mr. Hayes agreed.

"What are you two *conspiring* over there?" Mrs. McCauley asked, her voice loud.

"We're doing lunch tomorrow, away from the bugs," Ms. Sachs said.

"Oh, how nice. A fancy lunch for fancy children. That's positively *lovely*," Mrs. McCauley said. Mr. Hayes often wondered about *Mr.* McCauley and how he could marry such a horrifyingly awful woman. He had seen pictures of her in her youth, and she was certainly attractive, but her caustic personality would leave much to be desired, day to day. She was a lot of work, often high-maintenance, but the bugs in the lounge didn't seem to bother her. It was a strange duality.

"Would you like us to pick up a *fancy* slice of pizza for you tomorrow, Mrs. McCauley?" Mr. Hayes asked, trying to kill her with kindness, when in reality, he just wanted to kill her and be the hero of the Teacher's Association at Belvedere.

"Pizza is repulsive, Karl, and you could do with a salad slice," Mrs. McCauley said, rising and walking out of the lounge, a small cloud of gnats following her out the door.

"Pizza is delicious, and she's probably the biggest asshole I've ever met," Mr. Hayes said, after a moment, listening to her *click-clack-click* down the hall.

Ms. Sachs laughed. Mr. Hayes couldn't help but smile at her lighting up the room again.

***

That night, Mr. Hayes planned lessons, watched some television, and texted with Ms. Sachs. She sent him pictures of her cats. He sent her pictures of his computer workstation, which he spent way too much money on. He didn't have any pets or children or anything too remarkably fancy, but his workstation was pristine and well-organized, and it was something he was proud of outside of his work in the classroom. Ms. Sachs sent a lot of emojis, which Mr. Hayes had to decipher, but he thought of the challenge like an archeologist, unraveling hieroglyphics, often confused at the difference in meaning between an upside-down smiley face and a sideways smiley face with eyes closed tight.

There was a news report about the missing students, and Mr. Hayes still didn't recognize them. All he knew was what he had learned from his co-workers: they were average students from good families, and they tried hard. Their missing was strange, though, and some of the teachers worried that a prowler was on the loose. But they also noted that the missing children were friends, so it was entirely possible that they got lost together, maybe in the woods outside of town, and everyone hoped they'd be found soon.

Eventually, Ms. Sachs texted "goodnight, Mr. Hayes" complete with an emoji that had "Zzzzs" next to it, obvious in its meaning. He typed "goodnight," and sat in his favorite chair, watching *Seinfeld* reruns. Suddenly, another text came through. An emoji with a kissy face. He didn't know how to respond, so he didn't, and eventually he went to bed.

The next day at work was largely the same. Students and teachers, the usual. More gnats, suddenly in the gymnasium, swarming the large fans that were *never* turned on that rested on the ceiling. Mr. Hayes wondered why they were even there, for even in the harshest of summers, during summer school (which Mr. Hayes was sometimes asked to teach), the fans remained off, collecting dust and being completely useless. The gnats seemed bigger, but realistically, there were just more of them, moving in unison, a black mass zipping from fan to fan, fluorescent light to fluorescent light.

The only reason Mr. Hayes was down in the gym was that one of the teachers, Mrs. Daniels, texted him to come see the bugs. She wanted confirmation that she wasn't going crazy, and Mr. Hayes was happy to confirm that she was not, in fact, losing her mind. Mr. Hayes was always jealous of the gym teachers, since they got to wear shorts all year long. Hoodies and t-shirts, too. How hard could it be to tell kids to climb a rope or to run around the track? Mr. Hayes was busy dissecting the meaning behind imagery and language, and Mrs. Daniels was down in a huge space, yelling at her students while "teaching" them to play basketball. Didn't seem fair.

Mr. Hayes texted Ms. Sachs, and she came down to the gym before their lunch date. She was bundled in a red coat, the weather outside rather frightful that morning, snow starting to fall, the bitter cold season of Long Island starting to set in. She was wearing a knit cap that seemed almost too large for her, and Mr. Hayes teased her mercilessly about it, informing her that she'd grow into it eventually and that puberty would be rough but she can handle it. She laughed and teased him back, and by the time they got to the pizza place, he entertained the idea of ordering a salad slice. Ms. Sachs poked him when she noticed him checking his gut in the reflection of the display case, where a seemingly endless supply of pizza existed for the lunch crowd's desires.

"Don't listen to her. You look *fine*," Ms. Sachs said. "Lunch is on me, by the way."

"Oh, no no. I insist," Mr. Hayes said, taking out his wallet.

"You can buy next time, silly," she said. *Next time? More lunch dates? Maybe dinner?*

They got their slices and grabbed a booth in the back of the pizza parlor. The lunch crowd was heavy, but nothing too crazy, and the two enjoyed just being able to sit and chat, not worrying about being surrounded by their colleagues. They got to know each other more. Mr. Hayes thought about the kissy face emoji, and finally asked "Would you like to get dinner with me sometime? Maybe Saturday? There's a movie playing at the Cinema Arts Centre, a Japanese horror flick, supposed to be really psychedelic and nuts. I own it, but I've never seen it on the big screen. I'm not sure if that's your thing, probably not, but I figured --"

"Yes. To the dinner and the weird Japanese movie," she smiled.

So did Mr. Hayes.

***

That weekend, Mr. Hayes and Ms. Sachs had what they would both call their best first dates. Dinner at a local steakhouse was wonderful. Conversation didn't involve work, and the movie, a hallucinogenic ghost story set in the Japanese countryside, was both terrifying and hilarious. Ms. Sachs loved the movie, far more than Mr. Hayes imagined she would, and he couldn't have been happier. He drove her home and walked her to the door of her apartment building. The slight awkwardness of a first kiss vanished when she gave him a simple peck on the lips, catching him by surprise, and ducking into the building. He watched through the small window to the building as she ran up the stairs, to the second floor, disappearing down a hallway.

Mr. Hayes had one of those butterfly-type feelings, an injection of excitement he hadn't felt on a date, or in general, for a long time. The rest of the weekend was pretty lame in comparison. He found himself at lunch with a friend, gushing about the date the night before, his friends proud that he finally had the nerve to ask Ms. Sachs out. The two of them texted, pretty frequently, and Mr. Hayes soon found her use of emojis cute and started using them himself.

That night, there was a call from the school's emergency services line. It was snowing heavily, so Mr. Hayes assumed that Belvedere would have a delayed opening, or, the gift to every teacher on the planet, a mythical *snow day*, but instead, the typically robotic, long-ago-recorded message informing teachers and staff of a traditional emergency was replaced with a frantic message from their principal, Mrs. Crestwell, talking about an *infestation* of gnats and flies in the building. That word stayed with Mr. Hayes - *infestation*. He couldn't imagine how much it would cost to delouse and hit the entire school with bug spray. He imagined a massive circus tent covering the school, powdery smoke filling the hallways and classrooms, gnats and flies dropping from the light fixtures, gym ceiling fans, and dotted (most likely asbestos-ridden) ceiling tiles.

Ms. Sachs texted Mr. Hayes and asked if he wanted to have a "Bug Party," which sounded disgusting, but when he realized it was just the two of them getting together, eating food, drinking, and watching television, he agreed. She drove over, the snow beginning to fall harder, and when she sat down on the couch, glass of wine in hand, it wasn't long before the two were sharing their second kiss, their third, and more. At a certain point, Mr. Hayes lost track of how many times his lips met hers, and he wondered if she knew a mathematical formula to keep track.

***

Wednesday, the school reopened, and both Mr. Hayes and Ms. Sachs were depressed about it. They had spent Sunday night, Monday, and most of Tuesday enjoying each other's company (and bodies) and had exactly zero interest in returning to work. They would have to edit their lessons, having two days excised from their current plans, but that wasn't the bad part. Dealing with kids who just came off a four day weekend, *that* was a different story.

Mr. Hayes arrived at school, early as usual, and upon entering the teacher's lounge, he was still buzzing from the new romance in his life. He flipped the lightswitch in the lounge, but it wouldn't turn on. He could make out a form in the corner, by the window, the soft, gray morning glow creating an outline.

"Hello?"

The figure shifted in place and buzzed. Mr. Hayes stepped further into the room, trying to make out who it was. He thought it might have been Mr. Gregson. The figure was about the same height as the man. As he moved closer, he noted that the figure was heavier or was wearing an enormous coat that Mr. Hayes had never seen Mr. Gregson wearing.

"Hey hey," Ms. Sachs' voice caught Mr. Hayes' attention, and he spun around. She flipped on the light, but again, it wouldn't work. "Something up with the electricity?"

"I'm not sure," he said. He turned back to the figure and saw that it was gone. There was a light buzzing in the air, and he couldn't place it. It almost sounded like the squeaking of a school bus braking system, but further away, muffled. "You hear that?"

"Busses are arriving a little early because of the weather, I guess," she said, stepping to the refrigerator and putting her lunch bag inside. She then crept over to Mr. Hayes, looked around the lounge, and kissed him on the cheek. "Have a good day, Mr. Hayes."

He blushed. "You too, Ms. Sachs."

***

At lunch time, Mr. Hayes found himself in the lounge, by himself, as Ms. Sachs had a department meeting. Mrs. McCauley sat on the couch under the window, near where Mr. Hayes saw the figure earlier that morning. She stared into space, eyes glassy, almost watery. She didn't say a single word to Mr. Hayes when he entered the lounge, and he wasn't bothered by that in the least.

   Mrs. Linscomb came in and sat with Mr. Hayes, prodding him about Ms. Sachs. He spilled his guts, because he was happy to talk about his new romance. They mostly whispered because Mrs. McCauley was sitting not far from them and they worried about what she might say. Every once in a while, Mrs. McCauley twitched, and when Mrs. Linscomb left the room, Mr. Hayes could have sworn he saw a gnat slip out of her mouth.

***

Rumors spread quickly in a school like Belvedere. People only talked about Ms. Sachs and Mr. Hayes, but they mostly talked about Mrs. McCauley's dramatic change in personality. She was largely quiet, and her teaching had suddenly turned into showing movies and having kids write essays about the film. Gone was the fire-and-brimstone style that she was known for, and her pointed, often nasty comments somehow vanished. She still spent her free time in the teacher's lounge, alternating between sitting on the couch or staring out the window at nothing in particular.

When Mr. Hayes said goodbye to her before leaving, she simply twitched and he ducked out of the room.

***

At dinner that night, Mr. Hayes and Ms. Sachs talked about Mrs. McCauley. Ms. Sachs talked about how she saw her shuffling down the hallways, looking haggard and dirty, and Mr. Hayes said he didn't particularly notice, other than that she hadn't been her normal cheerful self. Ms. Sachs mentioned that there seemed to be dirt in Mrs. McCauley's wake, but again, Mr. Hayes didn't notice.

"What *do* you notice, Karl?" she asked, playfully.

"I notice *you*, Ms. Sachs," he said, and they finished dinner and made love. When she left, he didn't want her to, but he knew they both had to be up early the following morning for a staff meeting to discuss cleanliness in an effort to keep the gnats and flies away.

***

When Mr. Hayes pulled up to the school the next day, he was surprised to see a massive black cloud hovering above it. Other teachers were standing outside, in the cold, eyes locked on the cloud, which seemed to move. There was a buzzing in the air, loud, persistent. Mrs. McCauley stood directly beneath the center of the cloud, staring into it, mouth agape.

"What's going on?" Mr. Hayes asked when he joined the other teachers standing outside.

"That cloud … it came out of the vent behind the refrigerator. It's them, the bugs," Mrs. Daniels said, almost, whispered. "Been hovering above the school all morning so far."

"The kids'll be here soon. What are we going to do?" Mr. Hayes asked. He looked around. Ms. Sachs had just arrived and was walking over to the crowd.

"What's that crazy bitch doing?" Mrs. Linscomb asked, pointing at Mrs. McCauley.

Mr. Hayes turned to Ms. Sachs, kissed her cheek, and walked off toward Mrs. McCauley. As he approached her, he noticed a thin line of the gnats circulating around her. Her clothes looked filthy, confirming what Ms. Sachs had said the night before. Her clothes seemed to move, as though her body was tremoring beneath them. Gnats and flies swarmed from her mouth, all over her face, her hands, and body, from under her clothes.

"Mrs. McCauley, are you okay? Why don't you come with me?"

She didn't budge. Mr. Hayes could barely make out the whites of her eyes. There were tiny gnats crawling all over her. When he looked closer, her skin seemed cracked or chaffed somehow, her lips blistered and chapped. She was gurgling softly, and the line of gnats and flies streaming between her body and the sky buzzed with such intensity that the sky seemed to crackle and vibrate around her.

Mr. Hayes reached for her, now more concerned with her health and safety than anything else, but when his hand touched hers, she exploded. Literally, an explosion of meat, bone, blood, and bugs splattering everywhere. Mr. Hayes, now covered in what remained of Mrs. McCauley, recoiled and vomited. The cloud of bugs in the sky dispersed, and even the ones that crawled all over Mrs. McCauley's entrails had vanished. Snow started to fall, and Ms. Sachs, Mr. Gregson, and Mrs. Linscomb rushed over to Mr. Hayes to help him up.

"Are you okay?" Ms. Sachs asked. "Let's get you home."

***

Mr. Hayes showered, scrubbing harder than he ever scrubbed before. Mrs. McCauley's viscera washed down the drain, and he took an extra forty minutes than he needed, just letting the shower beat down on him. School was cancelled, of course, and even with Mrs. McCauley's death, the other teachers seemed more worried about the school closings impacting their spring break.

When administration and police examined the school, they paid specific attention to the vent behind the refrigerator. Inside, they found meat. Bags of it. Each with a name: Millie Mark, Dolores. Students who had been missing a lot of school, students who had fallen through the cracks, day to day, and vanished without much fanfare. Ms. Sachs had noticed, since two of the students were hers; however, most other teachers didn't notice, and the phone calls that called them in sick each week were traced back to Mrs. McCauley's phone.

The meat had caused the gnats. Mr. Hayes found a poetic justice in that. Mrs. McCauley, so buttoned up and in control, in the end was undone by her darkest secret. The rest of the children were never found, just these spongy, wet bags in the vent, but justice was done - Mrs. McCauley was gone, taken by the very creatures left over by her crime.

THE WORLD WHISPERS MADNESS

Depending on your point of view, aquariums, the big ones where exotic sea life is on display for school field trips, exhausted parents, and dating couples, are either a good thing or a bad thing.

One can either see them as a prison of sorts for the water-dwelling wildlife, or as a valuable educational and rehabilitative tool for injured animals. Either way, aquariums exist, and one of the largest, most popular ones is Adventure at Sea, built along the coast of Little Compton, Rhode Island.

The aquarium borders Sisson park, named after a Civil War colonel who invented the three-ring binder, and features a variety of sea life, from the ordinary great white shark to the somewhat-outrageous fifteen-foot-long green sea turtle, Adventure at Sea takes great pride in being on the cutting edge of research, rehabilitation, and educational programming. To that end, the aquarium is preparing to unveil its latest addition, an eighty-foot-long tentacled cephalopod, believed to be a mutated squid, possibly a Humboldt or even a Colossal, its beak extended, rows of jagged, sharp teeth inside, which, upon analysis by the experts at the aquarium, seem closely connected to pearls than to the typical chitin-based proteins of a normal cephalopod beak.

In place of the normal eight tentacles and two arms of a traditional squid, this particular specimen features two thick, mucous-membrane coated tentacles, impossibly powerful, that propel the creature through the water with relative ease. Two smaller arms, almost human in appearance be it not for the three clawed fingers, hug the sides of the beak, and the scientists of the aquarium imagine that they are primarily used for feeding, considering their size and location. Because of the close proximity to Sisson Park, and the terrible sense of humor of the staff of Adventures at Sea, internally, the cephalopod is referred to as "Sissy."

Acquired off the coast of Asia, lending credence to it possibly being related to a Humboldt squid, Sissy was caught in the propeller of a large transportation vessel. It nearly sunk the ship in its attempts to escape, but it eventually grew tired and passed out. Adventures at Sea was notified of the creature's rarity, after seeing it on a sailor's Twitter account, and sprang into action. They provided ships capable of storing the creature, while also providing trained staff to handle its recovery. Sissy was quiet during transportation, but upon arrival to the actual aquarium, the tentacled monster awoke, thrashing around in its enormous pool, its massive tentacles slamming against the ten-inch-thick glass of its enclosure, a double-pane hastily put together by the staff. It was secure, considering it was funded and assembled in a matter of weeks, about the amount of time it took to remove and transport Sissy from the waters of Asia to the east coast of the United States.

Almost immediately, Adventures at Sea began its promotion, both on social media and through traditional outlets. They took the angle of the "mysterious creature from the sea" and provided schools and news outlets with a treasure trove of pictures, videos, and more showing off Sissy. They didn't have an official name for it, so they came up with a contest in which a child could win a lifetime membership to Adventures at Sea, as well as a thousand-dollar college scholarship if a true name for Sissy was chosen. They received nearly ten thousand entries from students all over the country, and one was finally chosen - Pat. Since the staff at the aquarium couldn't find any evidence of sex organs (more evidence of it being some kind of mutation), the gender-neutral name Pat was perfect for Sissy.

Adventures at Sea had sold thousands of tickets for the official debut of Pat, and the staff and administration of the facility were incredibly excited to see people's reactions.

Crowds gathered outside the park, massive clusters of people waiting for their chance to get in to see this almost-mythical creature in the flesh. Lines of children and parents were all ready to be sold Pat t-shirts, hats, hot dogs with the bottoms split into legs to resemble the two tentacles, and other assorted items of varying absurdity.

Crowds flooded the park, almost all of the students making a beeline for Pat's tank, which was both inside the park and equipped with a viewing platform outside. A concrete ring with food vendors, toy stalls, and more surrounded the tank. In the center, floating, barely moving, was Sissy. The crowds gawked and stared. Children pressed and banged their smudgy pink hands against the tank, and everybody waited for the great creature to *do* something.

Sissy shifted in the water. The theme to *Jurassic Park* played loudly over the sound system. It was all the audio-visual crew of the aquarium could come up with, as one of the potential promotional concepts hyped Sissy as a lost primordial creature from the days of the dinosaurs.

Carbon dating proved this wrong; somehow, Sissy was far older. Analysis indicated that the creature was quite possibly the oldest creature ever discovered alive on Earth. This was added to the promotional material and was the main thing that drew in the protestors.

Adventures at Sea was used to protestors, granola-crunchy hippies screaming about the rights of whales and fish and whatever other injustice they held dear. Sissy (aka Pat) was no different. They shouted at the staff, the patrons, and the security guards about how the creature belonged in the ocean, in its home, and how humanity was imprisoning a rare and perfect being.

Some sang, some chanted, sometimes in English, sometimes in foreign tongues, their words sounding like a mouthful of mashed potatoes.

***

Weeks passed, and Sissy-Pat was still drawing crowds. The protestors began to dwindle, moving onto other causes. A core group, often wearing dark hoodies, remained, and they were the ones chanting, every day, outside the park. One day, fed up with the treatment of Sissy-Pat, they stormed the gates of the park, dozens of hooded figures quickly overpowering the guards and staff.

They rushed through and made their way toward the tank that held Sissy-Pat. Two hooded figures sprinted off from the main group, running down opposite ends, the main force of protestors serving as a distraction. The two protestors, both wearing backpacks, removed their hoodies, opened their packs, and began rooting through the various items inside. Parents with children passed them, ignoring them for the most part.

The two men worked quickly, an assembly of mechanical and hazardous items coming together in a MacGyver-like pace resulting in very crude explosive devices. The kind of explosive devices that could pierce double-paned aquarium glass. The kind you can look up how to build online, an assembly of manure, gasoline, and other odds and ends.

The security and staff were on the main cluster of protestors relatively quickly, but the other two, with the bombs, were able to work and apply their devices to the glass of the aquarium. The idea was to detonate the tank and hope that the water would flood out and propel Sissy-Pat out to the ocean, which wasn't far away. The aquarium was along a boardwalk, so, once through the gate, there was only about thirty feet of coast until the beach. The plan was half-baked at best, but it was the best the protestors could come up with. How else could they move the creature to the ocean?

***

Security surrounded the two men assembling the bombs and cleared the area of any bystanders. The confusion set in quickly, and even though the park had only just opened for the day, there were countless visitors. As clear as the area was, when the bombs detonated, dozens of people were injured in the explosion. Shards of glass and metal flew everywhere, and the two men who set the bombs were killed, if not in the first explosion then in the rush of water that engulfed them.

Sissy-Pat slid toward the ocean. Once to the boardwalk, it slowed, its mucous-membranous flesh leaving a deep trail along the wood of the crowded tourist area. The creature's great, hulking frame rose, pulling itself by its tendrils wrapped around trees in the park. Some protestors swarmed the beast, armed with bottles and buckets of water to throw upon its massive body. As they did so, Sissy-Pat pushed itself toward the ocean, scraping over rocks and the rest of the boardwalk.

Those nearby produced their cell phones to take videos and pictures of the event, but as they attempted to record, their phones died, the energy draining almost instantly. Sissy-Pat cast its eyes upon the crowd, a dark, amorphous cloud oozing from its flesh. The creature seemed to grow in size as it continued crawling into the ocean. The protestors continued to chant, shouting "scourge at hand, sun up high, our great Lord, our father!"

Dagon. The protestors repeated the name, over and over. *Dagon*, the father, *Dagon*, the scourge, *Dagon*, the corruptor.

Dagon continued into the ocean, leaving tracks in its wake. Its eyes darted all over, the protestors, the crowd that gathered, the police, the security. They watched as the great old one slipped under the waves, its tendrils whipping wildly, splashing, creating waves that spilled onto the sand. The protestors continued their chant as police made arrests and inquiries into what happened at Adventures at Sea.

***

The aquarium never reopened after the event, and the disappearance of the great old one was never verified, other than by those who watched it occur. Even then, the media took the stance of the protestors being more attractive than the apparent confirmation of an ancient god, and thus the event was largely forgotten, other than when people mentioned Adventures at Sea. And even then, the capture and display of a god was ignored.

Some protestors slipped away, escaping arrest, and they, along with their compatriots, knew the truth. The truth about the old ones. The truth that lurks at the bottom of the ocean.

THE FINAL GOODBYE

When Vanderbilt County installed red light cameras at nearly every intersection in Resting Hollow, the folks in the town were divided on how to feel.

On the one hand, it was important to enforce the law. Students from the local university often cruised through red lights late at night, and accidents could be high, especially in September when school was back in session. On the other hand, the tickets that were issued were around $175 a pop and were nearly impossible to fight. In the off-chance that one was actually innocent, he or she would be out of luck.

When a ticket arrived in Bradley Ellis' mailbox, he was surprised. He hadn't driven through any red lights as far as he could remember, but when he checked the addressee, he saw that it read *Bart Ellis*, his father.

The only problem was, Bart Ellis passed away six months ago.

It wasn't uncommon for Bart to get speeding tickets, and he certainly received his fair share of red light tickets since the program started. He always enjoyed taking a late-night cruise around Resting Hollow, first as a teenager in his two-door coupe, then as an adult in more sensible vehicles befitting a family man. He would drive Bradley around, as a baby, to help him sleep at night. He always drove to families' houses and always enjoyed taking road trips. He was also a careful driver, outside of a few tickets for minor offenses.

When Bradley opened the letter from the county, he studied the pictures that accompanied the ticket. There were three. One was of the rear of the car, his father's Subaru, long-since turned in to the dealership. Another was an extreme close-up of his father's license plate, attached to the back bumper of the vehicle.

The third picture, that was the one that rattled him. A clear view of the windshield, his father behind the wheel, wearing the suit he was buried in.

Bradley tucked the ticket into his back pocket and went inside. He had purchased his parents' home after his father passed away, and his mother had taken up residence in the guest cottage on the property, allowing Bradley to set up the house however he wanted.

He walked into the back yard where his mother was gardening. She had always worked in the garden, his entire life, growing kale long before it was trendy to do so and always having fresh tomatoes, cucumbers, and more. It was rare that she needed to buy the basic staple vegetables, as they grew plentiful for her during the seasons.

Bradley didn't know if showing her the ticket was a good idea or not, so he kept it to himself. He looked over the garden she was working in and thought it best to wait until he did some investigating into the ticket before revealing it to her.

***

That afternoon, Bradley sat at the kitchen table staring at the ticket. He looked at his father's face and checked the date the pictures were taken. According to the county's record, the pictures were taken only a month ago. His father had passed away by then, so Bradley took out his phone and called the county to verify whether the ticket was a mistake or not.

The woman on the other end of the phone was remarkably helpful and provided enough information to indicate that the ticket was, in fact, real. The pictures were taken at the stated time, on the stated date, and she was able to produce a short video clip, which she emailed to him. In the video, Bradley's father's car slipped through the light, late at night, with no other traffic in the area. The video even had sound, and Bradley was able to hear the familiar purr of his dad's Subaru's engine as the SUV rolled through the light. He had heard that engine a thousand times, a sharp contrast to the roar of Bradley's Chevy Tahoe.

Bradley watched the video of his dad rolling through the red light about thirty times that night, sitting on the couch and drinking his usual Miller Lite while watching *Hell's Kitchen* reruns on his Roku. He couldn't focus on Gordon Ramsey screaming at incompetent chefs; instead, he studied the photos and then watched the video, pausing when he could make out his father's silhouette in the car. The video was clear, but the close-up of his father wasn't as good as the still image on the ticket. When Bradley went to bed that night, he cried, thinking about his father, about the cancer that took him, and the possibility of life after death.

***

Bradley went to work the next morning and called the Subaru dealership at lunchtime. They informed him that the car was still on the lot, and they'd be happy to show it to him and provide paperwork and information to prove that nobody has driven the car, outside of the occasional test drive. They were actually a little surprised they hadn't been able to sell it yet.

"No one's driven it off the lot for anything *other* than test drives around the block?"

"No, sir. In fact, we can provide the mileage to you, as well," the salesman at the dealership told him. "Like I said, it's a bit of a mystery as to why it's still here. Our used cars typically fly off the lot."

"If you don't mind, could I come by and see it?"

"Sure, of course. I'm here all day until close."

"Thanks," Bradley said, hanging up and returning to work.

***

After work, Bradley headed to the Subaru dealership and met with the salesman he spoke to on the phone. Together, they walked to the Forester, which sat in a row of about fifty other SUVs, some

Foresters, some not. Many were the same color, and many were the same exact model as his dad's. The salesman handed Bradley the key, told him he'd give him some time, and headed off to chat with a pretty, young salesperson Bradley spotted on his way in.

In the Forester, Bradley settled in behind the wheel. The "new car" smell was there, but he picked up faint traces of his dad's cologne - Nautica Blue. Bradley stared off into the sea of vehicles around him, the Nautica overpowering him a bit. He felt his eyes welling up with tears and climbed out of the car. He walked quickly past the salesman, thanking him and telling him that he'd get in touch with him again if he needed to.

In his own car, Bradley cried for the second time in twenty-four hours. The way his dad's SUV was parked, in such close proximity to the other cars, it would be impossible to slip the car out. There was only a few feet of space between the rows, and Bradley couldn't imagine the headache of moving the other cars to get it out for test drives, let alone spectral cruises through red lights. He sat, paralyzed, and watched as cars pulled in and out of the dealership parking lot.

***

That night, unable to sleep, Bradley decided to go for a drive. He went over to where the camera ticket was taken, the corner of Orchard and Cicero, and waited. He checked his watch. He had about forty minutes until the time of night, 3:25 a.m., that the photo was taken. The area was empty. He sipped a bagged can of Miller Lite absently and waited.

"Come on, come on," Bradley whispered to himself. A car drove passed, going through the intersection slowly, and turned down Cicero. Cicero led to the older part of town where the houses were cheaper and land was being gobbled up by developers to turn into condos, apartments, and shopping centers.

He finished his beer then tore off a fresh one from the six pack he picked up at 7-11 before arriving at the corner. Popping the tab, he took a hefty swig, some of the cold contents spilling down the sides of his mouth, down his chin. He lowered the can and looked around. Down Orchard, an SUV approached. Bradley paused and waited, holding his breath, scared to make a noise. He always thought the term "waiting with bated breath" was nonsense, but here he was doing just that.

The SUV approached. It was the right color. The streetlights and businesses lit the area well enough that he could tell the SUV was the right shade of gray-blue to match his dad's. As it rolled closer to the intersection, Bradley strained to see the make of the car. A Ford? No. Maybe a Land Rover?

A Subaru.

Bradley's eyes went wide as the car slowly cruised through the intersection, casually running the red light. Bradley knew another ticket would be issued. He expected a flash of the camera but remembered that the cameras themselves didn't *actually* flash at all. Jumping out of the car, Bradley raced toward the intersection to get a look at the driver with his own eyes.

"Dad?" he said, spotting his father behind the wheel, gray-skinned, the same vacant look on his face.

Bart turned slowly and stared at his son as the car passed through the intersection. When their eyes met, Bart's expression changed. Bradley, a rage of emotion whipping through him, stood, hyperventilating, confused and scared. Bart raised his hand and waved to his son, smiling widely.

Bradley focused, and though his breathing was quick and frantic, fear and sadness taking him over, he raised his hand and waved back. He saw his father smile again, and nod, acknowledging his presence. Bradley watched as the Forester continued down the empty road, eventually vanishing into the night. He dropped to his knees and stared into space.

***

The next morning, Bradley thought about what had happened the night before. He took out the camera ticket, cut a check, and mailed it back to the county, thinking about his father's smile, and the simple moment they shared. That night, he decided to head back to the intersection at Orchard and Cicero.

He waited, patiently, sitting on the curb not far from his car, for the Forester to arrive. Time moved slowly, and his patience began to wear. 3:25 a.m. came and went, and Bradley felt that it was all over. He knew that he wasn't going to see his father again, and he treasured that the wave and smile they shared with each other, would be their final goodbye.

MISCELLANEOUS EPHEMERA

"I'm good, ma. I'm stuffed," Easton said to his mother, Nidia, while leaning back in his seat at the dining room table. Easton's twin sister, Becca, was next to him, and she was still shoveling forkfuls of spaghetti into her mouth. Becca was a bit thick in the midsection, and so was Easton, from years of pasta, pastries, and various other delectable treats homemade by their loving, doting, and oftentimes overbearing mother.

"Nonsense. You're skin and bones," Nidia said, putting another helping of pasta on Easton's plate. He looked down at the spaghetti and was intoxicated by the scent of the homemade sauce. His mother was half-Italian and half-Greek, and she was a master of both schools of culinary art. Becca was working on compiling their mother's best recipes to keep the tradition alive, but something was always missing when Becca made dinner and invited Easton and his girlfriend over. Even with the same ingredients and the same amount of care put into every dish, Becca's approach to their mother's recipes always fell flat.

"It's damn good, ma'," Becca said. She shook more grated Romano onto the pile of spaghetti and began twirling her fork in the mound. Absently, Easton followed suit.

"So what're you two up to this weekend?" Nidia asked, watching her pride and joy enjoy the food.

"I'm taking Rita to a carousel museum," Easton said, his mouth full of pasta.

"A carousel museum? Jesus. That sounds horrific," Becca said, pouring herself another glass of soda. "I can't believe how hungry I am."

"Rita's into carousels. It's weird. I know. But it's her one weird thing," Easton smiled, thinking of his girlfriend. He hadn't introduced her to his mom yet because he wasn't sure how she'd react. Rita was African-American, and Nidia was notoriously "traditional," to put it in her own words. "Anyway, we're going to the museum, then to dinner. Nothing too crazy."

"I hope I get to meet this Rita character soon. She seems to have you wrapped around her finger!" Nidia said, laughing. Becca laughed, too. "You, young lady, what're you doing this weekend? Any handsome young men taking you to a carousel museum?"

"Thankfully not," Becca said. "I'm just going to relax and work on the recipe book. I talked to a friend of mine who's an editor, and he thinks we could probably compile it into something folks might want to buy. Traditional recipes are big right now."

"That's great, honey. Good for you!" Nidia smiled. She patted Becca's hand. "More spaghetti?"

***

That night, after dinner and saying their goodbyes, Easton and Becca headed back to their respective apartments. Their weekly dinner with mom had gone well. Even though both felt sick from so much food, it was still nice to get together once a week. Nidia always enjoyed having her kids around, and even though both were in their thirties, they always made time for her and were always happy to sit around the dinner table like when they were kids and enjoy a meal.

Easton called his girlfriend to talk about the night and tell her how his mom asked about her again, and she laughed. "Well, your mom sounds sweet. Maybe she's not super racist after all?"

"I dunno, babe. Maybe you can meet her soon," Easton yawned into the phone.

"Aww. Is the baby tired? Too much time with his mama?"

"Yeah, yeah, yeah. Don't tease," he said, taking off his clothes and getting ready for bed. His studio apartment was in the center of town, above a bank, and he enjoyed the quiet of the town square at night.

"Whatcha' doin' now?"

"Just getting undressed and ready for bed, mentally preparing myself for all those carousels tomorrow," he said, with a chuckle.

"Ooooh, getting undressed, eh?" she said, a hint of flirtation in her voice. Rita wasn't shy about being flirty with Easton, which he loved. She was the one who asked *him* out, after all. He just kept stealing looks at her behind the counter at the coffee shop while he sat and pretended to work on his laptop. Rita was always very forward and aggressive, the total opposite of Easton, and it drove him wild. They were approaching their four month mark and knew it would have to be time to introduce her to Nidia soon, especially if he saw things going forward, which he wanted desperately.

"You're a creep, babe," he said, lying down in bed, the streetlights in the town square outside his window casting long columns of soft light across his ceiling.

"You love it," she said. "Go to bed, mama's boy. I'll be by around ten tomorrow morning for our best day ever."

"Goodnight, babe," he said. He heard her give him a kiss through the phone, and he returned it, then placed his phone on the charger, rolled over, and dozed off.

***

The next day, Easton and Rita enjoyed the carousel museum, which was the oldest museum in Resting Hollow. Rita scribbled notes on a yellow legal pad, and even though Easton didn't understand her obsession with wooden horses created to carry children in a circle while creepy music played loudly, he appreciated her enthusiasm and found it cute. Rita's glasses hung on the tip of her nose as she scribbled notes and drew sketches of the various horses. The museum didn't allow photos, so they couldn't use their phones to take pictures of anything.

The museum was connected to the town hall and contained a lot of Resting Hollow's history. There were numerous paintings of the various vistas in the mountains, as well as old photographs of the area that would become The Palisades, long before multi-million dollar homes were built. There was a lot of information from the local Native American tribes highlighting the region as holy land. Easton recognized a few of the photos from when he was a kid learning about the history of the town and the deep roots and ties to Native American folklore and customs.

The only thing that seemed out of place in the museum were the carousel horses. Frozen faces of wooden creatures, various expressions forever locked in place, all left Easton feeling uncomfortable. He wished they could spend more time in any other part of the museum, but this wasn't his day; it was Rita's.

"So when do I get to meet her?"

"Soon, I think," Easton said. "I think it'll be fine. She'll be fine."

"She better be; otherwise, I'll have to creep her out by bringing her here and demanding she let me keep seeing her baby boy," Rita said, tucking the pad under her arm and kissing Easton quickly. "Tell me about her."

"Not much to tell. After dad left me and Becca, mom became our world. We were still little, so, she had a lot to shoulder."

"You never heard from your dad after he left?"

"Nah. I tried finding him when I turned eighteen, thought maybe he'd want to meet his son and daughter, but I couldn't find any record of him online. No social media, no financial records, nothing. I even had a buddy of mine who's a cop in the city look him up, but he couldn't find anything either."

"That's weird. I'm sorry you couldn't find him," Rita said, taking Easton's hand. "He missed out on a great pair of kids. I can understand why you two are so close to your mom and why she's so protective of you guys. She's an impressive woman having to take care of you two."

"Couldn't have been easy, but she was always there. She worked her ass off. Two jobs. And we had everything we ever wanted. I don't know how she did it, honestly."

"So what if she's a horrible racist, right?" Rita said, laughing. Easton laughed, too.

"I'm sorry, babe. I know it's uncomfortable," he said.

"It's all good, sweetness, I'm just messing with ya. She'll love me, and if she doesn't, so what? It's not like I'm gonna stop banging you and dragging you to weird museums."

He smiled, and they kissed.

***

The next day, Easton called his sister and asked her to be there when he brought Rita to meet Nidia. Easton was jogging in the park, trying to work off the spaghetti from two days prior, and stopped to catch his breath on a park bench overlooking Serling Lake.

"Wow. The creepy museum went well, huh?"

"I guess so," Easton said, staring at the lake. "Can you make it?"

"Of course. I'm not one to shy away from a disaster. You know that," Becca said, laughing.

Easton spent the rest of the afternoon in various stages of worry, rehearsing over and over how he'd go about introducing Rita to his mother. He knew that a simple "Mom, this is Rita," wouldn't work, so he started drumming up ideas about how to get around Rita not being the type of girl his mother would approve of. He hated that he had to deal with his mother's old-fashioned way of thinking After all, Rita was amazing, and that's all that mattered.

Still, he imagined the looks his mother would give her, and they were similar to the ones Nidia gave him whenever he did something wrong as a kid. He remembered the first time he saw "the face" as he and Becca called it. Easton was playing in his parents' room and snooping around in their closets. Even though his father was long gone by that time, he still called it "his parents' room." His father's closet was empty, except for an empty shoebox, the thin paper used to hold the shape of the shoes still inside.

His mother's, however, was full of boxes, tiny ones, like jewelry boxes, and others still, larger. The box from his new Super Nintendo was on a high shelf that Easton couldn't reach, and even though he knew there was no SNES in the box, his curiosity was too much to handle, so he started climbing the shelves to try and see what was inside.

He couldn't quite get the footing he needed, and after he slammed to the floor he heard his mother charging up the stairs. When she got to the bedroom, he turned and saw the look. Her upturned lip and fierce eyes looked as though they could burn a hole straight through him, a perfectly bored tunnel of meat and bone where once his heart might have been. Easton did everything he could to avoid being on the receiving end of his mother's look, which danced somewhere between anger, disappointment, and hatred.

He checked his phone and texted Rita, letting her know that his sister would be at dinner, and she replied with a picture of herself giving a thumbs-up, a huge grin on her face. Easton smiled when he saw it, but he knew the work week was going to be stressful, and he prayed that Nidia wouldn't be too hard on him for bringing his amazing girlfriend to meet her. He decided that if his mother didn't like Rita, for whatever reason, it wasn't his problem, and certainly not Rita's, and this would be the moment Easton could stop being the mama's boy Becca always referred to him as, and stand up not only for his partner, but for himself, as well.

***

Rita spent the end of the week at Easton's apartment, and the two snuggled, made love, drank wine, and worked like normal. When they ate dinner, Rita would grill Easton with questions she imagined his mother might ask him, even throwing in a racist term every now and then just to trip him up. Hearing Rita use racial slurs made him uncomfortable, but Rita was persistent, saying "Hey, it's better coming from me than from her right?"

"I guess so."

"So, let's keep going, babe. What's your answer?"

"What was the question again?"

"What's your intention with this young lady? Is it purely a case of jungle fever or what?"

"Jesus. I don't think you can say that," Easton said, clearing his throat, uncomfortably. "I love her. She's pretty fantastic."

"Just 'pretty fantastic?' I thought I was amazing? What's the deal? Am I losing points already? No sex for you, mister."

He smiled and stared into Rita's eyes. They were a mix of gold and brown, and he fell into them easily. "You're literally the best ever. I love you."

"That's more like it," she said, rising and sitting in his lap, kissing him.

***

Eventually, Friday came, and when Nidia opened the door and saw Easton standing with Rita, she froze. Easton introduced his girlfriend to his mother, and Nidia, confused, shook Rita's hand and welcomed them inside. Becca was sitting on the couch, anxiously awaiting their arrival. When Becca saw Rita, she rose quickly and hugged her, right in front of Nidia, who continued to stare.

Then it happened. The cursed look. Directed squarely at Easton. His eyes locked with his mother's, and a wave of panic washed over him, sending his brain into a state of peril. His anxiety spiked, and he found himself paralyzed, still locked in her gaze.

"Mom, isn't Rita's sweater adorable?" Becca finally broke Nidia's gaze, and Easton took a breath.

"Lovely, dear," Nidia said.

"I knitted it myself. I can make you one, if you like," Rita said, sweetly. The girl was trying hard, smiling, beaming with positivity. Easton had met her family when they took a trip into Manhattan one weekend, and it went amazingly well, so Rita wanted this to work and knew that adding an extra layer of sweetness couldn't hurt.

"No, thank you," Nidia said, walking toward the kitchen. "Dinner's just about ready."

"Mom made chicken rollatini," Becca said, smiling.

"It isn't fried," Nidia said, almost quiet enough to not be heard.

"What's that?" Rita said, smiling. She stifled a giggle as Easton squeezed her hand and walked with her into the dining room. "It smells great, Nidia. Thank you for cooking."

Easton pushed Rita's chair in and sat next to her. Becca sat opposite Rita, and Nidia carried the food into the dining room. Nidia placed the large serving tray down in front of Becca, who started plating everyone's dish. Nidia took her seat at the head of the table and stared at Rita.

"How did you meet my son?"

"At my job. He comes in a lot," Rita said, smiling. "I'm a barista."

"What's that?"

"A barista? I work in a coffee shop, brewing coffee, making drinks, that kind of thing."

"Rita makes the best cappuccino in town," Easton said, his voice cracking with nervousness.

"Easton asked you out while at work?"

"Technically, I asked *him* out," Rita said, putting her hand on Easton's. "When I see something I want, I take it."

"My kinda' gal," Becca said, popping a forkful of rollatini in her mouth.

"Interesting," Nidia said, staring at Easton. "Eat up, kids, while it's hot."

Easton pulled his hand from under Rita's and started eating dinner. Rita put her hand on his thigh and squeezed, sensing his nervousness. Nidia caught Rita's hand slipping under the table and wiped her mouth with a napkin.

"If you'll excuse me," Nidia said, rising from the table and heading upstairs. "I'll be right back."

Becca placed another serving on her plate. "How do you think this is going?"

"I can't really tell," Easton whispered. "That fried chicken comment was pretty shitty."

"I've heard worse, babe," Rita said, kissing him on the cheek. "Just relax, okay? I love you and I'm here, right?"

Becca sighed. "I need to meet someone like you, Rita. Got any brothers?"

"Real brothers or *street* brothers?" Rita said, her voice dripping with sarcasm. The two girls laughed as Easton looked upwards, hearing his mother's footsteps above them. As a kid, Easton would pay close attention to everyone's footsteps in the house and was able to tell where people were based on their movement and sound. It's how he always caught Becca sneaking back into the house late at night, which he would always use as blackmail material to get her to do his chores.

"What's wrong?" Becca asked.

"Mom's in her closet," Easton said.

All three listened. The house was dead silent, and everyone held their breath expecting to hear something that never came. "Does she have a gun or something? Am I going to die tonight?" Rita finally asked, causing Becca to crack up.

"I wonder what she's doing." Becca said.

Easton suddenly felt his body heat ramp up, his forehead glistening with sweat. He wiped his brow and softly removed Rita's hand from his thigh. "I don't feel so good," he said.

"Did she poison you for bringing a black girl home?" Rita joked.

Easton leaned back in his chair and stared at the ceiling. He heard his mother walking again, heading toward the steps. When he saw her heading back down, his vision became blurry, his eyes painful. He tried standing up, but as he did so, his legs gave out from underneath him. Rita wasn't fast enough to stop him from falling, but she caught him enough to stop him from hitting his head on the table. Becca rushed over to him and started fanning his face.

Nidia, her face frozen, walked toward Easton as he lost consciousness, blackness creeping in from the corners of his eyes.

***

"Wake up, babe," Rita's voice echoed from what seemed like a distance away. When Easton's eyes opened, he was staring at the ceiling of his mother's living room. He sat up slowly and looked around. Rita was kneeling on the floor next to the couch, staring at him, her beautiful eyes helping him refocus. His sister was standing at the foot of the couch, and Nidia was next to her, a cup of steaming tea in her hands.

"What happened?" he asked, rubbing his head.

"You passed out. Dehydration, maybe. You feeling okay?" Becca asked, staring at him.

"A little queasy, I guess," he said.

"Here, drink this," Nidia said, handing him the tea. Easton noticed a small, dark pendant dangling from his mother's fingers. The shape of the pendant itself was like a tear, but thick and three-dimensional. A clasp was fastened shut, and it looked like it was made of lead.

"Thanks," he said, sipping the tea. It was bitter and pungent, clearing his sinuses immediately and waking him up. "This is pretty brutal, ma'."

"Maybe we should head home," Rita said. Nidia nodded, and the two younger women helped Easton up and to the door. "Thank you, Nidia. Dinner was great. I'm sorry our evening got cut short."

"Not to worry, dear. It was nice meeting you," Nidia said, smiling. Becca kissed her mother on the cheek, and the two women helped Easton out the door and to the car.

***

Easton sat in his apartment, Rita asleep in bed next to him. He was trying to replay the events of the evening in his head, but when he got to the dinner, his memories became fuzzy. He barely remembered waking up on the couch.

"Come back," Rita whispered, tangled in his blankets. He looked at her and smiled. He traced his hand along her shoulder and lay down next to her.

"Sorry about tonight," he said.

"S'okay. We can try again another time," she said, turning and tucking herself into him.

Easton's nostrils were filled with the smell of the tea from earlier. He was shocked that the scent was still with him, the pungent, almost meaty smell giving him a slight headache. He reasoned the smell was still on his tongue or his lips and kissed Rita's forehead before falling asleep.

***

The next morning, the smell was somehow stronger, and Easton hopped in the shower while Rita stayed in bed. He brushed his teeth vigorously and used two different body washes, and still, the smell of the tea remained. It had started to make him feel nauseous, and he found himself doubled over the toilet, spilling what little contents he had in his stomach into the porcelain bowl.

"Babe?" Rita called from the bedroom.

"Don't come in here," Easton groaned, examining the contents of the toilet. His vomit was greasy-looking, red, with flecks of black. He didn't remember eating anything that was black, so he immediately felt troubled.

Rita appeared in the doorway of the bathroom and tentatively reached out to Easton. He pushed her hand away and shouted at her to leave, and she backed out of the room, upset. He slammed the door and sat on the edge of the bathtub, holding his aching head, queasy from the smell that lingered in his nostrils.

"Do you smell it?" he asked, his eyes tearing.

"Smell what?" she asked, from the other side of the door. She sounded more annoyed than hurt about him throwing her out of the bathroom.

"It's that tea from last night. I can still smell it. It's making me sick," he said.

"I don't smell anything, babe. The bathroom smells like your body wash and, you know, puke," she said, chuckling. "I'll go get you some stomach meds. Maybe they'll help."

"Okay," he said. He heard Rita quickly get dressed and leave the apartment.

He sat on the edge of the tub for a moment longer, his headache starting to clear. He opened the window in the bathroom, and the smell started to dissipate. The queasiness in his stomach started to subside, and he rose, nude, and cleaned the toilet. He noticed that not all of his sick ended up in the bowl, so he cleaned the area quickly then hopped back into the shower to clean himself more. Once out, he brushed his teeth again, and the sickness had completely vanished. He felt perfectly fine and assumed the worst was over, so he got dressed and sat on the couch.

When Rita returned about forty minutes later, he met her at the door with a kiss on the cheek. She handed him the Pepto and he took a hearty swig. "Just relax a bit. I'll make you some soup to ease your tummy," Rita said as Easton walked back to the couch with the Pepto clutched tightly in his hand.

In what felt like minutes, the sickness washed over him again. He started to feel lightheaded and, though he was sitting, dizzy. He felt himself start to sweat and took a few deep breaths. He laid his head down on the pillow. When he closed his eyes, he saw spark-like flickers of light dancing around in the dark, and the sickness was relieved momentarily, but only slightly.

Rita made him some soup, but he didn't have the stomach for it so it sat on the coffee table getting cold for most of the day. It was late in the afternoon when Easton said she should probably head to her own place, because if he was contagious, he didn't want her to catch what he had. Rolling her eyes at him, she kissed him on the cheek and left.

***

A little while later, Easton began to feel better. He warmed and drank the soup Rita made for him and even went for a short walk around Resting Hollow. He sat on his favorite bench near the corner of the street where his apartment was and just watched the world go by. He sent a selfie to Rita, and she sent one back, a kissy-face along with a text saying she was glad he was feeling better. He promised to make her dinner in a day or two, and she replied saying "You better. Until then, you'll have to make do without my soup-making skills."

Easton sat for a while longer, people-watching until night fell upon the town. Resting Hollow was always beautiful at night. The storefronts, restaurants, and bars that lined Main Street provided a warm orange glow to the cool night air, and the stars dazzled in the clear sky above the mountains that framed the town. If one was to walk down to Serling Lake, where he often walked, there was a chance to encounter live music playing at one of the gazebos along the walkways in the park surrounding the area. Nidia would often take Easton and Becca to the free concerts in the park after their dad left. Easton liked to go even as an adult. Sometimes he'd go with Rita, other times with his friends or Becca. Becca wasn't always into the shows, but they were free and always had an assortment of food trucks around, so she was into that, at least.

Before he knew it, it was well into the night. The restaurants and bars got busy. Cars slowly drove past, and he remained on the bench, lost in thoughts about his mother and Rita and what to do about them. Nidia was his rock. She raised him. She loved him fiercely. She created a world of safety and wonder in the wake of his and Becca's dad disappearing. Part of that world was exploring all that their hometown had to offer. Easton learned a lot about Resting Hollow and gained a love for its history and folklore, from the original Native American settlers to the recent tragedy of a high school prom cruise that crashed into a cliffside late at night. The town had its share of ghosts and tall tales, like any other town in America, and Easton loved learning about it. Nidia instilled a lot of that in him, as she never shied away from taking her twins to local museums and the library for lectures about the town. "It's good to know where you come from," she'd say, often when Becca complained about being bored.

***

After about a week of on-again-off-again sickness, Rita urged Easton to go to the doctor, and when he did, he found out he was perfectly healthy, other than needing to lose a little weight. His blood test results would later indicate that he had a vitamin D deficiency, but according to his longtime physician, "everyone does." Easton couldn't figure out exactly why this intense sickness was coming over him, but the one constant was that it happened in the evenings, often after dinner with Rita. He wondered if maybe she was secretly poisoning him, and when he jokingly accused her of doing just that, she smiled and said "Poison is too long-haul. If I was going to kill you, I'd do it in the throes of passion."

"Not a bad way to go," he said, his head spinning and vision blurry as Rita drove them back to his apartment. "I'm sorry I haven't been feeling well. Maybe I'm allergic to something?"

"Well, the doctor did the allergy test, but he won't have the results for another week," Rita said, focused on the road. "Maybe it's my deodorant, perfume, hair stuff. I'll change it all and we'll see if that's what it is? Maybe you change your stuff, too? I'll go pick up a whole new line of products for us to use and we'll test it."

He nodded absently, the town passing by outside the car window blurry and out of focus. He had read that sometimes people develop allergies later in life, but such an adverse reaction to the normal, everyday things that Rita was mentioning seemed crazy.

***

Nidia's reaction to Easton's illness was more along the lines of "I told you so" than it was actual concern for her baby boy. "I always told you, those people will get you. She's probably got some weird African perfume that's giving you the shakes."

"I don't think Moschino is made in Africa, mom," Easton said, rolling his eyes. "Plus, she's Native American too, so, do you think she's doing a rain dance or some shit to make me sick?"

"A rain dance would only make it rain, Easton. You know that," Nidia said, placing a plate of spanakopita down in front of him, with a side plate of baklava. "Here. Eat. You need your strength to deal with this girl."

"What do you mean, ma?"

"You should break it off with her. She's making you sick, baby boy," Nidia said.

"All of a sudden? We've been together a while now, and I never got sick with her once before. It wasn't until we came here that night," Easton said, feeling annoyed at his mother's suggestion that he break up with Rita.

"Listen. You must make your own mistakes. That's the only way for your generation to learn. I guess you don't wanna listen to your mother, who *raised* you and *loved* you your entire life? That's fine, I guess," Nidia said, raising her hands in surrender. Guilt was a valuable weapon to be used sparingly, and Nidia knew that. She saved all her best salvos for her kids, using them more often with Becca who was more headstrong than Easton was, at least until her little boy started dating someone Nidia didn't approve of. "I'll be right back."

Nidia rose from the table and walked upstairs. Easton took his phone out and texted Becca, informing her that their mother was being a racist nutbag again. Becca responded with a .gif of Robert Redford from *Jeremiah Johnson*, nodding and smiling. Easton listened for his mother's footsteps and detected that she was in her bedroom again, in her closet. Curious, he rose from the table and moved to the steps. Looking up, he saw nothing, and he decided to sneak upstairs to see what Nidia was doing.

As he walked toward the bedroom he heard what sounded like stones being scratched together. He passed his old bedroom, and Becca's too, and as he reached for the doorknob to his mother's bedroom, she reappeared and jumped, dropping something that she quickly bent down and picked up. "What's that, ma?"

"What're you doing up here?"

"I heard a weird noise. I wanted to see if you were okay," Easton lied. He tried to get a look at whatever it was his mother had dropped, but she tucked it into her pocket quickly.

"Such a good boy," she said, patting his cheek. "Come. Let's head back downstairs."

Nidia walked down the steps, but Easton remained outside her room, staring inside at the walk-in closet, its slatted doors closed. "Mom, what were you doing in the closet?"

She paused, halfway down the steps. "I wasn't in the closet, Easton."

He stared at her. "Yes you were."

"Easton, my sweet boy. You're being silly. Come," she beckoned from the steps, her hand firmly in her pocket, wrapped around whatever it was she dropped moments ago.

Easton stared at the closet then turned and walked to his mother, down the steps and back to the table to finish the leftovers. Afterwards, he helped her work in the garden, digging new spots for plants and vegetables. He felt good and healthy, but his mind fixated on what was in the closet that was so important that his mother would lie to him.

***

"It was weird. It was like she got caught with her hand in the cookie jar or something," Easton said to his sister as they sat at the bar around the corner from his apartment.

"I can't believe you just used the phrase 'caught with her hand in the cookie jar,' Easton. You're unraveling," she said, finishing her vodka and club. "What do you think she was doing?"

"I don't know, but she got something out of there. Something small, because when she dropped it, she was able to hide it in her hand, then her pocket."

"What was it?"

He shook his head. "No clue." The music on the sound system changed from The National to The Police, and Easton bobbed along with the music.

She ordered another drink, along with a round of shots for the two of them. "Rumple Minze, if you have it."

"Jesus. You're in it to win it tonight, huh?"

"How's Rita?"

"She's good. I'm still feeling sick from time to time, so I don't know if changing our grooming products really helped all that much. This new deodorant I'm using is all-natural by the way, and it has to be re-applied like six times a fucking day."

"Is that why you smell like you've been dipped in Sriracha? Stings the nostrils a bit," Becca said, slamming the first shot of peppermint-flavored liquor, then the second when Easton waved it away. "Wuss."

"Well, we could always divide and conquer," she said, wiping a bit of Rumple Minze off her chin.

"What do you mean?"

"We run the Christmas-break gambit," she began. "I'll distract her while you sneak upstairs and investigate the closet. Easy peasy. I'll get a Greek book from the library or some shit and tell her I'm having a hard time reading it. She'll scold me for forgetting the language of *our people* and make me read it with her," Becca finished, doing her best Nidia impression to emphasize *our people*.

"That could definitely work," Easton said, nodding. "You should've seen how weird she got, Becca. It wasn't like her. There's something in there she doesn't want us to see."

"Maybe that's where dad is?" she joked, ordering two more shots.

***

"Are you like, actively avoiding me now? How am I supposed to feel?" Rita asked, annoyed. Her words became sharp and specific, enunciated perfectly. This was her normal tactic when she was upset about something, which was rare.

"It's not that. I'm not avoiding you, but there's something wrong, like, I don't know what it is. When we're together, my stomach goes crazy. When we're apart, I feel fine," he said into his cell phone. The pause in conversation was brutal. A long, dead silence that he knew meant she was reaching her breaking point with him. He had seen her this mad once before, when she found a text from his ex begging him to come back to her. He hadn't responded to the text, but Rita saw Easton's lack of candor as a betrayal. He agreed and apologized. "Rita, I'm sorry. This sucks, I know, but just give me a little time to figure out what's going on with me."

"What's going on is that you're pushing me away because your mom is a racist bitch, and you're a mama's boy who doesn't want to upset her," Rita said, angrily.

Easton thought about what she said. It was at least *partially* true. He hated the idea of upsetting Nidia. Easton loved Rita. She was sexy, funny, weird, and ridiculous in ways that he never found in another woman, but was she worth disappointing the woman who gave him life? Put him through college? Worked her ass off as a single mom to raise not one, but two weird little trolls?

"I'm sorry, babe. Please, give me a little time to figure out what's going on," he begged into the phone.

"You can have all the time you want, Easton. Fuck off," Rita said, hanging up on him.

Easton tucked his phone in his pocket. "Awesome," he said, looking out over the town through his apartment window.

***

The following morning, Becca and Easton descended upon their childhood home armed with a book in Greek, something about traditional Greek baking techniques. Becca would claim she couldn't understand some of the words, and Nidia would focus on helping her decipher them, allowing Easton time to investigate the closet. Becca spoke nearly-perfect Greek, so Easton a little worried that their mother would see through their plot.

Easton had sent multiple texts to Rita hoping that she would respond, but she didn't. He decided that she was running the "angry ex-girlfriend playbook" as he called it, and that she was in the stage of spending time with her friends who would all talk shit about him to make her feel better. Then he remembered that Rita didn't really have many friends, and most of her family was on the reservation on the other side of the mountains to the northeast of town. He thought about her a lot and missed literally everything about her.

"Entering the dragon's den," Becca teased as she knocked on the door.

Nidia answered, and they went inside. As usual, there were bowls of assorted delights on the table, and Becca popped many of them into her mouth. She was never shy about enjoying their mother's cooking, and Easton always got a kick out of watching his sister go to town on the things their mother made.

"Mom, so, I got this book. It's about baking techniques, and I'm having trouble reading some of the passages." Becca showed her mom the book. Nidia sat down next to her and the two started pouring over entries, Nidia taking the time to highlight and review the parts of the book that Becca was supposedly having trouble with. Easton wasted no time slipping up the stairs, removing his shoes to make less noise.

As he crept up the stairs, he got a text from Rita. It was a picture of the two of them from the Carousel Museum. She wrote "I miss this," and he smiled. At the top of the steps, he replied with "I miss you. Let me call you later?"

She replied with "Ok," and he tucked the phone into his pocket and slipped into his mother's bedroom. He took careful steps, imagining that if he could figure out other people's footsteps in the house, then his mother probably could too. When he reached the closet, he opened it slowly.

Other than Nidia's somewhat outdated clothing that hung on both sides of the walk-in, the closet was remarkably normal. Boxes of knick-knacks were on the shelves, and Easton looked through them quickly, trying to find what could have made that stone-on-stone noise he heard the last time he was spying on his mother. The boxes held old jewelry, old Playbills from Broadway shows and his and Becca's school plays, sea shells, clothing buttons, and more of the usual stuff a mom accumulates over the years.

On a middle shelf was a small statue of a woman with three faces, each roughly the same but her gaze cast in different directions. Her robed figure and hands bearing torches indicated to Easton that this was a statue of Hecate, goddess of the Moon.

On a high shelf, one that Easton could barely reach, and one that his mother most definitely couldn't reach without climbing on the step stool that was conveniently hidden behind some old winter coats, sat two weathered ADIDAS shoeboxes. Easton remembered those sneakers. He got them for Christmas one year, classic white ADIDAS shell tops. He wanted them for a long time when he was going through a Run DMC phase. He begged his mom for them, and come Christmas morning, lo and behold, there they were, under the tree. Easton remembered wearing them until they were ragged, smelly shells of their former glory, the once-pristine white of the shoes caked with dirt, mud, and God knows what else.

He pulled the box off the shelf and listened for Nidia and his sister. They were still talking about baking techniques, in smatterings of Greek and English. He pulled the top off the box and recoiled from the smack of a smell he couldn't explain. When he looked into the box, his eyes widened with confusion and terror. Inside, a collection of items he never knew existed. The largest, one of the ADIDAS sneakers he loved from his youth, pieces of it cut off at angles, the rubber frayed, the tongue of the sneaker all but gone. Along with the shoe, small bags of his baby teeth, yellowed, almost brown with age, some of them split, the halves missing. Locks of hair, tied neatly with a blue ribbon.

A small white envelope caught his attention. He picked it up, noting how light it was. Inside, tissues, parts of them stuck together, yellowed. It took Easton a moment to realize that these tissues were from private moments as a teenager, discovering his body in what he imagined to be the privacy of his bedroom.

Underneath the white envelope was a small Ziploc bag. Inside, a small black raisin-shaped piece of what looked like beef jerky. He opened the bag and realized where the smell was coming from. Disgusted, he zipped the bag back up and looked at the bottom of the box. Inside, a stone tablet with various etchings and shallow cuts. In the corner of the shoebox, a tiny, cold, metallic box that resembled a crude casket rattled around.

Removing the latch on the tiny metal box, which was heavy like lead, Easton peeked inside. The same smell as the Ziploc bag hit him immediately, and when he looked inside, he saw a piece of whatever was in the Ziploc, along with a baby tooth and a few threads of hair. The tooth and hair were tied together along with the black, meaty substance. He poked at it with his finger and immediately felt a pang of sickness run through his body. The inside of the metal box had more of the same kind of markings that were on the stone tablet. He realized that this small box could easily fit in the palm of his hand and could easily be hid in his pocket.

He charged down the stairs and into the kitchen, the shoebox held tightly in his hands. When he entered the kitchen, Nidia looked up, and when she saw what was in his hands, her eyes went wide. "Where did you find that?"

"Where do you think? What the fuck is this, mom?"

Becca's face recoiled at the smell coming from the box, even though it was about five feet away. "What is that, Easton?"

"Mom, tell us what this is."

Nidia looked down. Her surprise at Easton's discovery of the box changed to frustration, then to resignation. "There are things in there. Things from you, my sweet boy."

"What, like old gifts?" Becca asked, confused.

"In a sense," Nidia said.

"No. Not old gifts. My fucking baby teeth, my hair, all kinds of weird shit. Why do you have this? What's this metal box?" Easton threw the casket-shaped box on the table. It rattled around and Nidia grabbed it quickly, cradling it in her hands. Easton felt dizzy and braced himself against the kitchen table.

"Easy," Becca said, rising to help him.

"You don't understand," Nidia said. "You don't understand what I went through."

"What is this stuff, ma?" Easton shouted. "Why is this making me sick?"

"Because it smells like shit?" Becca offered, trying to break the tension.

"I had to protect you. Both of you. From your father. From yourselves."

"What does that *mean*?" Easton asked, the dizziness subsiding. He watched his mother cradle the tiny box.

"The old country offers many gifts to those of us who still observe the teachings," Nidia began. "I asked for help. When you were children. Your father, he was no good."

"How so?" Becca asked.

"Hit me. Yelled. Drank," Nidia said. "He was a cliché, and a pathetic one at that. I had to do something, so, after you were born, to protect you, to protect myself, I turned to her."

"Hecate," Easton said, sitting down.

"Wait. We're talking Greek gods and shit? I don't understand. We never went to normal church. Why all of a sudden would you be worshipping the old ones?" Becca asked, confused.

"She has a statue in her closet. On a shelf. Candles. Offerings of food and water next to her. Mom, what did you do? What's this?" Easton took the stone tablet out of the box, and Nidia reached for it, but he pulled it away.

"That's a curse tablet," Becca said, looking at it. "I've read about those online. Mom, what did you do?"

"I had to protect you. My sweet boy. My little boy. I don't want to lose you, not to that *girl*. I don't want you to go away," Nidia said, her eyes welling up with tears.

"Mom, I'm not going anywhere. I love her, but that doesn't mean I'm leaving you. I'll always be your son. Me being with anyone would never change that," he said, putting his hand on hers.

"This is fucked up, mom. You have to fix this," Becca said.

Nidia nodded slowly. "I know I do. I'm sorry."

***

When Easton proposed to Rita and she said yes, Nidia was happy. Becca was Rita's maid of honor, and they had a traditional Greek wedding, which Nidia catered herself. The entire affair was paid for by Nidia, who, along with Becca, prepared every dish, oversaw (with Rita's guidance) every aspect, and made sure Easton and Rita's guests were well taken care of.

After the father-daughter dance between Rita and her dad, who was an elder in the tribal community on the other side of the mountain, Rita wiped the tears in her eyes with a napkin from her place setting. It had been an emotional day for Easton, too, and he thanked his mother repeatedly, not only for lifting the curse, but also for taking care of their wedding. Rita placed the napkin down on her chair and headed to the bathroom to fix her makeup, Becca in tow.

Nobody noticed Nidia slipping the napkin into her purse soon after the two girls disappeared into the sea of people on the dancefloor.

About the Author

Robert P. Ottone is an author, teacher, and cigar enthusiast from East Islip, NY. He delights in the creepy. He can be found online at www.SpookyHousePress.com, or on Instagram (@RobertOttone). His collections *Her Infernal Name & Other Nightmares* and *People: A Horror Anthology about Love, Loss, Life & Things That Go Bump in the Night* are available now wherever books are sold.

About the Publisher

Spooky House is a small indie imprint dedicated to publishing elevated, quiet horror, speculative science fiction, and more.